Praise for Violet and Boy's first adventure

A PLACE CALLED PERFECT

Winner of the Crimefest Book Awards
Best Crime Novel for Children (8-12)

Shortlisted for the Waterstones Children's Book Prize
and the *Bord Gáis Irish Book Awards*

"A creepy, magical tale of bravery and self-belief."
Sunday Express

"This is one of those books that you think about when you're
not reading it and can't wait to find out what happens next."
Tom Fletcher

"A perfect choice for Waterstones Children's Book of the
Month and I will be recommending it to everyone,
including adults, that I can!"
Kelly Macdonald, Waterstones bookseller

"Helena Duggan builds an intriguing world
and tells a gripping story…"
The Scotsman

"A creepy adventure story full of twists and turns that
will ʜᴏᴏᴋ ʏᴏᴜ ɪɴ ꜰʀᴏᴍ ᴛʜᴇ ꜱᴛᴀʀᴛ ᴀɴᴅ ... essing

To Dad, for everything

First published in the UK in 2018 by Usborne Publishing Ltd., Usborne House, 83-85 Saffron Hill, London EC1N 8RT, England. www.usborne.com

Copyright © Helena Duggan, 2018

The right of Helena Duggan to be identified as the author of this work has been asserted by her in accordance with the Copyright, Designs and Patents Act, 1988.

Cover illustration by Karl James Mountford © Usborne Publishing, 2018

Map and A History of Perfect illustrations by David Shephard © Usborne Publishing, 2018

The name Usborne and the devices ♀ ⊕ are Trade Marks of Usborne Publishing Ltd.

A CIP catalogue record for this book is available from the British Library.

ISBN 9781474949514 04917-1 JFMAMJJ SOND/18

Printed in the UK.

THE TROUBLE WITH PERFECT

HELENA DUGGAN

USBORNE

CONTENTS

A HISTORY OF PERFECT

IN CASE YOU'VE FORGOTTEN

1.

DR EUGENE BROWN ARRIVES IN PERFECT WITH VIOLET.

2.

THE ARCHER BROTHERS ARE HIDING A BIG SECRET.

3. VIOLET RECEIVES A PAIR OF ROUND-RIMMED GLASSES THAT REVEAL BOY AND NO-MAN'S-LAND.

4. BOY AND OTHER ORPHANS IN NO-MAN'S-LAND HELP VIOLET UNCOVER WHAT'S GOING ON.

5. THE ARCHER BROTHERS USE TEA AND THEIR GLASSES TO CONTROL THE PEOPLE OF PERFECT.

THE WATCHERS WORK FOR THE ARCHER BROTHERS, GUARDING PERFECT AND STEALING IMAGINATIONS.

6.

7. IMAGINATIONS ARE STORED IN JARS AND HIDDEN AWAY IN THE ARCHERS' EMPORIUM.

8. VIOLET DISCOVERS THE GHOST ESTATE WHERE THE ARCHER BROTHERS GROW THEIR EYE PLANTS.

9. BOY'S MAM, MACULA ARCHER, IS A PRISONER IN A ROOM IN THE GHOST ESTATE.

10. WILLIAM ARCHER DEVELOPS THE REIMAGINATOR — A MACHINE TO GIVE PEOPLE BACK THEIR IMAGINATIONS.

11. PERFECTIONISTS AND NO-MAN'S-LANDERS UNITE TO DEFEAT THE ARCHER BROTHERS AND THE WATCHERS.

12. THE GATE BETWEEN PERFECT AND NO-MAN'S-LAND IS KNOCKED DOWN. ≷ WELCOME TO TOWN! ≷ AND SO OUR STORY BEGINS...

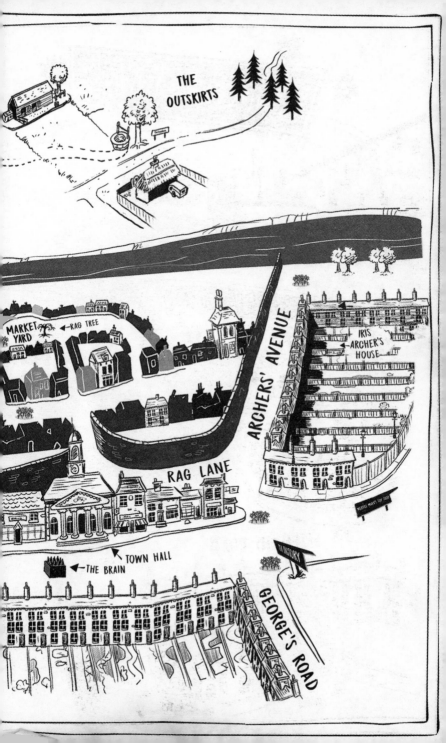

CHAPTER 1

HOME

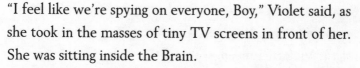

"I feel like we're spying on everyone, Boy," Violet said, as she took in the masses of tiny TV screens in front of her. She was sitting inside the Brain.

The Brain was William Archer's newest invention. Well, it wasn't that new, it had been around since just after Perfect fell, which was nearly a year ago. It looked like a black box from the outside and was around the same size as a garden shed. The Brain had black shutters on the sides, that could be lifted up to give easy access to the cramped space inside, for repairs. Hundreds of small black and red cone-shapes covered the flat roof.

It was situated just off the steps of the Town Hall, on Edward Street. The Town Hall was the centre of Town,

William said, and so this was the best place for the Brain to receive signals from all the eye-plant beds.

Since Perfect had fallen, William Archer had planted numerous beds of eye plants on the streets around Town. They acted as lookouts. "A Town security system," William said, when he first proposed the idea. The eye plants were living eyes and sent signals of what they saw back to the Brain, which converted those signals to pictures.

Boy looked at the screens too. "Maybe that's because we *are* spying, Violet," he joked.

"You know what I mean!"

"What are we really going to see in Town? Nobody ever does anything exciting around here – well, nothing they wouldn't want us to see, anyway. Though maybe you're right, Violet...I mean, we might see Mrs Moody putting out her washing, or what if we see Mr Bloom plucking his weeds!" Boy mocked. "Anyway, the eye plants spy on people all the time and you're fine with that!"

"Yeah, but they're doing it for a good reason – they're looking out for Edward, in case he ever comes back."

"And we're doing this to fix the eye plants. They won't be able to look out for Edward if they're broken, will they?"

"What's wrong with them anyway?"

"Well, Dad says they're acting up a bit. He's fixed the

rods and cones on the roof, and wants to see if that has worked. The electromagnetic sig—"

"Boy, I haven't a clue what any of that stuff means. Just say it in plain English!"

"I forgot you're not half as intelligent as me," he teased.

"Whatever. If it makes you feel better, you can tell yourself that," Violet said impatiently. "So what does your dad want us to do?"

"We've to look at the screens and check they're all working. Make sure none of them are blank or blinking on and off."

Violet jumped from her chair and began to walk around. Inside the Brain were lots of tiny TV screens, all clustered in the centre of the space like a giant spider's eyes. They were surrounded by a narrow walkway to inspect them from.

"Each screen is connected to an eye plant in one of the flower beds around Town," Boy continued. "The number on the top corner of the screen will tell you which bed. If you see a screen blinking, write down its number."

"They all look fine here." Violet's stomach churned as she watched Mr Hatchet pick his nose outside his butcher's shop on one of the tiny TVs. "It's a bit weird looking at people when they don't know, isn't it?"

"Oh, there's a new train in Merrill's toyshop window,"

Boy said excitedly, moving closer to the screen in front of him.

"Why do boys love boring things like trains?" Violet sighed, shaking her head.

"Why do girls love boring things like…talking?" Boy smirked.

"Any problems?" William Archer asked, poking his bearded face round the main door of the Brain.

"No, Dad," Boy replied. "Maybe the adjustments you made worked."

"Wouldn't that be great?" William smiled, ruffling his son's unruly hair. "It'd get Vincent Crooked off my back, anyway."

"Is the Committee meeting finished, then?" Violet asked.

"Yes, your dad is on the way, Violet. He was just having a word with Vincent."

"What happened this time?" she asked.

Her dad and Mr Crooked were always "having words", and most of the words weren't nice, her mam said. Her dad called it "a difference of opinion", but Violet knew that meant he just didn't like the man. She kind of agreed with her dad, though. If Mr Crooked was anything like his son Conor, then she wouldn't like him either.

"Nothing, Violet," William replied. "Vincent was just questioning how secure the eye plants are, after the recent problems. Your dad was trying to persuade him that everything is fine." He smiled.

"Right, Violet, are you ready?" Her dad stepped into the doorway, looking red-faced.

"Did you convince Vincent?" William asked.

"No," Eugene replied, "but I had fun trying. I don't know what it is about that man, but I just can't warm to him. He was saying something about robberies and how if the eyes weren't working properly, we wouldn't be safe in Town."

"Robberies in Town?" William laughed. "I wonder what he'll come up with next!"

"Anyway," Eugene said, stepping back out onto Edward Street, "it's Sunday night, time for your bed, Violet. Your mother will be wondering where we've gone to."

"But, Dad, can't I stay a bit longer?" Violet pleaded, looking at Boy.

"No, it's school tomorrow. Mrs Moody won't be happy if you fall asleep in class."

"Mrs Moody is never happy anyway, Dad!"

"Come on, Violet," Eugene said, squeezing her shoulders affectionately.

Violet sighed and said goodbye to William and Boy, then walked with her dad through the quiet streets of Town.

On the nights her mam went to cooking classes, Violet's dad brought her to Committee meetings. The

Committee was formed after Perfect fell, as a way to rule Town. It was made up of ten people. Her dad called it a demoncrosity or demoncr-something. Anyway, it just meant all decisions in Town were voted on, so everything was fair.

The meetings were boring and – unlike tonight when she helped with the Brain – normally Violet would have to sit through two hours of adults talking. The walk home with her dad always made up for it, though.

The skies in Town were usually clear, and Eugene Brown would point to the stars and ask her to name them. They'd done it so many times now that Violet knew them all by heart. Sometimes she forgot one on purpose, because Mam said her dad loved to show off all the stuff he knew about science.

"There's the Plough," Eugene said, pointing, as they neared their house.

She was following his finger, when all of a sudden something flew out of the bushes in front of her. Violet jumped, almost landing on her father's foot.

"It's okay, pet," he soothed, looking skywards. "It's only a bird. Strange it's out at this time of night."

Violet steadied her breath as they walked up their gravel drive.

"Do you think Town would be safe if the eye plants really stopped working, Dad?"

"Pet, Town is one of the safest places I've ever been. Perhaps one of the safest places in the world. We don't need the eyes, but they're William's indulgence. I think he wants to turn something bad into something good."

"But what about Edward Archer? What if he comes back and tries to steal everyone's imaginations again?"

"He's not coming back, pet. That man's long gone from here."

Eugene Brown opened the front door, flooding the yard with light as he walked into their house. Violet stopped on the steps for a moment, looking out at the clear dark night.

She used to hate this place, when it was called Perfect and everyone was controlled by the Archer brothers. But now, Town really did feel like home.

CHAPTER 2

TROUBLE WITH THE BRAIN

Violet's heart was beating loudly. She was following Edward Archer, the shorter, stocky twin, as he staggered up the hill, past the lamp post.

Her vision was foggy, as though a mist clouded the edges of her eyes.

She pushed open the turnstile to the graveyard, and shivered as the iron gate screeched.

Headstones lined the path that divided the cemetery. She couldn't see Edward in the thick, black night and ducked down behind a standing stone for cover.

"I know you're in here, Edward Archer!" she shouted.

His laughter echoed round her. Sweat pimpled Violet's brow.

Suddenly, a figure darted out from behind a grave. She tried to give chase but stumbled to the ground, bloodying her palms.

A sound like scraping stone filled the air, and her breath caught.

Violet rose and raced to where she'd seen the figure moments before. He'd vanished.

Where had he gone? She couldn't let Edward Archer get away.

She was standing by a tombstone, and rubbed moss from its surface, trying to read the engravings. Then a big black bird swooped down from the skies, its claws open, grasping.

Violet cowered, covering her face. Her screams pierced the night as the bird's wings beat the air above her.

"Violet, Violet, Violet," a voice called out in the distance.

Violet opened her eyes, her chest pounding. Where was she? Relief flooded her body as she took in the ceiling light in her bedroom.

She'd had that dream again. The one where Edward disappeared. Only this time it was slightly different. She'd been attacked by a bird.

"Violet, Violet…"

Somebody was calling her name. She bolted up. Something rattled against the glass in her bedroom window.

Cautiously, she crawled out of bed and over to her curtains, pulling them open just a little.

The large silver moon lit the night.

In the gravel yard below was a figure, his legs straddling a bike. Boy. What was he doing here now?

The bike was new, given to Boy by his parents, William and Macula Archer, as an early birthday present – though Boy's parents didn't need an excuse. Since they'd found their long-lost son, the Archers – including Iris, his granny – were always giving him gifts. Violet sometimes wished she'd grown up in an orphanage and then found her parents, at least that way she might get more than fleecy pyjamas and pink slippers for her birthday.

"Why are you standing in my yard this late? I only saw you a few hours ago," she whispered, after sliding open the window.

"You're such a moaner, Violet! It's not late," he replied, his breath sending small white puffs into the air. "It's early, nearly sunrise!"

"That's the same thing, Boy. I'm trying to sleep! Are you ever going to get used to proper hours, not the ones you kept in No-Man's-Land? Normal people sleep at night."

"Normal is boring. Now come on, get up. Dad needs us!"

"Again? For what? Can't it wait?"

"Too many questions… Come on!"

Violet huffed as she dressed. Then, as quietly as possible, she slipped out of her room and down the stairs. In a matter of moments, she'd opened the front door and was standing on the steps of her house.

"What took you so long?" Boy asked, as he turned and pedalled off. "Come on!" he called over his shoulder, heading quickly down the driveway.

Boys! They never wait around for anyone, Violet fumed, as she walked round the side of the house and pulled the bike she'd been given for Christmas away from the pebble-dashed wall.

What was up with Boy, that he had to drag her out of bed for?

She was just cycling out of her driveway when a big black bird flew down from a tree, right across her path, just as one had done earlier when she was with her dad.

Violet swerved, releasing an involuntary squeal.

"You're such a girly girl!" Boy teased, waiting by the bench just ahead.

"No I'm not," she puffed, catching her breath.

"It was just a bird, Violet."

"I know…" She fell silent as she pushed off once more. "It's just…well…I had that dream again. Only this time there was a bird in it, as well as Edward – so it scared me, that's all."

"I told you, Edward Archer won't hurt you or any of

us again," Boy said, pedalling up beside her. "You shouldn't be having those dreams any more."

"It's not like I have them on purpose," Violet replied. "I haven't had one in ages, either. I think it's because I was talking to Dad about Edward when we were walking home, and a bird frightened me then too. That's all. I can't exactly control what my head does at night, can I?"

"You can't control what your head does ever, Violet!" Boy teased. "Come on, Dad wants us at the Brain, ASAP."

"What does ASAP mean, anyway?" Violet panted, pedalling after him.

"It means *hurry up*!" Boy replied, taking a sharp angle onto Splendid Road and almost careening into a bed of eye plants.

"Well why didn't you just say that?" Violet laughed, as they whistled by what was once the Archer Brothers' Spectacle Makers' Emporium.

The Archers' Emporium had been at the heart of Perfect, and was where twins Edward and George had plotted and run their empire. When Perfect fell, Eugene Brown, Violet's dad, and William Archer had set up their own optician's business in the shop and it was now known as Archer and Brown.

The pair did normal optician stuff, like sell glasses and fix people's eyes, but they had a cool space too, where Violet's dad – who was an ophthalmologist, which is like a surgeon for eyes – did experiments that helped blind people see again. This research had been a passion of his since Perfect fell and it meant he got published in *Eye Spy*, a magazine about eyes, a lot more. Violet's mother, Rose, was very proud of her husband and told everyone about his "ambitious" plans for Archer and Brown.

Violet and Boy pulled on their brakes, stopping outside the Brain.

William Archer was muttering to himself as he rolled up one of the metal sides of the Brain, revealing the hundreds of small TV screens. "I've checked the cones, the wiring… What is it, what's going wrong? Some are blank on this side too." He tutted, tapping the glass. William seemed oblivious to Violet and Boy. "This just doesn't make any sense!"

"Erm…Dad…" Boy coughed.

"Great! You made it," William said, whirling around on the spot. "Hate to bring you back here so soon, Violet. Now off you go, be back here before light please. I don't want to alert all of Town to the fact this little beauty isn't doing her best again. We'll really have Crooked on our backs then. I told him everything was working fine after the meeting."

"What do you want us to do, Dad?" Boy asked, confused. "You haven't explained anything to us yet."

"Oh right, silly me."

He strode forward and awkwardly shook Violet's hand in hello. William Archer always treated kids the same as adults, which was why Violet liked him so much.

"Thank you for getting out of bed to help us, Violet. We'd be lost without you, as ever. We've the same problem as the one I thought I'd fixed earlier – some of the screens in the Brain have gone blank, and I can't get them to come back to life. I think if we work together – you two whizzing up and down between the Brain and the eye-plant beds on those bikes – we may be able to find out exactly what's going on, and fix it. We're a great team, us three. I know these hours seem unconventional, Violet, but I don't want to cause any alarm in Town, especially after Vincent's Committee questions. Hope you don't mind!"

"What are we checking the eye plants for, Dad?" Boy asked, trying to make some sense of his father's rambling mind.

"Loose transmitters or wires, foggy lenses, infections, that kind of thing. I'll check the wiring here again. Now don't split up – I know Town is safe without those Watchers patrolling our streets, but Rose and Eugene wouldn't be pleased if I allowed Violet to wander around in the dark alone."

"They won't know, William." Violet smiled.

"Nevertheless, Violet, please stick together. I know you two are more than capable of looking after yourselves, but I must at least try to act responsibly." He smiled. "Just go to the bed on Forgotten Road, the one in Market Yard and the one at the footbridge. They're the ones giving us trouble. See if everything looks normal, then come straight back."

Boy nodded, and turned his bike towards Archers' Avenue.

"Take this," William said, grabbing a strange, black rectangular device from the floor of the Brain and handing it to Boy. "Let me know if you see anything odd. Remember to say 'over' at the end of your sentences, otherwise I won't know when you're finished."

"Right, Dad," Boy said, rolling his eyes up to heaven, but so only Violet could see.

"What's that thing William gave you?" Violet asked, as the pair started to pedal down the street.

"It's a walkie-talkie. Dad just made a pair. It's for talking to him whenever I'm helping. They're really useful, especially if we're at different ends of Town, checking the eye plants."

"I'd love one of those." Violet grabbed it out of Boy's hand and placed it in her back pocket before sprinting ahead on her bike. "Bet you can't catch me!"

Violet could hear Boy over her shoulder, chasing her

down, as she wheeled left onto Archers' Avenue and then took another sharp left onto Rag Lane heading for No-Man's-Land, Boy's old home.

CHAPTER 3

IN THE BLINK OF AN EYE

When Town was called Perfect and under the Archer brothers' control, No-Man's-Land had been a prison for people who were different and didn't fit with Edward and George's plans for perfection. The No-Man's-Landers were outcasts, and their families still living in Perfect were robbed of all memory that they ever existed.

When Perfect fell, George Archer was captured and imprisoned in the clock tower of the Town Hall. The Watchers, who'd guarded Perfect under the Archers' control, were locked away in the basement of that same building. Edward escaped, disappearing in the graveyard beside the Ghost Estate.

The No-Man's-Landers and Perfectionists, who had

been living on different sides of a wall in the same town, united. The gate into No-Man's-Land was ceremonially knocked down, and the streets and buildings were renovated.

Forgotten Road was no longer forgotten – many of its buildings were already restored. Market Yard still held close to its roots, as a vibrant place where people gathered once a week to sell wares and exchange ideas.

Violet's mouth watered as she pedalled past Sweets for My Sweet, which had opened a few months before and was now one of Town's favourite shops.

Boy screeched to a halt as they neared the old orphanage.

The orphans had all gone back to their families, who'd forgotten they existed during Perfect, and now weren't orphans any more. The orphanage itself was left as it had been, and opened as a museum to Town's difficult history.

William told Violet, once, that the museum was so nobody ever forgot their Perfect past. She thought that was silly, since people wanted to forget about the horrible things that had happened in Perfect. At least, her mam did anyway. Rose got upset any time Violet brought it up. However, William had explained that sometimes the past was painful but, if you never wanted to feel that pain again, you needed to remember it. "People have short memories, Violet," he had warned her. "If we forget our past, it will catch up with us."

"These seem fine," Boy said, pulling Violet from her memories, as he examined the eye plants in the first bed they'd been sent to inspect, on Forgotten Road.

The beds were mounds of deep-red clay about two metres long and oval-shaped. They were edged with white-painted paving stones and lined with rows of knee-high eye plants. Beside each bed was a small tank of blood – supplied weekly by Mr Hatchet, the butcher – to feed the plants with.

Violet dropped her bike on its side and walked over, bending down for a closer look.

The red stem of one of the plants nearby pulsed as it fed from the deep clay. Its translucent skin-like petals were open and its eyeball centre watched Boy suspiciously, following his every move.

"Be careful, you don't want to annoy them," she warned her friend.

She remembered the last time the eye plants had screamed, on the night Edward Archer disappeared. The sound was eerily haunting and she definitely didn't want to hear it ever again.

"These things freak me out," she whispered, looking straight at a bloodshot eyeball as it surveyed her.

"These 'things' are keeping everyone safe, Violet,"

Boy said, as he crawled gingerly through the bed.

"Well, I don't see anything wrong with them," Violet announced, dusting off her trousers a minute later.

"Wow, you searched really hard!" Boy smirked, looking up from the clay.

"Yes, I did. As much as you did, anyway."

"Well, how come I'm the one still down here checking them, then?"

"Please...come on, can we just go? I can't look at the eyes close-up for much longer, they're disgusting!"

Boy laughed, jumping up from the ground to grab his bike. "Fine. They do all seem to be okay. Anyway, I thought you weren't scared of anything!"

"I'm not scared of the eyes," she huffed, "I just don't think they're nice to look at!"

Boy was about to say something, when he stopped and looked around. "Does this remind you of anything?"

Violet shrugged as she mounted her bike. "Does what remind me?"

"The silence and empty streets."

"No, why?"

"How about when we used to sneak through Perfect – when nobody else was about, only us and the Watchers?"

"Yeah, I suppose so," she replied. "I'm not sure I want to remember back then, though."

"It wasn't all that bad," Boy said, pushing down on his pedals. "Sometimes it was exciting! Town is so normal."

"There's nothing wrong with normal! Do you miss danger or something?" Violet asked, confused.

"No, but sometimes I do miss adventure. And doing bad things."

"'Bad things'? What are you on about?"

"I don't mean proper-bad things. I just mean things that weren't allowed, like climbing the wall into Perfect or tricking the Watchers. Everything feels really safe right now."

"Isn't safe good?" Violet asked, cycling behind her friend.

"Yeah, I suppose, but sometimes it's boring!" Boy called back as he disappeared down the laneway towards Market Yard.

"Maybe it's just you who's boring," Violet teased, speeding past him in the narrow space.

Boy put his head down and raced after Violet, the pair almost colliding as they skidded to a halt near the Rag Tree in the centre of Market Yard.

"I won!" Violet panted, throwing her hands into the air.

"No, I won! I always win – that's the rules!" Boy laughed, leaping off his bike and jumping around in mock celebration.

"You can't always win!"

"Yes I can, that's the rules."

"The rules you made up!" Violet retorted, pushing his shoulder.

"Rules are rules, Violet," Boy teased as he walked over to inspect the next bed of eye plants.

Violet was about to reply, when Boy looked up at her, his face serious.

"We need to get Dad! Give me the walkie-talkie."

"Why? What's wrong?" she asked, rushing over to hand it to him.

A large patch of eye plants was missing from the middle of the flower bed, as if someone had plucked them right out.

"They screamed earlier, gave me an awful fright," a voice called from across the yard behind them. "I was going to tell your father, in the morning, but now I've seen you two out here, saves me the bother."

Violet looked around. An old man was hanging half out the top window of a house on the edge of Market Yard.

"What time was it?" Boy asked. "Did you see anyone?"

"It was late, after midnight I'd say," the man replied. "The screeching was awful, worse than squabbling cats. I didn't see anybody, but it was dark, mind."

Boy spoke into the walkie-talkie, then looked at Violet.

"Dad's not answering. We better check out the next bed."

The pair got on their bikes and raced down Wickham Terrace, past Boy's house, towards the footbridge and the last of the beds William had asked them to examine.

"This one is the same – some of the eyes are missing," Boy panted, turning to look at his friend anxiously.

He tried the walkie-talkie again. A rustling sound, like leaves in the wind, rattled across the airwaves.

"Dad, someone's stealing the eye plants. OVER," Boy said. "Dad... Dad?"

Static fizzed out into the dawn.

"He's such a feather-head," Boy huffed, as he shoved the device into his pocket. "We'd better get back to him, quick, Violet!"

 **CHAPTER 4**

CHILDISH TRICKS

The sun was just rising over Town, as Boy and Violet swerved onto Edward Street and pedalled furiously back to the Brain. William Archer's nose was almost touching one of the screens as he fiddled with some dials.

"What's happened?" he asked, looking up. "Did you find something?"

"We met a man who told us the eyes screamed last night. There's some missing from the bed in Market Yard and the one at the footbridge," Boy panted.

William seemed confused. "What do you mean? Have they died, or fallen over? I don't understand."

"No, gone, Dad, like someone has pulled them up and taken them," Boy said bluntly.

"Oh dear. Are all the plants in those beds gone?" William asked, scratching his head.

"No, just some of them," Violet replied.

"Surely if someone took the plants, they should have been spotted by the other plants? Why can't I see it on the screens? This is very strange, very strange indeed…"

Violet and Boy watched as William Archer strode forwards and backwards, muttering to himself.

"We need to tell the Committee. It's probably just someone playing a trick, though I wish they wouldn't play it with the eye plants – they're delicate."

"Delicate? More like disgusting," Violet whispered.

"Crooked will have a field day with this! Violet, will you tell Eugene I'll be over a little later this morning, to fill him in?"

"What's going on, Dad?" Boy asked.

"I don't know, son, but as I said, I'm sure it's just someone playing a trick." William looked straight at Boy. "Let's not talk about this in front of your mother, though. At least, not until we figure it out a bit more. She's got enough on her plate already."

Boy nodded.

"Is it okay if I cycle back with Violet?" he asked.

"Okay, then come straight home," his dad replied, over his shoulder.

Boy nodded, then quickly cycled off down Edward Street.

"I *can* go home by myself, Boy," Violet insisted, as she caught up to him.

"I know you can – I just don't want to go back yet!" He smiled, pedalling ahead again.

"Why did your dad say that about your mam?" Violet asked catching up once more.

"Say what?"

The sun was just popping out behind the clock tower of the Town Hall as they passed Archer and Brown, on the corner of Edward Street and Splendid Road.

"Not to tell her about the eyes, that she'd enough worries?"

Boy didn't reply. He looked a little sad, not like his normal self.

"Is there something wrong?" Violet asked, feeling worried this time.

"No... Well, I don't really know..."

"You can tell me, I'm your best friend."

"I know, Violet, I just don't know what to tell. Mam is acting weird. She's sneaking around a lot and always seems kind of upset. It's like she doesn't listen, like her head is somewhere else."

"Did you ask your dad?"

"Yeah, he got awkward and said something about her finding it hard being free of the small room the Archers kept her in. I don't believe him, though. I think he knows what's really going on. I've heard them whispering, sometimes. I don't know why adults whisper like that."

"I know." Violet sighed. "It's like they don't think kids have ears! Maybe she's just stressed? Adults get that a lot. I think it's like the flu, or something."

"I don't think that's `what stress is, Violet!" Boy laughed.

"William might be right, though," she continued, ignoring him. "I was only in Macula's room for a few minutes, but I think living in it for all those years must have been really hard. All your mam did was sit there and write letters."

Violet remembered the deep-red carpet and dark mahogany furniture of Macula Archer's room, the luxury a complete contrast to the derelict house that encased it in the Ghost Estate. She remembered the wild paintings that looked like freedom, and sitting in Macula's chair reading one of the hundreds of letters to her boys.

"She never talks about that time." Boy sighed.

"Mam always tells me I've to talk about things, especially bad things. She said that if you don't talk about the bad things, they can get stuck in your head and get much worse. Then they turn into really bad things, when they were probably not that bad at all to start with."

"I feel sorry for the things that get stuck in your head!" Boy joked.

"Very funny!" Violet smiled, stopping outside the entrance to her house.

"Right, I better get back home. I'll see you in school."

"Hey, Boy!" she called, as he turned to cycle away.

"Yeah?"

"Your mam will be okay. Remember, my mam lost her imagination and was totally under the Archers' control in Perfect, and she's fine now. Parents are always okay in the end. They just like to worry about things."

"Thanks, Violet." He half-smiled.

She watched until Boy disappeared round the corner, then climbed off her bike and pushed it up the gravel drive, to the side of her house. She was just climbing the steps when there was a rumble of thunder.

Violet jumped, her heart pounding as clouds gathered in the sky above.

The sun had perpetually shone in Perfect – or, at least, people thought it did – but since the Archers' downfall, lots of things, including the weather, were back to normal. The weather in Town was good. It was sunny a lot of the time, broken up by the odd rain shower – but Violet had never heard thunder in the skies here before. She'd almost forgotten what it sounded like.

"Violet, what are you doing up already?" her dad asked, as she went inside. He was standing in the half dark at the bottom of the hallway.

"Did you hear the thunder, Dad?" she asked, eyes wide.

"I thought I heard something, pet. Thank goodness it wasn't my stomach!" Eugene Brown smiled. "What were you doing out there?"

"Boy called for me."

"At this time?"

"Yeah, William needed help. There's a problem with the eye plants."

"I thought he fixed that last night?"

They walked through to the kitchen and Violet sat down at the table. She had filled her dad in by the time William Archer knocked on the door a little later that morning.

"Any news on the eye plants?" she asked, as William strode into the kitchen.

"No, Violet, I searched for footage in the Brain's memory stores again, but there's no information at all. The other eyes didn't pick up any attack. It's very strange, almost as if something is disturbing the signals."

"Violet told me what happened, William," Eugene said, looking up at his friend. "Sit down, I'll make you a cup of tea."

Tea hadn't been a favourite in Town for a while after Perfect fell, because the Archer twins had poisoned their brew to steal everyone's sight. Then Violet's dad and

William had come up with the idea of reopening the tea factory. They called it a "cross-community project". When Violet asked her dad what that meant, he said it was something that the No-Man's-Landers and the Perfectionists could work on together, so they could see that they weren't so different. In the beginnings of Town, some people had still been a little suspicious of each other.

The factory was reopened a month after Edward disappeared. It had taken Town a while, and a lot of work, but gradually people began to trust each other and the tea factory again.

Now *UniTea* was a favourite on all kitchen tables. Eugene was particularly pleased with the tagline, "Bringing Town Together", which was displayed proudly on every purple packet and over the factory gates on George's Road.

Violet loved having the tea back. It was made from the same Chameleon plant the Archer brothers had used and tasted like anything she wanted it to, but was minus their blinding potion, so it didn't rob her eyesight.

"Thanks, Eugene," William said, looking worried as he sat down. "I'm at a loss as to what's happening. I'm sure it's someone playing a trick, as I can't imagine anyone in Town stealing anything – especially not those plants."

"And nobody saw a thing?"

"Mr Eton said he heard the plants screaming and looked out, but whoever it was had gone. A few others heard them too, but nobody spotted anything. One person said they saw Boy when they heard the screams, but they must have confused their times. Boy and Violet weren't down there until after the eye plants were taken."

"It's very strange," Eugene said, shaking his head. "I'm sure Vincent Crooked will be raving about this at the Committee meeting tonight. Of course, you'll have to call a meeting, given the circumstances."

"I can ask about the eye plants at school, Dad," Violet said, feeling excited. She missed investigating stuff. "It could be kids. They might think it's funny?"

"It's alright, pet. We'll figure it out," Eugene said. "Do you think it could—" He stopped abruptly, looked at his watch and turned to face his daughter.

"Pet, you need to get ready for school or you'll be late again."

"But, Dad, I want to stay and hear!"

"Violet!" Her father's tone was serious.

Slowly, she got up from the table and walked out of the kitchen. Eugene closed the door behind her. Then, after a few moments, she carefully placed her ear against the cream-painted wood.

"Violet's having bad dreams about Edward. I thought they'd gone, but I heard her have one again last night,"

Eugene said, from the other side of the door. "I didn't want to talk about him in front of her."

"Edward?" William asked.

"Yes. Do you think he could have come back?"

"Violet Brown!" Her mother's voice rang down the hallway towards her.

The kitchen door swung inwards and Violet stumbled forward, off balance.

"Violet!" her dad exclaimed. He looked disappointed, and she hated when he looked at her like that. "What have I told you about eavesdropping? Go get ready for school."

"But, Dad, if Edward's come back, I want to know! You can't keep it a secret from me."

"He's not, pet. I just asked the question, that's all."

"My brother is not coming back. It's not him, Violet," William said, standing up and walking to the door. "He wouldn't need to steal the eye plants, they're his invention after all."

Eugene coughed. "Not entirely his…"

Even though the eye plants were invented because of a terrible idea, Violet's dad was still a little proud of having helped develop them. He said they were a good thing, just put to a bad use by awful people.

William nodded and looked back down at Violet. "And if my brother ever does return, you and Boy will be the first people I inform," he said seriously. "You saved Perfect. You defeated my brothers, Violet. We're a team, like I told you before."

"Thanks," she said, smiling proudly.

Violet got dressed and rushed out the front door, bidding goodbye to her parents and William in the kitchen. Then she climbed onto her bike and headed towards Town.

The sun was peering round the clouds as she pedalled the streets to her school.

CHAPTER 5

LIES

Violet sped down the tree-lined avenue and turned left onto Splendid Road, towards the centre of Town. She waved at Mr Hatchet, the butcher, sweeping up outside his shop door. He waved back warmly as she cycled past and swung up right off Edward Street to her school.

Everybody was friendly in Town these days – not falsely friendly, like they'd been in the old Perfect days, but proper friendly.

Violet propped her bike against the school wall and headed for the entrance.

"You better get a lock for that," somebody said, behind her.

Violet turned and was greeted by Beatrice Prim –

possibly the most annoying girl in school, or at least in Violet's class.

"Nobody locks their bike in Town," Violet said dismissively.

"They do now," Beatrice said. "Haven't you heard the news?" The red-haired girl lowered her voice, as though she were about to tell Violet a massive secret. "Lucy Lawn's bike was stolen from outside her house last night. Her mother told my mam at the school gates. Lucy's so upset that she couldn't come in today!"

"Oh," Violet replied in surprise. So it wasn't only the eye plants that were taken last night. She'd never heard of anyone stealing in Town before now.

Violet's dad said Town was one of the safest places in the world – but real safe, not Perfect safe, where everybody did what the Archers told them to, without question. For the most part, since Perfect fell, people had a new respect for each other, Eugene Brown had said.

"Maybe somebody just borrowed Lucy's bike, and they'll drop it back later," Violet answered.

"You would say that." Beatrice smirked.

"What's that supposed to mean?"

"You're his best friend – of course you'd cover for him."

"What are you talking about?" Violet asked, feeling a little frustrated.

Beatrice smiled and stepped back.

"Lucy said she saw Boy take it last night, right around the time those disgusting eyes went missing. She heard a noise and looked out her window. She swears it was him!"

"Well, it wasn't," Violet said, shocked. "I was with Boy last night and he didn't steal anyone's bike. In future, Beatrice, get your facts right before you tell lies about people."

"Ask Lucy," Beatrice said, as she turned in a swoosh of hair, and swiftly disappeared into the school.

How could anyone accuse Boy of stealing a bike? He'd be really angry when Violet told him. Beatrice was annoying, sure, but saying something like that was going too far, even for her.

Everyone was already at their desks when Violet entered the classroom.

"Good of you to join us, Ms Brown!" Mrs Moody said, in a tone that didn't sound as if it were "good" of her at all.

Violet nodded and kept her head down, as she walked to her seat. Boy was in his place already and she squeezed in beside him.

"You'll never guess what Beatrice said to me this morning," she whispered across the desk.

"Violet Brown," Mrs Moody called, "classroom time is classroom time!"

"Classroom time is classroom time," Violet mimicked as Boy tried to stop himself from laughing.

46

"You two, I will split you up!" the teacher warned, as she looked over again.

Then Mrs Moody told everyone to take out their homework and she began to correct it, writing the answers on the board.

"I thought she'd be a bit nicer, since Pippa came back," Violet whispered, shaking her head. "If she was my mam, I'd want to be back in No-Man's-Land!"

Mrs Moody's daughter, Pippa, had been taken into No-Man's-Land years before and was reunited with her family when Perfect fell. Violet remembered watching her teacher cry as she held her daughter. The whole thing made her kind of like Mrs Moody a bit more. That changed quickly when school started again, though.

"Pippa said that's just her mam's way, Violet. She said Mrs Moody is soft underneath," Boy whispered back.

"Her clothes must be made of stone then!"

Boy smothered his laughter again.

"What did Beatrice say to you, anyway?" he prompted, a little later.

Violet looked over at the red-haired girl, then dipped her head a little bit as she whispered. "She said Lucy Lawn saw you stealing her bike last night."

"She what?" Boy's eyes almost popped out of his face.

"I know," Violet said, nodding. "I couldn't believe Lucy would say something like that either."

"But why would Beatrice say that? Was Lucy's bike really stolen?" Boy asked.

"Beatrice says it was. I think that's weird, though – nobody would steal anything in Town. I mean, except the eye plants."

"Lucy lives on Forgotten Road, doesn't she?" asked Boy.

"Yeah, I think her family moved into the house her dad had when he was living in No-Man's-Land," Violet replied.

"So, near one of the eye-plant beds... Maybe the person who stole the eyes took Lucy's bike too?"

"But why would someone do that?" Violet asked.

"Because they wanted to get away quickly!"

"Not that," Violet huffed. "I mean, why would someone from Town want to steal in the first place? Almost everybody knows each other. It's not like the person who stole Lucy's bike can cycle it around without being seen."

"I suppose...but why would Lucy say I took it?" Boy replied, thinking out loud.

"You two have had enough of a warning," Mrs Moody said over her shoulder. "Violet, come here."

The teacher pointed to a desk in front of her. Boy tried not to laugh as Violet, red-faced, picked up her books and sat down right under Mrs Moody's large nose.

With no one to talk to, she stayed in total silence for the rest of the day, apart from lunch, and was itching for conversation when the bell tolled to signal the end of school.

Boy rose quickly from his desk. "Come on!" he said, pulling his bag over his shoulders.

"Where are we going?" Violet asked, gathering up her stuff.

"To Lucy's house. I want to ask her what she saw. It might help us figure out what happened to the eye plants."

"Okay," Violet said, running excitedly after him. "We're on an adventure again!"

"Relax, Violet, we're only going to Lucy's."

"I know, but we are kind of trying to solve another mystery. Like the olden days!"

"You really do get excited pretty easily…"

The pair pedalled their bikes up Edward Street and turned onto Rag Lane, racing down to Forgotten Road.

Violet was remembering, back in Perfect, when the buildings in No-Man's-Land were in disrepair. Lucy's house, although she didn't live there then, had always been kept nice, though. This was because Larry Lawn, her dad, was a carpenter and great with his hands.

Mr Lawn had been locked in No-Man's-Land while Lucy and her family, having forgotten he ever existed, lived in Perfect. Her dad had made good use of his time, repairing the house with leftover materials. Larry created all sorts of beautiful household things, such as patchwork curtains, lampshades and even kitchen stools from old buckets he added legs to.

When both sides of Perfect came together and created Town, Lucy's family moved into Larry's house and Mr Lawn opened a shop in Market Yard, selling his unique creations. Rose Brown, Violet's mam, was one of his best customers.

Violet and Boy pulled on their brakes outside Lucy's house.

Boy left his bike against the wall and walked up to the purple door, knocking solidly, with Violet beside him. Mrs Lawn opened the door.

"Oh, I knew it had to be a mistake, Boy." She sighed. "I told Lucy you probably needed her bike for something and would return it."

"Erm…" Boy looked at Violet, wide-eyed. "I didn't take the bike, Mrs Lawn, that's why I came. I wanted to ask Lucy what she saw."

Lucy stepped out into the hallway from a room off it.

"Hi, Boy," she said, her face stern.

"Hi, Lucy," he replied. "We heard about your bike and came to see if we could help. Some of the eye plants have been stolen in Town too, and we were wondering if maybe it was the same person. Can we ask you some questions?"

"It was you," the girl said firmly.

Boy shook his head. "I didn't take your bike, Lucy," he replied, a hint of red skin showing at the base of his neck.

"But I saw you…"

"Where did you see him?" Violet asked.

"I saw him out the front. My bike wasn't locked, but it screeches when you pull the brakes. I meant to get Dad to fix it. I heard it screech, so I ran to the window and saw Boy."

"But it wasn't me," he said again, the blotchy red skin now highlighting his cheeks.

"It was you, Boy, I saw you! You even turned around and looked straight at me when I called your name."

"Wasn't it dark?" Violet asked, confused.

"My daughter wouldn't say it if she hadn't seen you, Boy," Lucy's mother interrupted. "I don't mean to accuse you, you seem very convincing, but she doesn't lie."

Lucy blushed and hid behind her mother.

"Neither do I, Mrs Lawn," Boy replied.

"This is not getting us anywhere," the woman said, closing the door a little as her daughter began to cry. "I'll bring this matter to William and see how he takes care of it. In the meantime, Boy, if you do remember what happened and return Lucy's bike, an apology will suffice. We just want to sort this out. I know you're not a bad child, all children make mistakes."

"But I didn't…"

Mrs Lawn forced a smile.

"I'll be speaking to your mam and dad, Boy, and, as I said, if you remember anything…"

The purple front door closed firm. Violet looked at Boy's red face.

"What was that about?" she almost whispered.

"I don't know," he said, shaking his head. "I didn't take her bike, Violet."

"I know you didn't, Boy, but it's strange. I don't think Lucy would lie…"

"What's that supposed to mean?" Boy asked quickly.

"Nothing. I just meant that—"

"That Lucy doesn't lie, so I must be?"

"No, Boy, I didn't mean that at all."

"I'm sorry, Violet," her friend said, picking his bike back up. "It's not your fault. I'm just annoyed. Lucy seems so convinced, but how could she think I'd take her bike?"

"Don't worry. Do you want to come back to mine for dinner? We can try and work it out. Maybe she saw someone who looks like you, like Bobby Broderick or something."

"Bobby Broderick doesn't look like me," Boy said, shaking his head.

"I know, but he's your height and has the same colour hair and stuff. Maybe, at night, she might think…I don't know. Bobby is the type of person who might take Lucy's bike."

Bobby Broderick was one of the school bullies and if anyone would steal a bike, he would.

"We can't go around accusing people too, Violet!" Boy shook his head. "Anyway, I'd better go home. Mrs Lawn is going to tell Mam and Dad, and I want to speak to them before she does. The way Mam is at the moment, I'm not sure how she'll react."

"It'll be fine. You didn't do it, and Dad says the truth always comes out," Violet said, picking up her bike. "I'll see you tomorrow!"

"Yeah." Boy didn't look at her as he pushed down on his pedals and headed for Wickham Terrace.

Violet cycled back through Town, her head spinning.

Lucy Lawn really seemed to think Boy had stolen her bike. Violet knew Lucy from school, not really well as Lucy was a year ahead, but she'd always seemed nice, not like someone who would lie. Or, at least, that's what Violet thought before now. But Boy definitely wouldn't lie either, so what was going on?

Violet wanted to ask her dad about it that evening, but her mam said he was going straight to the Committee meeting after work.

"It'll be a long one this evening." Rose sighed as she set down a plate of bacon, potatoes and cabbage in front of her daughter. "Vincent Crooked is creating a fuss over the plants and Lucy Lawn's bike."

"You heard about that too?" Violet asked, unable to stomach much of her food.

"Yes, pet, it's all over Town today."

"Lucy is telling everyone Boy took the bike, but he didn't, Mam," Violet insisted, pushing her food round the plate.

"She's just upset, and needs someone to blame—"

"Well, she shouldn't blame Boy!" Violet interrupted.

"I know, pet, but don't worry. It'll all be sorted soon."

Violet sat playing with her food a while longer, before sliding away from the table and heading up to her room.

She waited on her window seat, watching the yard for her dad, but her mam was right – when night had long fallen, he still hadn't returned.

Violet climbed into bed in a muddle, and fell into an uneasy asleep.

CHAPTER 6

NEW FRIENDS

"How did the meeting go last night?"

It was the first thing Violet asked as she joined her parents at the kitchen table the next morning. "Did William find out anything about the eye plants?"

"No, unfortunately not." Her dad shook his head.

"And now this missing bike," Rose replied, scrambled egg falling from her fork. "It's a bit strange, really. Town is normally such a safe place. I can't imagine anyone—"

"Lucy said it was Boy, Dad," Violet cut across her mother. "We went to her house yesterday and she seemed really convinced."

"You didn't tell me you went to her house. Oh, Violet, don't go bothering the Lawns like that." Her mother tutted. "Better to leave this to your father and William."

"I heard you paid a visit, Violet," her dad commented. He sounded a little annoyed.

"How?" Violet asked.

"Lilly, Lucy's mother, came to the meeting last night," Eugene said, looking up. "She put in a complaint about Boy, and wants the Committee to look into the theft."

"But it wasn't Boy, Dad. He was as shocked as I was when he heard. That's why we went there, to ask her about it!"

"I know, Violet, but please just let it all blow over. Once the eye plants are back up and running properly again, things like this won't be in dispute. Anyway, the Committee have to handle it now, but I'm sure Boy has nothing to worry about."

"Are you going to check up on him?" Violet asked, her spoon stopping millimetres from her mouth.

"We have to, pet, but, as I said, I'm sure Boy has nothing to worry about."

"He doesn't," Violet said, swallowing the last spoonful of cereal, before packing her school lunch to go.

"Violet!" her mother called, as she raced out the door.

"Yeah?"

"I know how you get, pet. Leave the Lawns and the eye plants alone. The Committee can figure out what's going on here, they don't need your or Boy's help."

"But, Mam, they think it's Bo—"

"No buts."

Violet didn't respond as she closed the front door behind her. She knew better than to disagree with her mam and she wasn't able to lie to her either. After school she was sure she'd go investigating with Boy, so it was better to say nothing at all – technically that meant she wasn't lying to her parents.

❉   ❉   ❉

Boy was at his desk when Violet arrived in school.

"Any news on the eyes?" she asked, slipping in beside him.

"No." Boy shook his head. He seemed a little distant.

"Is everything okay?"

"It's nothing," he said, looking over his shoulder as a flying pencil hit his back.

"Who did that?" Violet whizzed around in her seat.

"Give me back my pencil, Archer," Conor Crooked laughed, from the back row of the class. "Stop stealing everything!"

"Stop it!" Violet said, glaring at him.

Conor Crooked, Vincent's son, was Bobby Broderick's best friend, and he was also a bully. Conor was an undercover bully, though – the type who all the adults loved because he smiled at them and said polite things.

Boy grabbed her arm. "Leave it, Violet, I'm able to take care of myself!"

"Yeah, but he's saying stuff about you..."

"Leave it, I'll handle Conor myself." Her friend half-smiled. "I was an orphan, remember?"

Violet turned back around, ignoring Conor's sniggers.

"Did you find out anything else about Lucy's bike?" she asked.

"No." Boy shook his head. "But Lucy's mam put in a complaint at the Committee meeting last night. Dad wasn't happy."

"With you?" Violet asked.

"No, with himself. He said if the eyes were working properly, none of this would be happening. Anyway, it'll be fine, Violet. I just don't like people saying things about me that aren't true."

"I know." Violet sighed as Mrs Moody walked into the classroom.

"Take out your maths books," the teacher instructed, straightening her blue pencil skirt.

Violet and Boy spent the rest of the day in relative silence. He didn't seem in the mood for joking, and Violet racked her brains for some sort of solution to Boy's problem.

"I know," she whispered, as the clock neared home time. "Why don't we go and knock on all the doors in

Market Yard? William only talked to a few people. Someone must have seen something."

"Someone already told Dad they saw me in Market Yard at the same time that the plants were taken. That'll only cause more trouble."

"Well, not if you didn't do it."

"*If…*? Thanks, Violet!"

"Argh, I didn't mean that – you know what I meant."

"It doesn't matter anyway." Boy shook his head. "I've to go straight home today."

"Why? It won't take long. You can go home after."

"No, I can't." He sounded definite and upset.

"Okay," Violet replied sheepishly. "I'll see you tomorrow then."

Boy didn't look at her. He threw his bag over his shoulder and raced from the room.

"He's probably off to steal another bike," Beatrice said, smirking as she passed Violet's desk.

Violet didn't respond. She was a little annoyed with Boy. All she was doing was trying to help him…

Stop, she scolded herself. He was upset. She would be too, if people were telling lies about her.

Maybe she could still help him. She could go to Market Yard alone. It might even be better if she went and asked the questions herself, without Boy there.

Violet packed up the rest of her stuff and buckled

closed her bag, ignoring her mother's voice in her head. Boy needed her help right now, and she was going to prove to everyone that he had nothing to do with Lucy's stolen bike.

She left the school and pedalled right onto Edward Street, heading for Archers' Avenue, then onto Rag Lane and Forgotten Road. She was just nearing Market Yard when she pulled on her brakes.

Boy was on the other side of the square, heading down Wickham Terrace.

He wasn't alone. He was walking with his bike, beside Conor Crooked.

Violet couldn't believe her eyes. What were those two doing together?

She cycled through Market Yard, avoiding a few near-collisions, and rounded the top of the terrace. Boy and Conor walked straight past number 135, Boy's home, heading for the footbridge on the edge of Town.

The pair were laughing, but Violet was sure Boy didn't even like Conor, especially after what had happened in class today.

Boy had said he was able to handle Conor on his own, so maybe that's what he was doing now…? Violet didn't like it, though. Something felt wrong. She was about to call Boy's name, when he stooped under the footbridge and pulled out another bike.

The bike was purple with a white saddle and tyres. Conor stood back and laughed, then high-fived Boy, before grabbing the handlebars and jumping onto it. Then the pair cycled over the bridge, to the other side of the river, and along the road towards the Ghost Estate.

Violet felt a pang of something, deep in her stomach. Why had Boy lied to her? He said he had to go home. And whose bike had he handed to Conor? A thought formed in her head, but she shook it off. It couldn't be Lucy's. It just couldn't be.

She decided to follow them. Maybe there was a good reason for this whole thing?

Maybe Conor knew something about the eye plants? Maybe he was helping Boy and Boy couldn't tell her, because...well, she didn't know why Boy couldn't tell her anything. They'd never kept secrets before – at least, none that she knew about.

Violet pedalled over the footbridge, which had been restored to its glory since Perfect fell and now spanned proudly over the roaring river. It comprised a mixture of delicate wire, woven steel rope and wooden floorboards, strung between elegant silver-and-blue painted iron pillars.

Nothing else had been renovated on this side of the river, though – at least, not yet. Nobody had gone near the Ghost Estate and its derelict half-built homes, or fixed a single pothole on the tarmac road that led to it.

Violet's dad said the Committee were still in talks about what to do with the estate. Not a single thing had been decided about it, though it had almost been a year. A year since Edward disappeared in the old graveyard nestled on the hill above the half-built homes of the Ghost Estate.

Violet was sure nobody wanted to go near the place because of the ghost stories, and the dreadful fear that hung over every person who set foot inside its entrance.

Taking a deep breath, Violet followed the tarmac road and stopped under the billboard of a happy family, which was next to the pillars into the Ghost Estate. The image was even more faded than the last time she'd seen it – the night Edward Archer disappeared. The dad's teeth were now black and his wife's skin a tinge of damp green. Their children had all but disappeared.

As quietly as possible, Violet laid her bike on the ground. She was just peering around the pillar to get a view into the estate when a large black bird flew down, landing on the stone-capped pillar beside her.

She shivered, remembering her latest dream.

The bird turned its head and stared at Violet, its dark bead-like eyes boring into her. Its shiny coat shimmered in the light as the bird displayed its wings, revealing glimmers of deep blue amongst its feathers. Then it opened its hard black beak and cawed, sending lonely echoes through the estate.

Violet's stomach churned. Maybe she shouldn't have come back here.

She tried to shoo the creature away, but it didn't move, standing just millimetres away, unblinking. The bird didn't seem afraid of her. She was just reaching towards it again when it opened its wings and soared into the sky.

Violet followed its flight path over the green in the Ghost Estate, which had once been lined with eye plants, then out above the building debris and half-built homes that rested at the edge of the unfinished road.

She couldn't see Boy or Conor anywhere.

The sky darkened. More clouds hung heavy in the air, blocking the low sun.

It was getting late, maybe she should go home?

Movement caught her eye. She froze to the spot, afraid she'd be seen. Two figures darted out from one of the half-homes and sprinted up the hill towards the graveyard.

Her heart pounded. What were they doing?

Boy and Conor laughed and jeered, as though having great fun. Something stung inside Violet as she watched them. The pair then disappeared over the horizon. She already didn't like the idea of going into the Ghost Estate alone, but she definitely wasn't going to the graveyard. The thought made her queasy.

Feeling a little hurt, Violet turned to go home. It didn't feel right, watching in secret.

Maybe there was some kind of a normal explanation for all this? She'd ask Boy at school tomorrow.

Violet picked up her bike and propelled her way back to Town. She was turning onto Forgotten Road when, just ahead, she saw Lucy Lawn at her front door.

"Hey," she called, pedalling faster.

The older girl pretended not to see her.

"Lucy!" she shouted, louder this time.

"Oh, Violet," Lucy said, looking around as Violet skidded to a halt. "I didn't see you there."

"I just wanted to ask you a question about your bike," Violet panted.

Lucy nodded, but didn't say a word.

"Erm, I just…I just wondered, what colour is it?"

She felt bad even asking, it almost felt as if she was betraying Boy.

"It's purple, with a white saddle and wheels. And I know you're his friend, but it was Boy I saw!" Lucy huffed before disappearing quickly inside her home.

Violet's stomach churned as she set off again. That was the exact colouring of the bike Boy had pulled from under the footbridge and given to Conor. Could Boy really have taken Lucy's bike? Maybe Conor made him do it…but how, and why? Violet couldn't imagine anyone making Boy do anything he didn't want to.

Her parents were sitting in the kitchen when she arrived home, her head in a muddle.

"What happened?" her mother asked, looking up from her seat. "Are you okay? You look upset."

"I'm fine, Mam!" Violet said, sitting down at the table. The truth was, she wasn't sure how she felt. She couldn't make sense of anything she'd seen, but she couldn't tell her parents. Not yet, not until she'd spoken to Boy.

Dinner was bacon, potatoes and cabbage again. Of all the foods in the world, why did someone invent cabbage? Anyway, she couldn't eat right now, not after everything. She pushed the food around her plate.

Her dad was reading the *Town Tribune*, a newspaper that had been set up in Town by Robert Blot after the Archer brothers' downfall. Violet's mam called Robert Blot "a self-appointed know-it-all".

"This article is laughable!" her dad said.

DISAPPEARING BEFORE OUR VERY EYES was written in huge black letters across the front page, over a picture of a half-empty bed of eye plants.

"What does the paper say, Dad?" Violet asked, curious and glad of the distraction.

"Blot's writing about the eye plants going missing. He says there is an epidemic of robberies in Town. He talks about young Lucy Lawn's bike too. I'd hardly call it an epidemic."

"What's an epidemic?"

"Oh, he's just trying to say that there have been loads of robberies, Violet, as though it's a huge problem in Town."

"Have there been more robberies?"

"No!" Violet's mother exclaimed. "Robert is always trying to make everything sound bigger than it is. I think he gets bored writing about everyday news. This recent spate of activity must be very exciting for him."

"Yes, but it's hardly responsible journalism, Rose. I'm not sure William will be happy with the tone of this piece."

"Why not, Dad?"

"Blot's picked up on the idea that Boy is involved. He seems to be suggesting that Boy took the plants *and* Lucy's bike. Utter nonsense."

"Oh." Violet almost choked on her potato.

"Boy, a thief?" Rose laughed. "It's ridiculous. And why would he want to steal those awful plants, from his own father? The idea of a thief in Town is rubbish anyway! I'm sure it's just a trick gone a little wrong. The culprits will come forward."

"I hope so." Violet sighed.

Her parents began to chat again, so she slipped quietly from the table and discreetly emptied her food in the bin.

"Is everything okay, Violet? You don't look well," Rose asked, standing up to feel her daughter's forehead.

"I'm fine," Violet lied, pushing away her mother's hand. "I just have lots of homework to do."

She disappeared out the door, followed by her parents' whispers. Violet was sure they were talking about her. She went upstairs to her room and collapsed onto the bed.

Boy, a thief and a liar? She felt sick at the thought.

CHAPTER 7

MORE LIES

Dark circles rimmed Violet's eyes the next morning as she made her way to school. She hadn't slept at all well, and was the first in the yard waiting for class to be called.

Boy was early too. He walked towards her, and Violet could feel her body tense. A rumble of thunder filled the skies and she looked up. The clouds were thick, the sun now barely visible behind them.

"If the wind changes, that face will stick," he teased, sitting on the bench beside her.

Now that Boy was here, Violet wasn't sure what to say to him. She'd been going over the previous afternoon's events all night in bed, and still hadn't figured a way to broach the subject.

"How's Conor?" she asked. The words were out before she'd realized.

"Who?" Boy asked, furrowing his brow.

"Conor Crooked!"

"How would I know how Conor is?"

"I saw you with him yesterday afternoon. I followed you two to the Ghost Estate."

Boy laughed. "Very funny, Violet. I almost fell for it!"

"Fell for what? I saw you. I went to Market Yard to question people about Lucy's bike. Remember? You wouldn't come with me because you had to go home." She emphasized the last few words. "I saw you going down Wickham Terrace with Conor, so I followed you. I was going to say hello until…"

She stopped.

"Until what?" Boy's neck was red again, his eyes narrow.

"Until…well…"

"Violet!"

"Until I saw you hand Lucy's bike to Conor."

Boy looked more serious this time. "Very funny, Violet, but I'm not in the mood for weird jokes."

"Boy!" Violet said, frustrated. "I'm not joking, I saw you. If this was you 'sorting Conor out', like you said in class yesterday, then just tell me. I want to know what's going on."

"But I did go straight home," Boy said, standing up. "What's going on with you?"

"With me? Stop it, Boy. I saw you with Conor! If something's up, I can help. Did Conor make you steal Lucy's bike?"

"Conor Crooked, make me steal something? What are you on about, Violet?"

"Boy, please," Violet said, getting upset. "I'm your best friend."

"Yeah, I thought you were too," Boy replied sharply. He stared blankly at her, his face a deep red.

The bell rang, and Mrs Moody appeared at the school door to call in the class. Violet stood up quickly, her eyes glassy. She avoided looking at Boy as she walked away.

"Morning, Violet, you get your homework done?" Beatrice called, skipping after her.

"Oh morning, Beatrice." Violet forced a smile.

Boy remained on the bench as everyone filed inside, chatting loudly.

"Good morning, class," Mrs Moody said, her face looking a little more wrinkled and cross than usual.

"Good morning, Mrs Moody," everyone replied.

Boy walked in and took his seat beside Violet. He didn't look at her.

"You're late, Boy!" Mrs Moody said.

"Sorry," he grunted at the floor.

Mrs Moody glared down at their desk and Violet looked away.

If everything was normal, Violet would have made a joke right now, but things felt awkward. She'd never not known what to say to Boy before.

"Class, I'm afraid I have some bad news to report. Conor Crooked didn't return home after school yesterday. As you can imagine, his parents are extremely worried."

Violet stiffened.

She glanced across at Boy. He was fidgeting with his sharpener, twisting a pencil against its blades. A small pile of wooden shavings had gathered on the desk.

"Does anyone know where he might have gone after school?" Mrs Moody asked, eyeing each and every student.

Violet flushed as the teacher's gaze swept by her. Should she say something? Boy should, but he was too busy rubbing parings off the desk onto the floor.

Why wouldn't he speak up?

"Anyone?" Mrs Moody asked. "I know some of you are Conor's friends. Come on, class. If anybody knows anything, please say it. You won't get into trouble. His parents just want to find him!"

Conor had friends, but Boy wasn't one of them. His friends were other bullies, like Bobby Broderick. Violet stabbed her eraser with the tip of her pencil and glanced over at Boy again.

Why wasn't he saying anything? Why was he putting her in this position? Boy was still her friend, though. She couldn't tell on him, could she?

Her dad always told her to be honest, and Violet wasn't being at all honest right now. She avoided Mrs Moody's glare as it swept by once more.

Tension mounted in the room.

Violet felt like she was sitting under a spotlight. Heat rose up her neck and into her cheeks. Surely Mrs Moody would know something was up?

The teacher kept her eyes on the class. Everyone was silent, except for the awkward sound of children shifting in their seats. Boy didn't look up, not once. His face was red now too.

"I'll let you all think about it for a while," the teacher announced, "and if anyone has anything to tell, you can come to me in private. You won't get into trouble."

Yeah right, they wouldn't get in trouble! Violet imagined Mrs Moody hanging her upside down from the Rag Tree.

She looked out the window into the schoolyard. A big black bird sat on the bench. She was sure its beady eyes were staring straight at her. Violet shivered. Black birds were everywhere these days.

"Do you know anything, Violet?" Beatrice whispered across the desks.

Violet shook her head; her first lie. At least she hadn't lied to Mrs Moody yet – she just hadn't said anything. Beatrice turned back around, ignoring Boy.

By lunch, suspicion seeped into all conversation, and the whole school was speculating over what had happened to Conor. Boy didn't talk to Violet as they left the classroom, and spent his break with Jack and some others.

Jack was an ex-orphan too, and one of Boy's best friends from No-Man's-Land. He'd found his family again when Perfect fell. Now, instead of the orphanage, he lived on George's Road, out towards the tea factory. He was a year or two ahead of them in school.

Violet sat alone on the bench, eating her lunch.

"I saw Conor leave school yesterday," Beatrice told the girls sat in a semicircle round her spot on the ground, "but I didn't see where he went."

Violet nudged nearer to the group.

"Was he on his own?" she asked, butting in.

"Yes, I think so, Violet…" Beatrice continued, "or no, maybe he wasn't. Actually, Bobby was with him."

Everyone gasped and looked over at Bobby, who'd just elbowed past a small blond boy.

Bobby Broderick was a good friend of Conor's. It would make much more sense if he were the one with Conor yesterday, but Violet was sure she hadn't seen him.

"Imagine if Bobby killed Conor!" a girl in the circle gasped.

"Bobby kicked my cat once!" another girl cried.

Everyone started talking very excitedly about all the bad things Bobby Broderick had ever done.

"Bobby wasn't with Conor," another girl said, interrupting the gossip. "He was at my house yesterday evening, with his mam. Our mams are best friends."

Then somebody else came up with another explosive claim, and the group continued their gossip.

Violet turned her back on them. Hanging around with Beatrice and her posse would be more painful than hanging around on her own.

She watched Boy. He was eating alone now too, while the others played football. Violet stood up and walked across the yard, making sure not to awkwardly catch his eye from a distance as she approached.

"Can I sit down?" she asked, standing above him.

"It's a free country," he mumbled, not looking up from his lunch.

They sat in silence for a minute, until Violet couldn't hold her tongue any longer.

"Why didn't you tell Mrs Moody about Conor? You won't get into trouble."

"Because there's nothing to tell?" Boy sounded puzzled.

"But I saw you!"

"I don't have a clue what you're talking about, Violet. I wasn't with Conor yesterday!"

"Well if it wasn't you, then who was it?"

"How am I meant to know? You're the one who said you saw me!"

"Did something happen? Is Conor hurt? Has it got something to do with Lucy's bike?"

"What are you on about, Violet? Have you gone crazy? If you don't believe me, that's fine, but don't go around accusing me of things I didn't do!" Boy sounded angry.

He stood up, and was about to walk away, when he stopped and looked back down at her.

She waited for him to say something, silently pleading him to tell her the truth.

Then he shook his head, smirked, and joined his friends playing football. Boy was acting as if nothing had happened. How could he just pretend like that?

Violet looked around, hoping nobody had seen them fight. She caught Beatrice's eye and the red-haired girl turned away quickly.

The bell rang, sounding the end of lunch. Violet stood up from the bench and filed back inside with the rest of the school.

She didn't talk to Boy for the rest of the day, not even when Mrs Moody mentioned Conor again, asking everyone to think long and hard about the last time they'd seen him.

At the end of school, Violet walked to her bike alone.

The clouds were thick and heavy, almost ready to burst. The low sun only peeked through in part, so the streets of Town were unusually dark as she pedalled towards home.

Posters of Conor Crooked now hung from every lamp post. He was wearing a smart black suit, and his normally wild hair was brushed cleanly to one side, with only a single curl visible, right in the middle of his forehead. He looked a picture of innocence and was almost unrecognizable without that bullish grin.

CHAPTER 8

WHISPERINGS

Violet rose the next morning a little worse for wear. She'd slept badly, again. Her fight with Boy played over in her head. Groggily, she put on her uniform and trudged down the stairs. Her dad was sitting at the kitchen table, also looking worn out.

"You okay, Dad?" Violet asked, as she opened the fridge in search of milk.

"Fine," he said, but he seemed distracted.

"The Committee has ruled there's no school today," Eugene continued, his voice a little softer. "We're searching for Conor, and need everybody's help."

"Okay," she said, as a sickly feeling filled her stomach. Violet wished it was all a dream, but Conor was still missing and, somehow, Boy was involved.

"It's an unfortunate situation but we have to stay strong." Her dad sighed. "We'll be searching the Ghost Estate and that side of the river today."

"The Ghost Estate… Really?" Violet replied, trying to keep an even tone. "Why are we searching out there?"

"Vincent Crooked got a tip-off, and a search party went out there last night. We found a few things in one of the old houses," her dad said, looking straight at her. "Now we need to expand the search."

"Oh." Violet felt a little breathless.

She looked away, and put some bread in the toaster.

"Are you okay, pet?" her dad asked.

"Uh…yeah, I'm grand," she stuttered.

"If you have anything you'd like to tell me, Violet, I'm all ears. Conor's parents are very worried, you know."

"I know, Dad, but I don't know anything, I swear," she said, staring at the toaster. Violet hated lying to her father.

Her toast popped, in a wisp of smoke, breaking the tension, and she busied herself buttering it. Then she dropped the cremated bread on a plate and headed back upstairs to her room, leaving her dad to grumble over the latest edition of the *Town Tribune*.

Violet ate looking out of her bedroom window, and watched the darkening clouds. Every day now, they seemed to threaten a storm. There were never storms in Town.

A black bird was there again, sitting on the branch of a tree across the gravel yard. She was sure it was staring at her. It couldn't be the same bird, could it?

Squinting, Violet tried to study the bird's markings for anything that might single it out from all the other big black birds that circled the skies.

"Violet, are you coming to look for Conor? We're almost ready," Rose shouted up from below.

"Coming!" she called, quickly getting changed.

Her mam and dad were waiting at the door, as Violet bounded down the stairs into the hallway.

"Do you think we should bring coats?" her mother fretted, looking out the window. "I've never seen clouds so angry over Town. What does the forecast say, Eugene?"

"Nothing about rain, Rose," Violet's dad answered. "It does look like we might have a storm coming, though."

"Grab your jackets, just in case. Here's me fussing about the weather, when the poor Crookeds must be out of their minds with worry. I couldn't imagine it," Rose said, wrapping an arm protectively round her daughter.

"Right, everyone ready?" Eugene half-smiled, opening the front door onto the grim, grey day. He had just closed the door and descended the steps to their gravel yard, when he looked up and muttered, "Well, isn't that strange?"

"What?" Rose asked.

"I know it sounds mad, but I get a funny feeling that bird is stalking us. I've seen it perched on that spot a few days in row. Haven't you noticed it?" he asked, pointing up across the yard.

The black bird was sitting in the same place it'd been in earlier, when Violet watched it from her window.

"What kind of a bird is it, Dad?" she asked, curious.

"I think it's a raven, Violet," he replied. "There's lots written about those particular birds – people seem to be fascinated with them. I've always thought they look a little threatening. Perhaps it's their size and their tiny black eyes. Popular folklore says they're the carrier of ill omens."

"'Ill omens'?" Her mother smirked. "Aren't you meant to be a man of science, Dr Brown?"

"I was simply answering Violet's question, Rose!"

"What's an omen, Dad?"

"It means a sign of the future," he replied.

"So a raven can tell the future, like magic?"

"No." Her dad shook his head. "The bird was just seen as a sign of bad luck to come. It's folklore though, pet, not fact. I never believe that nonsense."

The hairs on Violet's arms stood on end as they passed it, onto the tree-lined avenue towards Town.

Edward Street began to fill up as they walked past Archer and Brown. A big crowd had turned out to search for Conor. People looked serious and spoke in hushed tones. There was an unusual tension in the air.

As they turned onto Archers' Avenue, Violet's parents fell into conversation with Merrill Marx, the toymaker. He had helped them save Perfect, and was a Committee member and one of William Archer's best friends.

Merrill now had a toyshop towards the bottom of Edward Street, and it was everyone in school's favourite place in Town. Violet sometimes spent hours there with Boy, asking Merrill a million questions about anything she could think of. He never got cross or told them to go away, and seemed to enjoy their company while he carved his creations.

The toymaker was standing by the bed of eye plants just at the corner of Archers' Avenue and Edward Street. It looked like a big chunk of the plants had gone missing from the middle of this bed now too, and Townsfolk whispered to each other about it as they filtered by.

Violet slipped quietly past her parents and followed the crowd down Rag Lane into No-Man's-Land. The chatter distilled to a low hum.

She spotted William Archer through the crowd. He was walking beside a man who seemed to be angry.

"If your Committee was any good, William, we wouldn't be having this trouble," the man said, loudly enough for everyone around to hear. "There's been a spate of robberies, and now a child is missing! The Brain is clearly not working."

"We're doing our best, Peter, I assure you. We will catch whoever's doing this. Please don't be afraid, Town is not a dangerous place."

"Not a dangerous place? You are mad, Archer. A child has disappeared!"

"I know, and we will find Conor," William replied calmly. "I promise we're doing our best!"

"Your best is not good enough!" the man said, as he grabbed his child's hand and strode through the crowd.

William's face was glowing bright crimson. Everyone was looking at him, and some were whispering. Violet heard one woman say something like, "Boy's dad...should be ashamed of himself."

"Violet!" William called, spotting her across the sea of bodies.

People were looking at her now and, embarrassed, she pretended she didn't hear Boy's dad. Instead she sped forward, pushing past everyone, out onto Forgotten Road.

A pang of guilt hit her.

How could she have ignored William like that? Why was Violet embarrassed to be seen with him, after everything he'd done for her, her family and for Town?

But people were whispering about him. Lucy's bike

and some eye plants had been stolen, and, even worse, Conor was missing.

Maybe William deserved people to be just a little annoyed with him. After all, he and the Committee were in charge of Town, and his invention, the Brain, was meant to stop anything bad like this ever happening, but it clearly wasn't working.

CHAPTER 9

A MAGPIE FOR DETAIL

When Violet arrived the Ghost Estate was full of people searching for Conor Crooked.

Stepping through the pillars that marked the entrance, she allowed the weight of awful feelings to overtake her, just as they had done every time she'd previously been in the estate.

When it first happened, about a year ago, she'd been cocooned in mist, huddled under the old lamp post that overlooked the estate, at the top of the hill near the graveyard. She'd felt worse than she ever had in her life – her mind had been taken hostage by worry and fear. Boy had comforted her then, telling Violet it was just the effects of the estate. He'd explained how it happened to everyone who walked inside its entrance, and that people believed it was because the place was haunted.

After Perfect fell, Iris Archer had explained to Violet that Macula's dad, Oliver Lashes, had been in the middle of building the Ghost Estate when strange things began to happen. First, shovels went missing and tool belts disappeared, then windows were broken and the builders started to hear whispered voices, telling them to leave the place.

Iris said it was when Mr Lashes was found dead on the green in the middle of the estate one morning that all work stopped and the place was abandoned.

Rumours began to circulate that souls from the ancient graveyard on the hill above haunted the place. So, people stayed away. That is, until the Archer brothers used the Ghost Estate for their gruesome plot to control Perfect.

Violet's dad said ghosts didn't exist. He told her there was "no scientific evidence to support them", though she thought ghosts were weightless and didn't need support. He insisted they were only a figment of the imagination, and Violet had imagination in buckets. Eugene said it was people's belief in ghosts that brought on fear, and this fear conjured their awful feelings any time they entered the Ghost Estate. He believed people made themselves feel bad and it had nothing to do with ghosts at all.

Whatever it was, Violet felt terrible every time she passed inside the stone pillars. Her mind clouded over in worry, until she was almost paralysed.

Last year, she'd developed a tactic to combat the estate's awful effects. She told herself the feelings weren't real. They were only thoughts, bad thoughts that made her sad and scared, and she didn't need to believe her bad thoughts if she didn't want to.

Violet tried the same tactic now, as she stood looking round the derelict homes. It worked – the weight of the world played just round the fringes of her mind, and she was able to relax, if only a little.

She spotted Macula Archer across the green. She was pale and looked sick, just like Boy had said.

"Violet, where have you been? We were worried!" Her dad interrupted her thoughts as he strode towards her.

"Oh…um, sorry. I just went ahead with the crowd, Dad," Violet replied.

"Don't do things like that, pet," Rose said, looking around anxiously. "This place is not safe. Stay close!"

"I'm fine, Mam," Violet replied, a little sharply.

Rose jumped and cowered as if she was frightened. Her hands were shaking, and she nervously put them in her pockets.

"The thoughts aren't real, Mam," Violet insisted.

"They'll go when we leave the estate."

"I know, pet, I know. Your father told me I'd feel like this, but it really is awful. Poor Conor, the poor boy, his poor parents…"

"Rose," Eugene said, grabbing his wife's shoulders. "Relax, just breathe…"

Violet noticed a table in the middle of the green – the large grassy area that had once been home to the eye plants. Madeleine Nunn was sitting behind the table and people were hovering around it, inspecting something. Madeleine Nunn, as Committee head of public safety, was leading the investigation into Conor's disappearance.

Curious, Violet snuck away across the green, while her dad tried to convince her mam to calm down.

As she got closer, she could see Lucy's bike resting against the table.

"Ah, Violet," Madeleine Nunn said, standing to greet her. "How are you holding up? I know Conor is in your class."

"And in mine," someone else added quickly.

Violet looked to her right. Beatrice Prim's lower lip quivered as if she was upset. Beatrice didn't even like Conor, but she really liked attention.

"Oh, of course he is," Madeleine soothed, reaching across to comfort the red-haired girl. "We'll find him, I promise."

"I hope so," Beatrice sobbed.

The purple bike with the white saddle and wheels seemed to glare at Violet, making her stomach churn. It was definitely the same bike she'd seen Boy pull from under the footbridge and give to Conor, the evening he'd disappeared.

She felt sick and her head swam with worries. What if Boy really had done something to Conor?

She thought about the raven and the ill omens her dad said it brought. What if the future was full of terrible things?

"Are you okay, Violet?" Madeleine asked. "Do you recognize anything?"

The woman gestured to the table in front of her. On it were two see-through plastic bags. The first held a school bag that she recognized as Conor's and the second held a watch. Her stomach flipped once more.

"Ahem… No, no, I don't. I, um…I'm just in shock about Conor…"

"Are you sure you don't recognize anything, Violet?" Beatrice smirked, picking up the bag with the watch.

"Put that down, Beatrice!" Madeleine commanded. "Evidence must not be tampered with."

"Oh, I'm so sorry," Beatrice said, innocently dropping the plastic bag under Violet's nose.

The watch was Boy's. He'd gotten it as a birthday

present from Macula. Violet felt sick, and steadied herself against the table.

"Do you recognize the watch, Violet?" Beatrice probed. "There's something very familiar about it, don't you think? It's as if I've seen it before. They found it on the handlebars of Lucy's bike, and Conor's bag was beside them."

"Yes, you're right, Beatrice," Madeleine said. "Lucy has indeed confirmed that it is her bike. Some good news, in all of this mess."

"I've never seen the watch before, Beatrice, but I'm not good at noticing things," Violet lied.

"I notice everything. Mam says I'm like a magpie for anything that's shiny," Beatrice said, locking eyes with Violet.

Violet looked away. "Well, you're just great, Beatrice!" she snapped sarcastically.

"I'm going to find Boy and ask him if he recognizes the watch. I'm like Sherlock Holmes, Mam says. I've a nose for mystery, and I'm always right!" Beatrice continued. "It's not nice to lie, Violet!"

Why couldn't Beatrice just leave things alone? She was forever trying to get people into trouble – like it was her job, or something. But maybe this time she was right. It was Boy's watch, after all; it proved he was involved somehow. Maybe somebody needed to say something, since Violet couldn't bring herself to.

Violet hated lying. Her dad said it was one of the worst things a person could do, and that she'd never get in trouble if she told the truth, no matter how bad. But she couldn't tell on Boy – this was his truth, and he needed to own up to it himself.

"Everything okay, girls?" Madeleine interrupted, glancing at the pair.

"Oh yes, Mrs Nunn," Beatrice replied politely.

Then she turned on her heels, flicked her red mane and strode back across the green.

"How about you, Violet?" Madeleine enquired. "You're looking at that watch a lot. Do you recognize it?"

Violet's hands trembled. Quickly, she shoved them into her pockets and shook her head.

"No," she mumbled, then turned and walked away.

Violet had to find Boy before Beatrice did. If she could persuade him to own up to everything, he might not get in as much trouble. He needed to tell the truth – whatever that was.

"Violet," her dad panted, reaching her, Rose just behind him. "Stop running away like that, without telling us! Are you okay? You're white as a ghost, pet."

"I'm fine," she said dismissively.

"What was that about with Madeleine?"

"Nothing!"

"You're shaking!" her mother said, wide-eyed.

"Stop it, Mam!" Violet snapped, edging away. "It's just this place!"

What she'd said was partially true. Her head was racing with all sorts of terrible thoughts.

She scanned the estate, looking for Boy. There was a huge crowd on the far side of the green, searching houses and back gardens. He didn't appear to be among them.

She turned around and surveyed the houses on the other side, and spotted him. He was standing on the sparse grass of a house a little way away, staring at the weather-worn door.

Violet took a deep breath and tried to stay calm. It was strange, feeling nervous about talking to her friend – her best friend ever. At least, that's what she'd thought he was, only a few days before.

But just as she was about to walk towards him, Boy disappeared inside the house.

She followed, jumping the low wall into the garden, then hesitated before pushing open the door.

The house was quiet. The only sound was the thump of her heart.

She could hear Rose calling her, outside.

Violet looked round the concrete-grey ground floor, but there was no sign of Boy. A sudden chill engulfed her as she checked up the dark stairwell, its neglected wooden steps patterned by watermarks. She could see the plastic sheeting billow in the window cavity upstairs.

A memory wrapped around her.

She'd climbed inside the top window of a house just like this one before. It was the day she'd rescued Boy from George Archer, her first time in the Ghost Estate. She remembered her heart pounding as she crawled across the landing and found him tied up with a leash. She remembered the Watcher, how he'd mounted the stairs to check on Boy and how, in a panic, Violet pushed open a door on the landing and was saved by Macula.

Could this be the same house?

Forgetting her mission to find Boy, Violet climbed the stairs. Everything felt a little too familiar. She reached the landing, and without thinking, turned right, followed her feet to the door and turned the handle. The door brushed open over the deep-red carpet now greyed by dust. She stepped inside.

The familiar mahogany writing desk was on the far side of the room in front of her, with Macula's chair empty beside it. Everything was exactly how she remembered it.

Violet walked across to the desk. A single piece of dusty paper rested on its wooden surface. One of Macula's letters – there'd been hundreds of them before.

Her beautiful handwriting traced elegantly across the mottled cream paper.

Dear Boys,

I sat and thought of you today. There wasn't a moment in twenty-four hours where you were not all of my thoughts. My fragile mind holds on to your sounds, your smell. You are my world, and though my wings are clipped, you both allow me to fly...

The letter seemed so sad. It was written from another time, a time when Macula was on her own, her husband and son lost.

At first, Violet had thought Macula cowardly. She'd given up her only child, Boy, to the orphanage and surrendered herself to the Archer brothers, becoming their prisoner for twelve years. Though the room wasn't locked, she never left it.

Violet asked her mam once if she would ever do something like that.

"For you, I would," she'd answered. Rose said it took huge courage to give up a child in order to protect them. She said a mother's love was so strong that keeping Boy would have been a much easier, but selfish, option.

"What Macula did was selfless," her mother told her.

"She did it to protect her son from the Archer brothers."

Until that point, Violet had never thought about it like that before.

"Being nosy, again?"

She jumped, and Macula's letter slipped from her grasp.

"Boy!" she gasped.

Drawn into her memories, she'd forgotten she was meant to be looking for him.

"You scared the life out of me!"

Boy was sitting on the carpet, his back against the wardrobe – the one Violet had hidden inside when the Watcher came knocking last year.

"Why didn't you say anything when I walked in?" she asked breathlessly.

"Because I didn't want to talk to you. I thought you might leave without noticing me, but you were taking ages!"

"Oh…okay. Anyway, I wasn't being nosy," she said, looking for something to say.

"What would you call it, then?"

"I was just…I was just…"

"Just being nosy!" Boy was blunt.

"Fine," Violet snapped. "Then you were just being creepy, not telling me you were there. Still sneaking around, hoping I won't see you!"

"What's that supposed to mean?"

"Your watch was on the handlebars of Lucy's bike. They found it by Conor's school bag, in the estate. Madeleine has it on the table outside and Beatrice is going to tell on you."

"Tell on me?" Boy's eyes were piercing. "I had nothing to do with it! I lost my watch a few days ago."

"So you're saying someone put it there on purpose?"

"I don't know, Violet, you seem to be the one with all the answers."

"But I saw you with Conor! Please, you have to own up to it. It's the only way to avoid getting into more trouble. Dad says the truth—"

"I don't care what your dad says!"

Boy looked away and ran his fingers roughly over the red carpet, making lines in the dust.

"You can tell me," she encouraged him, trying to hide the upset in her voice, "no matter what happened. I know you wouldn't do anything bad on purpose."

"On purpose? I've done nothing, Violet! Why won't you believe me? I went straight home after school that day."

"You didn't. I followed you both down the street to the footbridge. I saw you hand Conor the bike. I'm not making it up! It was you, the same as you're here now, lying to my face. You're meant to be my best friend," she said, louder than intended.

"And you're meant to be mine."

The pair stayed silent for a bit, leaving a sharp tension in the air, then Boy stood up and walked out into the hall.

Violet wanted to say something, anything, but she couldn't. Why wouldn't he just tell her the truth? Boy had to be in some sort of trouble.

Her body shook as he stomped down the stairs and banged the front door, rattling the half-finished house.

Violet cried.

Then she waited for her eyes to dry before rejoining her parents and the search outside. They checked out every inch of the Ghost Estate, but by late evening there was still no sign of Conor or any clue as to what might have happened to him.

Her dad stayed behind to keep looking, as Violet and her mam trudged out of the estate towards home. Passing back through the pillars, relief flooded her body and most of her worries floated away on the evening breeze.

She still felt sick, though – sick at the thought of losing her best friend.

CHAPTER 10

THE CHILD SNATCHER

It had started to drizzle, the next morning. The clouds that gathered over Town were finally releasing some of their moisture, as Violet pedalled to school feeling very anxious. The pit in her stomach had grown overnight. Beatrice must have told on Boy by now.

She was early and waited at the gate, hoping to catch a glimpse of either one of them, to find out what had happened. By the time the bell rang, neither Boy nor Beatrice had arrived. It wasn't unusual for Boy, but Beatrice was never late.

The pit grew even bigger – there had to be something up.

"Violet Brown, I'm speaking to you!" Mrs Moody

called across the classroom as Violet scribbled some ideas in her notebook.

Snapped out of her terrible theories, she looked up.

"Have you spoken to Boy Archer today? Will he be joining us?"

"Ahem, I don't know, Mrs Moody. I haven't seen him. Maybe he's sick?" Violet shrugged, trying to act normal.

"My dad says he's sick in the head," somebody sniggered behind her.

"And has anyone seen Beatrice this morning?" their teacher asked, now looking concerned.

Everyone remained silent and a ripple of fear swam through the room. Violet could hear it in the whispers of those around her.

No one was allowed outside at lunchtime. Mrs Moody had said it was because of a burst pipe, but Violet didn't see any water in the yard as she looked out the window. Teachers whispered secretly to each other as they popped in and out of the classroom. Unlike Beatrice, Violet didn't need a Sherlock Holmes nose to figure out something was up.

When the bell rang to signal the end of the day, Violet raced from the classroom. She needed to get home, quickly, to see if her parents had heard anything.

Throngs of parents crowded round the school gates, grabbing their kids in a panic. They huddled in groups, whispering above their children's heads, just like the teachers. Why did adults always seem to think that kids had no ears? Violet pushed her way past them.

There was a strange tension in the air – people seemed unusually angry. Violet felt it too as she elbowed through the crowd and climbed onto her bike.

Town seemed strangely empty as she cycled home.

"Mind where you're going, Violet!" Mr Hatchet said, a little impatiently. The butcher was perched halfway up a ladder. Violet swerved quickly to avoid a collision.

Mr Hatchet was about to attach a poster of Beatrice Prim to the lamp post, above a poster of Conor Crooked. Beatrice was smiling, a picture of perfection.

"You shouldn't be out on your own, Violet," the butcher huffed. "Did Eugene not pick you up? He's a head like a sieve, that man! If you wait a minute, I'll just hang this and drop you home."

"Oh no, I'm…I'm fine cycling," Violet stammered, still staring at the poster. "Why are you putting a picture of Beatrice up there?"

"Didn't you hear? I thought all of Town knew by now," Mr Hatchet replied. "She's disappeared, just like Conor Crooked. An awful thing. It's strange times for this Town, strange times indeed!"

Violet's mind was spinning. "What do you mean? Beatrice is missing?"

"She didn't come home yesterday after the search. It's an awful business, terrible really."

Beatrice didn't come home? She was going to talk to Boy, she'd told Violet that in the Ghost Estate. She'd been going to confront him about the watch, and now she was missing too. He couldn't have... He wouldn't have done anything?

Violet felt faint, and reached out to steady herself against the lamp post.

"I...I better go, Mr Hatchet," she mumbled, pushing down heavily on her pedals. "Mam will be worried."

"Oh no, wait there, Violet. I can't let you go off alone!"

"I'm fine, I promise," she called over her shoulder.

The darkening sky rumbled as the rain fell lightly around the streets.

Violet's heart thumped. Her legs took on a life of their own and she whizzed down Splendid Road. Her mind raced and time blurred.

Just as she turned the corner onto her driveway, a hulking figure stepped out onto the gravel in front of her, blocking the path. She snapped on her brakes and skidded to a halt.

The man was large, slightly stooped and shabbily dressed. He was half-hidden by the shadow of the trees that lined the driveway and Violet couldn't see his face properly.

He grunted and moved towards her, limping as he dragged one leg behind him. Violet froze, petrified. The man was just upon her when she sprung back to life.

He grabbed her sleeve. She squirmed and tried to struggle free as a horrible stench engulfed her. She opened her mouth to scream, but nothing came out. His arm was around her chest, locking Violet tight against him. In the frenzy, she caught sight of his face.

He seemed barely human. His skin looked like it had melted in places, revealing raw bone beneath. His eyes were too big and protruded from his face. They were rimmed by flaps of thin skin, like petals, that closed when he blinked. One eye drooped down from its socket and, with his free hand, the monster picked up the eyeball and shoved it back in place. His eyes looked exactly like eye plants, the very ones that grew in the beds around Town!

Violet wriggled harder to free herself.

The monstrous man held tight. She kicked out as hard as she could. Something cracked and he collapsed to one side. Violet bit into his arm to loosen his grip. The skin was wet and soggy, coming away in her teeth. She gagged and spat it out. Her stomach churned, the smell engulfed her, and the world began to spin.

The edges of her vision faded.

Then Boy was there, standing in the entrance of her driveway. He was shouting something, but she couldn't make it out. His voice sounded far away, as though Violet were underwater. He was running towards them now, yelling at the disgusting man to stop. Boy would save her, she knew it. She knew he was her friend.

Then everything went black.

CHAPTER 11

ILL OMENS

Violet's head hurt. She opened her eyes and dark dots danced through her vision. Her sight was fuzzy. Slowly, a flowery lampshade hanging above her head came into focus.

She was in bed, in her room. She looked under the covers and discovered she was wearing her pyjamas. What had happened? Had it all been a dream?

She tried to sit up, but everything spun and her stomach was queasy. She lay back down for a few moments and steadied herself, before gingerly getting out of bed.

A thin line of light was cast across her carpet from between her almost-closed curtains. She made her way to the window and peered outside. The clouds were dark and she could just see a corner of the sun poking out from behind them.

What time was it?

As she walked onto the landing, muffled sounds of a radio reached up from the bottom of the stairs. She held tight to the banisters and slowly made her way down.

"Violet!" her mam said, rushing over as she entered the kitchen. "You're awake. You shouldn't be up!"

Rose pulled out a chair for Violet to sit on.

"How're you feeling, pet?"

"Um, I don't know," Violet replied. "What time is it?"

"Saturday lunchtime, pet. You've been out for the count all night and half the day. You had us worried sick!"

"What happened?" she asked.

"I was going to ask you the same thing. You didn't come home after school and, what with these kidnappings... Well, I don't like to think about what was going through my head, pet. I could have killed your father for not collecting you. He promised he would."

"But how did I get home?" Violet interrupted.

"Well, I went looking for you, when you didn't arrive back after school. I found you unconscious at the bottom of our driveway." Her mother felt Violet's forehead. "Did you faint, pet? Were you feeling unwell? Do you remember anything?"

Violet filtered through the fog of her mind. She remembered something. The hair on her arms rose.

"I was attacked, Mam, by a…by a…monster!"

"What?" Rose turned ghostly white, and she grabbed the back of a kitchen chair.

"But Boy…Boy saved me. Where is he? Is he here?"

Her mam sat down.

"Let's not talk about Boy now," Rose said. Her voice had changed. "Just tell me what happened. Just as you remember it, Violet."

"Is Boy okay? Why can't we talk about him? The man must have kidnapped Beatrice and Conor, and he was trying to kidnap me too, except Boy stopped him. Please tell me he's okay, Mam?"

"What man?" Rose asked, avoiding Violet's questions.

"The monster. He was a man, but not a proper one… It's hard to explain. His skin was falling off and I could see some of his bones, and his eyes were the eye plants!"

Rose felt her daughter's forehead again.

"Are you sure you're feeling okay? The doctor said you might be a little delirious when you woke. He said you probably hit your head in the fall."

"I'm fine! Where's Boy? You're not telling me something," Violet insisted.

Rose released her daughter's arm and stood up. She turned her back and walked to the far end of the kitchen.

"What is it, Mam? What's happened?"

"William got the Brain working again, and some of the footage recorded his own son stealing the eyes from one of the beds," Rose almost whispered. "There are rumours he's involved in Conor and Beatrice's kidnappings too. Town is not happy, Violet. People are growing very angry."

"What do you mean?"

"Robert Blot reported in the *Tribune* that it was Boy's watch found on the bike in the Ghost Estate, right beside Conor Crooked's school bag. Lucy Lawn said the bike is hers and that she saw Boy steal it. Beatrice Prim told her parents that she believed Boy was involved in the kidnappings, and there are witnesses who saw Beatrice with Boy in Town, just before she vanished too. It's awful, Violet. I wouldn't believe it, only the facts seem to line up. Madeleine went to William's house to question Boy, but he's disappeared. She suspects he's run away."

"But Boy saved me, Mam. I'm sure of it. We need to find him."

"We'll talk about it when your father gets home from Town," Rose replied, her tone a little sharp.

"But, Mam…"

"No buts, now, Violet. You're not well. We'll talk about it at dinner, when your dad gets home. Now go back to bed and I'll bring you up some lemon and honey."

"But I'm not sick!"

Her mother raised an eyebrow, and Violet stepped back out of the kitchen. What was the use in talking to grown-ups when they never listened?

She walked up to her room and sat on the window seat – it was her thinking spot.

What was going on? She'd seen Boy with Conor and then he'd disappeared, and someone had seen Beatrice with Boy and then she'd vanished... But Violet had been attacked by the monster, and Boy had saved her. She was sure she hadn't made that up.

All sorts of ideas swam round her mind, her imagination firing at full whack.

What if the monster was following Boy, for some reason, and attacking anyone he talked to? Or maybe the monster was making him do bad things? Like maybe the monster threatened to eat all of Boy's family, if he didn't help him catch children...but then why would Boy save Violet? Anyway, why would the monster want children? And the biggest question of all: who, or what, was the monster?

There was one thing Violet knew for certain: Boy was missing and in trouble. Perhaps he'd been taken, like Conor and Beatrice. But nobody was going to hang a poster of him in Town – at least not now that everyone thought he was behind the kidnappings.

As Violet invented scenarios, a movement caught her eye in a tree opposite. A black raven, perched on the same high branch directly across the yard, stared straight at her.

CHAPTER 12

THE NIGHT VISITOR

Night was approaching as Violet watched her dad arriving home. He walked across the gravel yard and bounded up the steps to the house. His feet pounded the hallway, then the stairs, until finally her door flew open.

"Violet," he said, striding across the room to wrap his daughter in his arms. "We were so worried!"

"It was Boy, Dad, he saved me!" she mumbled, squished against his shoulder.

"We can talk about that later. I'm sorry I couldn't come home until now, things are a little mad in Town, what with all these goings-on."

He squeezed her even tighter, as though afraid to let her go.

"No, I want to talk about it now. Boy saved me, Dad!"

Eugene pulled back to look at her.

"You know he's been seen, by the Brain, stealing the eye plants?"

"Are you sure?"

"Yes, Violet," her dad snapped, before catching himself. "I'm sorry, pet, it's been a tense few days. Anyway, I didn't believe it myself, until I saw the evidence. Merrill was with William when they watched the footage this morning. I've seen it now too. It was definitely Boy. No one has been able to track William down since – he's gone missing too; I expect he's looking for his son. It's a horrible business."

"But why would Boy steal the eyes? It doesn't make sense."

"I don't know, pet."

"A man attacked me in the driveway. He was a monster, Dad. His skin was falling off and his eyes were the eye plants! I promise I didn't imagine it. Boy saved me from him!"

Eugene Brown sat down on the edge of the bed. A long, low sigh escaped his lips. He looked tired and troubled. Violet hadn't seen him like this since the days of Perfect.

"What if it's the monster-man doing all these bad things?" she continued, trying to convince him. "Maybe

Boy was just playing with Conor when I saw them, and then after Boy left, Conor met the monster and was kidnapped by him. Maybe it's just a coincid...cociden... whatever you call it, Dad!"

"Coincidence, Violet. But what do you mean, you saw Boy playing with Conor? You never told me that before."

Her dad sounded upset. Violet looked away, red-faced. She hadn't meant to tell him like that, or even tell him at all.

"I couldn't tell you, at least not until Boy owned up to it. I saw him give Lucy's bike to Conor, and then I followed them to the Ghost Estate. I didn't see anything after that, but the next day Conor was missing."

"Violet, you shouldn't keep secrets like that! What have I told you about telling the truth?" he said angrily.

Her cheeks burned red.

"And are you sure it was Boy you saw?" her father continued.

Violet nodded, reluctantly.

"But he didn't kidnap anyone, Dad, I'm sure now. I think it was that monster-man – he tried to kidnap me, but Boy stopped him. Boy saved me, but now he's been taken and no one will search for him because everyone thinks he did it!"

"Slow down, Violet." Her dad was losing patience. "Who is this monster-man, again? What do you mean?"

She steadied herself before speaking. The story sounded crazy.

"He, um…he attacked me… His skin was peeling off, kind of like he was melting or something. He smelled awful, and his eyes were the eye plants, the petals closed when he blinked…"

"Violet, your mind is trying to make sense of it all, right now. You're trying to protect your friend. I understand that."

"No, I'm not imagining it, Dad. I thought it was Boy for ages too, but now I'm not so sure. Maybe the monster is attacking people and made Boy steal the eye plants."

Violet started pacing the room – she could think easier on her feet.

"Maybe the monster needed more eyes, in case he lost one, or something. One of his was falling out when he attacked me. I saw him push it back in! Think about it, Dad, why would Boy need to steal the eyes? William has loads of them."

"Town is growing uneasy, Violet. People are fearful. They need answers to what's going on, and, at the moment, all fingers seem to be pointing at Boy. Sleep on it tonight, see if you remember anything else. I'll speak to William when he reappears," Eugene said, standing up and giving her a hug. "We'll get to the bottom of it all, I'm sure."

"Thanks," she replied, trying to smile, though she

didn't feel very cheerful. Maybe she had managed to convince her dad, a little.

Violet crawled into bed and watched him leave. Then she climbed straight back out and went over to her window seat. She needed to think more.

The sky had darkened further. A loud clap of thunder filled the air, and the clouds, which had been drizzling for a while now, exploded. Rain streamed down Violet's window. She had never seen anything like it in Town before.

She was looking out, mesmerized by the downpour, when the bulb in her room flickered. A flash of lightning lit up the yard below, and she saw him, watching her.

Violet's breath caught, as Boy beckoned her outside.

He was okay? The monster hadn't caught him? What was he doing here? All of Town was probably looking for Boy right now.

Violet stood up and faltered. She couldn't go downstairs to get outside, her parents would surely hear her. So, on the next clap of thunder, she opened the window and climbed out.

Rain bulleted off the rooftop. The tiles were running wet, making it really easy to slip. Violet felt a sudden surge of fear as she looked down the sloping roof to the yard far below. The branch of a tree reached in over the house. She edged her way across and grabbed it, pulling herself along its length towards the trunk. A niggling worry hung round the back of her mind that she couldn't quite grasp.

Slowly, Violet worked her way down branch by branch to the garden.

"Boy," she whispered, reaching the soggy ground. "You're safe!"

"What did you expect?" he snapped.

"I just thought maybe the monster caught you. How did you get away?"

Lightning brightened the sky.

"Why would I need to get away?" he answered, as thunder boomed overhead.

A sudden anger grabbed Violet.

"To escape the monster… The one you saved me from!" she snapped back.

"I didn't save you, Violet! You're nothing to me. I was helping that 'monster' to catch you." He laughed. "I told the Child Snatcher to hold you tight, to squeeze your insides until your lungs burst."

Feeling uneasy and confused, she stepped back.

"Stop messing, Boy, it's freezing out here." Violet's teeth chattered as the cold engulfed her. Her pyjamas were now soaking wet.

"I'm not messing! You're too ignorant to understand, just like the rest of Town."

"What do you mean? You're making no sense! What's

going on? All of Town is looking for you. Everyone thinks you kidnapped Conor and Beatrice."

"Took them a while to figure that out. Witless fools!"

"What are you saying? Did you do it? Did you kidnap the others?"

"What do you think?" He stepped closer and glared at her.

Her heart pounded, she wanted to move away but didn't step back.

"I...I don't think you did it... I know you, Boy, you wouldn't do anything like that. The monster must be making you."

An intense fear gripped her body. Her breath was short and sharp as her chest tightened.

"That 'monster' works for me, Violet. He's another of my father's inventions. We christened him the Child Snatcher. You clearly don't know me as well as you think you do."

"What...?" Violet was shaking as she stepped back. "No, it's not true. You didn't kidnap anyone. That monster is not yours. Please say you're joking..."

"That'd be a fib, Violet, and I know how you hate liars. I did kidnap Conor and Beatrice, and I'll kidnap more wretched children."

Boy pushed Violet, sending her tumbling backwards onto the muddy patch of lawn.

"I am not your friend. I never was, and never will be. William and I are taking over Town. We will succeed where my uncles failed."

"You're scaring me," Violet stuttered, as Boy loomed above her.

"Good," he stated, rubbing the driving rain from his face.

Boy grabbed her pyjama top and yanked her up so they were face-to-face, close enough for Violet to see the anger in his jet-black eyes.

He'd never acted like this before.

"Watch yourself, or your poster will be hanging on lamp posts with Beatrice's and Conor's," he whispered.

Something rustled in the trees and Boy's eyes darted towards the sound. He was so close to Violet that she noticed a strange, thin streak of ice blue, almost white, edging his left iris. When he looked back, it had disappeared.

Another clap of thunder filled the night. Boy laughed, then pushed her back down onto the lawn before running off through the trees.

Violet didn't try to chase him. Her mind swam as she pulled herself from the muddy lawn and stumbled towards the house, calling for help.

Everything felt like a blur as she watched her parents rush down the steps in the driving rain and grab her tightly.

"Boy…Boy said…said he did it. He kidnapped the others. I don't…understand. I don't…" she spluttered.

Eugene led her inside and sat Violet down at the kitchen table. Rose raced round the house, grabbing piles of towels and dressing gowns, as her dad held her tight.

"Rose, just sit down!" he barked angrily, as her mam rushed back into the room. "This is not a time for panic."

"Don't speak to me like that, Eugene," her mother replied sternly. "I will take care of my daughter as I see fit!"

"Your daughter? She's my daughter too!"

"Stop it!" Violet chattered angrily. She'd never heard her parents argue like this before.

As they both calmed down, she told them everything. Her mam nodded nervously, but her father looked enraged.

Violet wished she'd said something earlier. This was all her fault. She had seen Boy with Conor and hadn't told anyone.

That night, she lay awake petrified as she listened to her parents fighting. They were saying awful things about each other, things Violet didn't want to hear. She covered her ears with her pillow.

Though not cold, she had an uncontrollable shiver. Her heart thumped loudly and her mind raced so fast she couldn't grab her thoughts. She felt like she did the first time in the Ghost Estate, multiplied a thousand times.

When she closed her eyes to sleep, she saw Boy, standing above her, his jet-black iris edged in ice blue, like the sliver of a winter's moon.

CHAPTER 13

A LITTLE HELPER

Violet climbed out of bed and got dressed, glad it was Sunday. Her head had stopped spinning, but she definitely wouldn't be able to face school. She couldn't face her parents either, so she slipped past the kitchen, where they were sat in stony silence, and out of the house before either of them noticed.

It was still raining outside, and she pulled the hood of her jacket over her head.

She was heading up Splendid Road and had just crossed the street when, from the side of her eye, she spotted a new poster on the lamp post nearby.

Boy's image sat under the words WANTED in red capital letters. His face was contorted and his usual smile was replaced by a grimace. His dark eyes stared out at her menacingly.

Violet recognized the picture. It was taken in school a few months before. Mrs Moody wanted a class photo but, as a joke, instead of smiling everyone had pulled scary faces. Part of Violet felt it wasn't fair to use this photo. Her friend didn't normally look scary like that, but now part of her wondered if maybe this was the real Boy.

She felt so angry that her whole body shook. How could Boy do any of those things he said he did? Did it mean everything he'd ever told her was a lie?

"The picture doesn't look like Boy, does it?" a tiny voice whispered.

"Who said that?" she snapped, turning around.

Anna Nunn, Madeleine's young daughter was standing just behind Violet.

"It's me," Anna replied, her tone also a little sharp.

"Oh, I'm sorry, Anna," Violet said sheepishly. "What are you doing out alone?"

"I'm old enough to take care of myself, and I'm not going home. You can't make me!" The seven year old stamped her foot in a tiny protest.

"But where's your mam? She'll be worried!"

"No, she won't. She doesn't notice me any more." Anna sounded angry. "She's too busy looking for the missing kids. She thinks Boy is napping them and she won't listen to me. But I know it's not him!"

"It's called kidnapping, Anna," Violet said impatiently. Her anger rose again. Violet wasn't cross with Anna, but as the little girl stood before her, all she felt was overwhelming fury. She struggled to control it.

"You don't have to get cross with me, Violet," Anna fumed, her face red. "I was only saying that Boy didn't nap any kids."

"*Kidnap*, Anna, the word is kidnap. Anyway, how do you know he didn't?"

"Because he told me he didn't KIDNAP anyone," Anna replied sharply.

"Well, he told me he did!" Violet snapped, allowing another swell of anger to sweep through her.

She closed her eyes and took a few deep breaths, trying to calm down. When she opened them again, the little girl was still standing in front of her.

"When were you talking to Boy?" Violet asked, her tone a little more even.

"I talked to him just now. I had a fight with Mam and I was really sad and angry, and I was thinking all bad things – like, how could Mam forget about me when she was in Perfect and I was in No-Man's-Land, but not forget about my sister? So we had a big fight, and I ran away to our secret place and talked to Boy."

"You and Boy have a secret place?"

Anna nodded.

"And Boy told you *this morning* that he didn't kidnap Conor or Beatrice?" Violet probed, feeling very confused.

The little girl nodded again.

The night before, Boy had stood in Violet's garden, said he had taken both Conor and Beatrice, and that he'd kidnap more children. This morning, he'd apparently told Anna he didn't do anything. Something very weird was going on.

"Is Boy there now, Anna, in your secret place?"

Anna looked at the ground and scuffed her foot against a stone. Then, slowly, she nodded.

"Can you take me there?" Violet desperately needed to speak to Boy.

Anna shook her head. "I can't. It's a secret."

"But Boy's in trouble. I want to help him!"

The little girl stayed silent.

"Please, Anna," Violet said, trying not to lose her cool again.

"Do you promise you won't tell on him, Violet?" she asked, a few moments later.

"I promise. I just want to help him...if I can."

Anna's eyes were now rimmed with tears. "'Cause he didn't do any of those bad things people are saying, and I think he's scared."

"I believe you, Anna."

"But you have to believe *him*. Promise!"

Violet was angry again. She grabbed the bottom of her jacket and pulled it tight, trying to stop herself from snapping.

"I can't promise. I want to believe him, but he told me something very different, just last night. Boy scared me, Anna. I still feel scared. But I can promise that I want to help him, if I can."

"Okay," the little girl whispered. "I know you're his friend."

Without another word, Anna darted across Splendid Road and up Edward Street. Violet raced after her, past the Town Hall, by the tea shop and into Archers' Avenue, before ducking into Rag Lane.

People tutted as the two girls ran through the wet streets of Town. No one seemed friendly this morning.

Anna continued along Forgotten Road until she reached the door of the old orphanage, which, as an ex-orphan, used to be her home. She held up a hand, signalling Violet to stop a distance back.

The little girl checked the coast was clear, then pulled a key from her yellow coat pocket and stood up on her tippy toes. After a little struggle with the lock, she pushed the door open and vanished inside.

Unsure whether to follow, Violet waited until a small hand poked out between the double doors and waved her forward. Inside, Anna looked tiny in the cavernous entrance hall of the orphanage museum.

"It's closed today," the little girl said, "but we still have to be quiet – sometimes the ladies who work in the museum come in to clean on a Sunday."

"Do you come here a lot?" Violet whispered.

"Shush!" Anna scolded, shooting her finger to her lips.

A little red-faced, Violet followed behind, down the hall to the side of the ornate wooden staircase.

A small door was cut into the wall of the stairs, under the steps, barely noticeable. Anna knocked on the wood.

"Boy, it's me. Open up," she whispered.

Nothing stirred. Anna grabbed a small cream-painted knob and pulled it back. The door popped open, and she bent down a little and ducked inside. Violet got onto her hands and knees and crawled in after her.

The space was dark and tight. The ceiling was low above Violet's head, but grew higher as it travelled back, mirroring the stairs above. Most of the place was stacked with boxes, and a nest of blankets rested in amongst them, just out of sight of the door, as though somebody was sleeping there.

"Boy's gone!" Anna said, a slight whimper in her voice.

A small cardboard box was open on the floor by the blankets. Violet crawled forward and peered inside it. It was full of photos of the orphanage and the orphans.

Most of the pictures seemed old, a yellow haze of time shadowed them.

"Boy must have been looking in the boxes. They're normally all stacked up there," Anna said.

Violet was just putting back the photos when she noticed a loose picture poking out from under the box and pulled it free.

Freeze-framed were almost thirty orphans, all looking a little ragged. In the middle of them was a tall, thin woman who grimaced more than smiled.

Dark shadows rested under her cheekbones, as though she hadn't eaten in weeks, and her wire-like hair poked out in all directions from beneath a strange white cap. The woman wore a white pinafore, hidden under a dark cape that was tied high at the neck. She held a young boy in her arms.

Violet gasped.

Though the picture was a little grainy, she was sure the child was Boy. He hadn't changed much at all and had the same jet-black hair and pale complexion.

Violet turned over the photo. There were two lines of handwritten text on the back. One was scrawled in an adult's fancy joined letters and read: *Nurse Powick on her retirement day*. The other line Violet was sure was written by Boy. It simply said: *Two of me?*

CHAPTER 14

NURSE POWICK

Violet sat in the semi-dark under-the-stairs cupboard, staring at the picture. What on earth did Boy mean by *Two of me?*

The woman in the uniform had to be the Nurse Powick, though she looked a little young to retire. Violet was sure only old people did that. Lots of other kids filled the background behind the nurse. Violet recognized a few faces, but it was hard to make out anything clearly in the dim light.

"We better go," Anna whispered, "before anyone catches us here."

Violet put the photo in her pocket, then crawled out behind the younger girl, into the hallway. She pushed the door shut and followed Anna as she snuck across the hall and out the main door.

"How did you get a key?" Violet asked curiously, as Anna locked the door behind them.

"Mam always leaves her bunch of Committee keys on the table, and never notices when one of them is missing. I can go anywhere in Town!"

As it was a Sunday morning, Forgotten Road was quiet. A pair of women passed quickly out of the laneway beside the orphanage and scurried across the road. They had linked elbows, and whispered nervously as they hurried along. A strange tension hung in the air.

A child was playing with a stick, a little away, and Violet watched as a man rushed from his home, grabbed the girl by her wrist, and yanked her back inside, all the while scolding her for being out.

Violet had just moved clear of the doorway when she noticed a raven perched on the lamp post opposite. Surely it wasn't the same bird again? The creature was really beginning to give her the creeps.

As she looked away, she saw a hooded figure moving quickly towards her from the bottom of Forgotten Road. He was trying to hide his head but she was sure it was Boy.

He hadn't noticed her as he ducked down the furthest laneway, towards Market Yard.

Quickly the bird launched into the sky, diving for the laneway as if following after Boy.

Violet grabbed Anna's arm and the pair raced after him, stopping to watch as he emerged into Market Yard. The large, black bird swept out behind him, landing on his shoulder.

Then Boy rubbed its head gently, before shooing the creature away. The bird flapped its wings and took off, landing on the roof of a house at the start of Wickham Terrace.

Anna was about to speak, when Violet put her finger to her lips and shook her head. She waited for Boy to disappear across Market Yard before turning to the little girl.

"Go home, Anna, your mam will be worried."

"But what are you going to do?"

"I have to follow Boy."

"Why don't we just talk to him, like you said?"

"Something feels wrong. I want to see what he's up to. I won't tell on him, like I promised."

"But…"

"Please, Anna. Go home!" she snapped, feeling her anger rise again.

Violet didn't wait for a response – there was no time. She left Anna in the laneway and had just reached the Rag Tree when she heard a noise behind her.

"He's my friend too!" Anna insisted.

There was no time to argue.

The pair slipped onto Wickham Terrace and were just nearing the footbridge when Violet caught sight of Boy again. He was far ahead on the tarmac road, almost at the entrance to the Ghost Estate.

"We have to hurry!" she whispered.

The pair raced over the footbridge, following his path. On reaching the estate, Violet stopped and pulled Anna behind one of its cement pillars, before peering round it.

Boy was sat on the kerb of the footpath that lined the green. He rubbed his eyes vigorously before putting a small box into his trouser pocket. The large black bird was flapping its wings by his feet, as if excited. It looked like he was having a game with the creature, picking up small stones and throwing them for the raven to fetch.

But Boy didn't have a pet bird. He liked animals and loved Merrill's mouse friend, who lived in the shavings of his toymaking room, but he definitely didn't have a pet of his own – especially not a big black bird.

After a few more games, the raven flew onto Boy's head and began to peck his hair. He laughed and pulled the bird back down before rubbing its crown playfully and placing him onto his shoulder. Then he stood up and headed for the hill to the graveyard.

Violet's dad had said ravens brought bad luck, but this

bird seemed friendly. All it brought to Boy was a much-needed smile.

"I wish I had a pet bird," Anna said, looking longingly at the pair. "Would Boy let me play with his, if I asked nicely?"

"I don't know, Anna," Violet answered, distracted, as she watched their friend mount the hill.

Was it the same raven Violet had thought was following her? She'd seen it in her yard the night Boy turned up and she'd seen it now, just before he arrived outside the orphanage. A strange thought hit her. Maybe the bird followed Boy, and every time she'd seen the raven, Boy was there too, watching her. But why would he do that?

"We better hurry!" Violet said, pointing up the hill as Boy neared the top.

He stopped under the lamp post and shooed the bird away, before heading in the direction of the graveyard.

Violet and Anna raced inside the Ghost Estate, heading for the hill. The place didn't have its normal effect on her mind now, but maybe that was because she was feeling horrible anyway, worse than she ever had before.

As they neared the lamp post, Violet heard a turnstile creak loudly. The hair on her arms stood up. Boy had gone into the cemetery.

Though she'd visited many times in her nightmares, the last time Violet had physically been inside those walls was on the night of Edward Archer's disappearance.

She struggled for breath, as fear took hold. Anna tugged on her sleeve.

"You told me before that the scary thoughts here weren't real. Are they real this time?" the little girl asked, wide-eyed.

"Of course not...of course they're not real," she stuttered, grabbing the little girl's hand and squeezing it.

Violet knew she was making herself afraid, believing all her scary thoughts, when she could choose not to listen to them. Edward was long gone; he wasn't waiting for her in the graveyard.

Anna stumbled bravely forward, heading for the turnstile.

"Not that way," Violet whispered, shaking her head, "he'll hear us!"

A loud gravelly sound, like crunching stone, filled the air. Violet froze. She'd heard that noise before, the night Edward Archer disappeared.

She willed herself onwards, holding tight to Anna's hand, then helped the little girl over the graveyard wall before following close behind. Using headstones as cover, the pair shadowed Boy as he moved through the mist.

A muffled voice carried on the wind, and their friend stopped abruptly.

Violet pulled Anna down behind a mound of overgrown weeds as two figures approached Boy. One seemed to be dragging one of its legs.

"Put those back in, you fool!" a woman said, stepping forward.

"But there's no one around. It's uncomfortable wearing them all the time," Boy protested weakly.

"You can't be too sure and, I assure you, it'll be very uncomfortable if you're caught."

Boy pulled the same small box back out of his pocket, opened it and took something from inside. Then he began to fiddle with his eyes.

"Good," she barked. "Don't let me catch you without them again."

The woman was tall and wide with thick arms and legs. Her hands were huge and her fingers were as fat, brown and crusty as fried sausages. Rose Brown would call them "working hands".

She wore a small white cap and grey wiry hair poked from beneath it. A navy cloak hung over her shoulders, sheltering a starched white uniform beneath.

Violet reached into her pocket and pulled out the photo they'd found in the orphanage. She studied the image in disbelief. Nurse Powick, the woman who'd held Boy on her retirement day, now stood before him in the graveyard.

CHAPTER 15

THE TUNNELLED TOMB

"I've been looking for you." Nurse Powick said to Boy. "You failed to capture that Brown girl, again, I see. I checked the cell. What are you playing at?"

"Nothing! I promise I tried. She hasn't left her room. People in Town are apprehensive, they're not allowing their children outside," Boy replied.

"Nonsense. Don't give me that – it's not meant to be easy. You know he needs another child, to stir the fear that's brewing in Town," she snarled. "If they're not allowed outside, then you should have gotten inside. Lateral thinking! Fail to prepare, prepare to fail. Have I taught you nothing all these years, or are you simply half-witted?"

All these years? Violet was confused. Boy must have kept in contact with the nurse since she'd retired. But he'd never mentioned her before.

"I'm not an imbecile," he answered quietly. "It's just taking time."

"Time? Time's run out, young man – you know that well. If this goes wrong, all fingers will be pointing in your direction. You should have just taken the Brown girl when you were meant to the first time."

"I told you, I couldn't. Her…her father happened upon us. He almost captured me," Boy protested.

"Imbecile" and "happened upon us". Boy had never used phrases like those before, at least not to Violet. He sounded like Beatrice when she was trying to impress Mrs Moody by talking like she'd swallowed a dictionary. And why was he lying about her dad almost "capturing" him? Her mam had said that *she* was the one who found Violet unconscious on their driveway.

Nurse Powick pursed her lips. "There is no redemption for liars! Deceit is not the language of the decent."

"I'm not being deceitful." Boy quivered, lowering his head.

"That better not be another lie on those lips, or I might have to cut off your tongue and give it to Hugo."

The nurse walked forward, so they were almost nose to nose.

"I reared you as my own, because he sees things in you. You'll make him great again, he tells me." She wrapped her thick fingers around Boy's neck. "But I don't see anything! You're cowardly. Sometimes I wonder if I took the wrong child."

A long, slow groan passed through the tombstones, as if someone were in pain. The nurse looked up and released her grip.

"Hugo, where is he?" she called, anxiously scanning the graveyard. "Where is he? That dumb creature is always wandering off alone. You better find him," she snapped, turning back to Boy. "He's my greatest creation so far."

Boy began to search the graveyard, and Violet had just pulled Anna down a little further behind the weeds, when an awful stench grabbed her nose.

A shadow moved across the top of the grassy mound that shielded the two girls. Something dripped onto Violet's head. She patted her hair and a dense wet liquid came away on her palm.

She willed herself to look up.

Thick saliva dripped on her from a gaping mouth that was framed by greenish, cracked lips. Above the lips hovered two large hairy nostrils, either side of a partially eaten-away nose. Bloodshot eyes glared down at the pair.

The Child Snatcher stood above them.

Anna opened her mouth to scream, but Violet quickly muffled it. The monster looked down at the girls, unblinking, and his top lip lifted up at the side, like a dog mid-snarl. He raised a bony hand and reached towards them.

"Hugo!"

The monster stopped, and looked to his left. Boy stood metres away, glaring straight at Violet. As she held his gaze, her body turned cold.

"Hugo, here, now!" Boy ordered.

The monster grunted and stomped away towards their friend.

Violet's heart pounded, her eyes still fixed on Boy. She stayed deadly still, waiting to be given up. But Boy turned away, as if he hadn't seen them, and headed back to the nurse.

"You ugly thing, don't do that again!" Nurse Powick scolded the monster.

Hugo winced a little.

"Take him back to the Outskirts," the nurse ordered, glaring at Boy. "He'll need to recharge his batteries before the festivities begin."

"But what about the Brown girl?" Boy asked. "Don't you want me to get her?"

Violet froze.

"So you're interested in helping now?" Powick snarled.

"Well, it's too late. We'll just have to do without her. The opportunity has passed."

Violet and Anna held their breath and watched as Boy walked silently to the side of a large, rectangular stone tomb just a few metres away.

The loud scraping sound they'd heard earlier filled the graveyard again. The front stone of the tomb moved down into the ground as if it was slowly being swallowed by the clay.

"Home, Hugo!" Boy pointed into the black hole that had opened in front of him.

The Child Snatcher stomped ahead, Boy followed, and both disappeared into the ground, as if walking down a set of steps.

The nurse surveyed the place suspiciously, then snorted and vanished into the tomb after them. Violet heard the scraping once more and the front panel of the tomb moved back up into position, leaving the two girls on their own in the graveyard.

Speechless and alone in the mist, they stayed hidden for a while, unable to move a muscle.

"He didn't tell them we were here," Anna whispered.

Violet didn't reply, her head was swimming again.

"Is Boy working for that woman?" the little girl continued. "I don't understand what's going on."

Violet stood up.

"Neither do I, Anna, but I'm going to find out."

Goose pimples prickled Violet's skin as she walked over to the tomb they'd all disappeared inside. There was something familiar about this spot. She trembled, trying to remember. Was it where Edward Archer had disappeared, all those months before?

Quickly, her head filled with images of that awful night. Her weakened father; Edward Archer holding a gun; Macula at the window; Boy's blue lips; the book. She had been sure Boy had died – that was why she'd chased after Edward, unthinking. She remembered her rage, how she wasn't going to let the stout twin get away with hurting her best friend. It was the first time she'd thought of death as happening anywhere else than in a film.

The tomb she now stood before had a solid stone lid, carved with words. Violet ran her fingers across the engraved letters, but many were too worn by time to read. She pushed against the stone cap but it was much too heavy to move. So she traced her fingers under the lid, hoping to stumble across a lever or button that, once triggered, might open it. Having no success, she bent down onto her knees and crawled around the base, inspecting the stone sides, but there was nothing to indicate how the tomb opened.

"Look, over there, Violet!" Anna whispered, pointing across the graves.

Violet followed the little girl's finger and her eyes fell upon a stream of white mist rising out of another tomb, a little way away. Curious, she picked herself up from the ground and walked towards it.

The closer she got to the mist, the more enraged and fearful Violet became. At just steps away, her body shook, and her heart beat rapidly. Every fear she'd ever had raced round her mind until she felt overwhelmed and longed to cower into a tiny dark corner, forgotten.

The stone lid of this tomb was shoved a little to the side, and the strange fog was streaming out from its dark interior.

Some of it wafted around the tombs, creating the mist that was a constant in the graveyard. The rest formed small, unusual clouds that floated up into the sky.

Violet felt physically sick. Her body convulsed, and it screamed at her to run, as fear tried to grab hold of her mind.

She willed herself to stay put. There was something odd about this mist.

"Violet, can we go? I don't feel good. Please can we go, please?" Tears stained Anna's cheeks.

"In a second."

Slowly, Violet forced herself further forward into the fog.

She retched as she gripped the stone sides of the tomb

to look inside. It was dark, much too dark to see the source of the vapour, so, resting her stomach on the front stone, she dipped forward. She was now half-inside the tomb, her legs dangling off the ground.

A huge swell of anger then overtook Violet. Her whole body shook rapidly. For a second she lost her grip on the stone edges and tumbled forward.

Violet gasped as she fell at huge speed down a dark, metal pipe full of mist. The last thing she remembered was a bright white light.

CHAPTER 16

THE WHITE ROOM

Violet felt woozy. Her head hurt a little as she opened her eyes. She was lying on her back on a white tiled floor. A strange hissing sound played round her ears and her vision was cloudy.

Panicked, she sat bolt upright.

Her eyesight immediately cleared. She looked down to see that her legs had disappeared into a dense fog that covered the bottom of this strange room. The floor, walls and ceiling were a stark, bright white and there wasn't a door or window to be seen anywhere. The brightness of the walls was dazzling, and she closed her eyes for a moment.

The space was really warm. Her cheeks felt flush and

sweat pimpled Violet's skin, causing her clothes to stick. The mist she'd been lying in was rising and had now reached her chin.

Her body shuddered as though electricity coursed through her veins, and her heart thumped wildly. Everything felt intense. She wanted to scream or hit something, or somehow release the pressure that was building inside her.

Suddenly her ankle erupted in pain, as though something had bitten her. She winced, pulling it back, and looked through the fog at her foot. The bare skin between her sock and jeans was burned and blistered.

She felt around the space where her ankle had been. Quickly she moved her fingers away as they stumbled upon searing hot steam streaming from a tiny white pipe in the wall, filling up the room.

The vapour was so thick now she was finding it hard to breathe. Afraid she'd choke, Violet clambered up from the floor, and frantically searched for a way out. Everything looked smooth and white; she couldn't see a window or door anywhere, or the pipe she'd fallen down.

In the midst of her panic, a tiny round beacon high up on one of the white walls started to flash. It turned the place a ghoulish green colour. A large hatch slid open in the wall beside the flashing light, releasing a burst of cold air down into the room.

Then the green light turned red and a small pipe high on the opposite wall sprayed something into the space.

Overwhelmed, Violet backed up against one of the walls and slid down onto the floor, before curling into a ball. Her head and heart pounded, and tears streamed down her face.

Her mind swam with worries. She thought about Anna alone in the graveyard. Violet had abandoned her. What was she doing? Why couldn't she just be a good friend? She'd abandoned Town too, and Beatrice and Conor. Then she thought about Boy and her blood boiled, as the fog engulfed the room in a white haze.

She felt woozy and gasped for air. Then suddenly the ceiling of the white room parted above her, and all the fog was sucked right out of the space into what looked like the funnel of a metal pipe. Most of her fear and anger vanished with it.

Moments before, she'd felt awful. It was how she usually felt in the Ghost Estate except much, much worse. Now she was okay again. What was this place?

Violet climbed up from the floor. She needed to escape. She'd gotten in, so there had to be a way out.

The pipe in the ceiling, the one that just sucked out the vapour, had to be the same one she'd fallen down. From the brief glimpse she'd gotten, it looked vertical and

143

much too steep to climb back out – even if she could reach it.

She looked to the cold-air hatch, high in the wall to her right. It would be big enough to climb inside. That was when she noticed a column of white metal bars, almost invisible against the wall – they reached, like a ladder, up to the hatch. Though she didn't know where it led, it seemed to be her only opportunity for escape.

Hissing passed through the room once more, as the pipe in the bottom of the wall pumped out steam. Then the beacon flashed green and Violet watched the cold-air hatch zip open. Over the next few minutes, the red light flashed, the gas was released, the vapour built up, the ceiling parted again and it all disappeared up the metal pipe above her.

The sequence of events seemed to work on a cycle. If she could time it right – and be at the top of the ladder when the cold-air hatch opened – she could climb inside and try to escape.

Violet waited. When the steam started again, she sprung to life, ignoring the pain in her blistered ankle. Quickly she climbed the white ladder, and was at the top of the steps when the hatch opened.

Struggling against the blast of cold air, she wriggled through the opening, into a metal pipe just like the one she'd fallen down, except this one wasn't steep at all, it was horizontal. The space was tight and Violet had to shimmy along a short distance to a huge turbine, which had to be what created the blast of cold air. Its propeller blocked her escape.

The propeller was like something from the bottom of a ship and whirred to a stop when she reached it. The space between its blunt metal blades was just big enough to squeeze through, but she'd need to move quickly before the cycle started again.

She poked her head in the gap between the blades for a look. On the other side of the turbine was a storage room filled with brown cardboard boxes.

Violet moved back into the pipe and wriggled around in the tight space, so she was facing the propeller feet first, which would make it easier to drop onto the floor on the other side.

The turbine clicked. Her heart jumped.

Nothing happened.

Quickly she shoved her legs through the gap, but her right shoe got caught on the edge of a blade. She tried to release her foot, as the turbine clicked once more. This time, the blades rocked a little.

She grabbed at her shoe but it wouldn't budge. Panicked, Violet pulled her legs back inside the pipe. Her right shoe fell off into the storage room.

Thinking quickly, she yanked off her sock, spun back

around and planted her feet on either side of the pipe. The toes on her right foot gripped the cold metal. There was a small ledge round the rim of the turbine. She held onto it, and braced herself for the blast of cold air.

The blades came alive. Violet ducked as far as possible down in the pipe, trying to avoid their full force. The propeller picked up speed. Cold air washed over the back of her head and body, as she clung on for life.

Her fingers slipped from the ledge and she began to slide back down the pipe. The skin on her right toes ripped against the small metal rivets.

Just millimetres from the hatch, the propeller clicked and slowed, the whirring silenced, and the force of the cold air stopped.

Violet scrambled forward and flung herself through the propeller, into the storage room below. She landed with a thud on a stack of brown boxes, sending a clatter of small metal canisters across a stone-flagged floor.

Clambering to her feet, Violet stumbled through the squashed cardboard, wincing in pain, and found her shoe before gently easing it on.

She was standing in a vaulted stone room full of cardboard boxes. The boxes were marked with the letters OA in large red print. Violet opened one. It was full of the same small canisters she'd just sent scattering across the floor.

Shaking one of the cans, she pushed the nozzle and sprayed a little of its content into the air. Immediately her fear and anger flared, and she felt just like she had in the white room. What was this stuff?

Violet had to get out of here and find help. She had no idea what time it was, her parents were probably worried and she had to find Anna.

There was a stone arch at the far side of the room. Violet limped across the space, out the door, and passed into what appeared to be an underground tunnel. It was just like the one she and Boy had discovered last year that led from the Archers' Emporium to the graveyard. She'd been told that because it was really old, Town had lots of similar passageways winding underneath it.

The floor of the tunnel was flagged in large stones and the dirt walls were roughly cut. Bulbs were strung along it, dimly lighting the space.

"I thought I heard a noise, and now I see we have a visitor," a voice sneered from the darkness in front of her.

Violet stiffened as a shadow walked forward into the light. It was Nurse Powick.

"How did you get down here, young one?" the woman asked, her voice high-pitched.

"I, erm…I…" Violet trembled, unable to speak.

"Cat got your tongue, girl? You're lucky I haven't got it…yet!" The nurse cackled. "Now, tell me how you wriggled your way in here. We don't take kindly to nosy parkers."

"I, erm…Boy caught me," Violet stuttered, thinking on the spot.

Something told her not to tell the nurse she'd found the white room.

"He did, did he? That young man's a mystery to me sometimes." Powick grimaced, shaking her head as she walked forward.

Violet turned to run in the other direction, but slammed straight into the Child Snatcher, who was silently standing behind her in the tunnel.

"Hugo, we've another visitor," Nurse Powick snarled. "Grab her!"

The huge monster lifted Violet by the collar, into the air. She kicked and squirmed, but he wrapped one arm round her flailing legs, stopping them dead, and threw her roughly over his shoulder.

"Put her with the others," Nurse Powick spat, "while I find this obstinate boy!"

CHAPTER 17

FALLING FOUL

Hugo was horrible. The night he'd tried to kidnap Violet in the driveway outside her home, she'd noticed his eye-plant eyes, and in the graveyard she'd seen his melted skin. But now – as she hung upside down over his shoulder – she wasn't sure if he was human at all.

His clothes were dirty and tattered, and huge holes in the material revealed much of his body underneath.

Running along the length of the monster's spine was a curious metal bar. Tiny holes pierced the bar at regular intervals, and from these snaked small wires that appeared to be attached to his skin. Similar bars also traced the back of his arms and legs, like some kind of mechanical outer-skeleton.

Hugo's skin was mainly grey, blue and purple, as though badly bruised. It looked almost melted or eaten in places but in other places, like the back of his leg, it was pink and hairy and looked soft. The Child Snatcher was also dotted in bits of coloured fur, which seemed to be stitched onto him like patchwork. One of the fingers on his left hand was missing too, replaced by what looked like part of a toy doll's leg.

The monster was covered in stitch marks. A line of rough stitching traced his left wrist. More ran up the side of his leg, and others over his feet. He looked just like the rag dolls Mrs Moody had tried to make the girls sew in school one day. Violet had refused because the boys weren't doing it, but Mrs Moody had said boys did other things, like carry stuff. Violet said she'd carry stuff too, then, and got extra homework that night.

Gradually, the sound of whispering voices reached along the tunnel and Hugo ducked through a narrow archway to his left into a small stone room, a little like the one with the cardboard boxes.

The voices stopped.

The Child Snatcher threw Violet roughly down onto the flagstone floor and she winced as her sore foot hit the stone. The monster then rested a hairy bare foot on her stomach to stop her struggles as he searched his torn pockets for something.

In front of Violet was a row of black iron bars, blocking off what looked like a prison cell behind. Light didn't penetrate far enough into the small stone space to see what was locked inside. Violet shuddered as the Child Snatcher pulled a set of large rusted keys from a tattered trouser pocket and slotted one into the iron lock.

There was a loud click, and the cell door screeched open.

Something shuffled about in the furthest corner of the cell and Violet panicked as the Child Snatcher grabbed her jumper, dragged her roughly across the floor, and flung her inside, locking the door behind her. Then the creature grunted and stomped back out into the tunnel.

Violet shuffled up against the iron bars, afraid of what lurked in the darkness.

"Hello…?" she whispered, her voice weak.

"Shush!" someone replied sharply.

A shadow moved towards her.

"Beatrice!" Violet gasped, relief flooding her. "You look, you look…"

"She looks awful, doesn't she?" Conor Crooked croaked, crawling out of the dark.

Beatrice burst into tears, curling up by the iron bars. For the first time ever, Violet reached forward and forced herself to hug the red-haired girl.

"What are you doing here?" Conor asked. Deep navy circles shadowed his eyes. "Did he get you too? I thought you were meant to be his friend!"

"I...I don't know what I'm doing here." Violet shook her head as she sat back against the bars. "I fell into a tomb in the graveyard, and landed in a weird white room; then the nurse caught me, and..."

"Nurse, what nurse?" Beatrice sniffled, looking up.

"The one who owns the monster?" Violet answered, taking in their blank faces. "She wears a white uniform and a strange hat...I think Boy might be helping her?"

"Boy!" Beatrice cried, yanking Conor's sleeve. "Don't talk about him. I never want to hear his name again."

"Get off me," Conor said, pushing Beatrice away roughly. "Now that Violet's here, the girls can do all their moaning on that side of the cell, thank you very much. This side is for boys, and since I'm the only one of those here, it's all mine."

The heavyset boy stood up and traced his foot along the floor, from the back wall to the black iron bars of their prison, creating a line in the dirt. Then he pushed Beatrice over onto Violet's side of the space.

"Don't cross that line!" he said, pointing to the freshly-made divide.

Suddenly the light bulbs that hung in the main tunnel went out, and the place was plunged into total darkness.

"Great." Conor sounded like he was smiling. "Now I won't have to look at your two ugly faces any more."

"Means we don't have to look at yours either," Violet snapped.

She'd never liked Conor Crooked before, and now she knew why. Even being kidnapped didn't make him a nicer person.

"You never said who the nurse is," Beatrice whispered across the darkness.

Violet's eyes were adjusting to the lack of light and she could just about make out the girl's features. Beatrice's cheeks looked hollow, as though she hadn't eaten in a while. Her once glossy hair was dull and lifeless, and her clothes were filthy.

"Have you really not met Powick?" Violet asked, confused. "She told the Child Snatcher to bring me here. I think she owns him or something. She called him her 'creation' in the graveyard."

"What do you mean, owns him? Like he's her slave or something?" Conor snorted.

"I'm not sure," Violet said, a little nervously. "Have you seen him up close? I know it sounds weird, but he looks like he's been pieced together – like the rag dolls Mrs Moody made us sew in class."

"Like he's dead or something, like a zombie, you mean?" Conor gasped, stepping across his own line.

"Get back, Conor, this is our side," Beatrice barked, finding her voice, "and he's not a zombie, Violet said he's a rag doll. Zombies don't exist!"

"Neither do walking rag dolls," Conor said.

"So you've never seen the nurse?" Violet quickly asked.

"No," Conor stated drily. "We could do with a nurse, though, Beatrice's farts are pretty awful. There has to be something dead in her stomach."

"Conor!" Beatrice roared. "I told you, I don't do disgusting stuff like that."

"Everybody farts, B – just not everyone's smell as bad as yours."

"Stop it, Conor," she fumed.

"I know...maybe that's how we'll escape. When Boy comes back with another kid, Beatrice can fart and knock him out. We will call her Farticus. You know, like Spartacus, the fella Mrs Moody said saved all of Rome or wherever. You'll be a hero, Beatrice!"

Violet tried not to laugh.

"So, who have you seen down here?" she asked, to distract Beatrice, who was clearly upset with Conor's continuous teasing.

"Just Boy and the...the rag-doll man, sometimes. Boy talked about William too. Why? Are there others, Violet?" Beatrice asked shakily.

"I'm not sure, I've only seen the nurse," Violet replied.

"I think Boy might be working for her. She used to work in the orphanage."

Violet took out the picture and tried to show it to Beatrice, though it was very hard to make out in the darkness.

"But why would a nurse be keeping us here?" Beatrice asked.

"Don't listen to Violet," Conor said angrily. "This is all Boy's fault. He's a No-Man's-Lander and they were all locked up for good reason. Dad says so. The No-Man's-Landers are all crazy. If Town had stayed Perfect, none of this would be happening."

"What?" Violet said, wide-eyed. "There's nothing wrong with No-Man's-Landers."

"Well, that's not what Boy told us," Conor exclaimed. "He said that the No-Man's-Landers were put in No-Man's-Land by the Archers for a good reason, because all of them are crazy. He said William wants to take revenge on all the Perfectionists, for keeping him locked up."

"The No-Man's-Landers aren't crazy!" Violet said angrily.

"It is true," Beatrice said quietly. "Boy told us that yesterday."

"William is going to lock us all up, Violet." Conor's voice was high-pitched. "We're just the start of it!"

Violet fell silent. What Conor said sounded a little like

what Boy had told her only the night before, on the lawn outside her house. But Anna had met him the next day and he hadn't said any of that. He had seemed normal, like the old Boy.

William had gone missing too; her dad had told her as much. Were William, Boy and the nurse all working together to take revenge on the Perfectionists?

None of it made sense, and lots of things didn't add up. Boy had told her that the Child Snatcher was William's invention, but in the graveyard the nurse said Hugo was her creation. Violet knew loads of No-Man's-Landers too, and they weren't crazy – well, at least not in a bad way.

Although she hadn't thought Boy was mad either, but he was beginning to prove her wrong.

The three children sat in silence for a while, but Violet's head was full of unanswered questions.

"What happened after you met Boy at the footbridge, Conor?"

"How did you know about that?"

"I saw you. I asked Boy about it, but he denied everything."

"He would, wouldn't he!"

"He's a liar," Beatrice spat.

"Boy asked me to go to the graveyard," Conor continued. "He said he had Lucy's bike and I pretended

I wanted to see it so I could get it back for her."

"Yeah right, you were just upset you didn't steal it first," Beatrice barked.

Conor glared at her before continuing.

"Anyway we went in the graveyard gate and somebody hit me, that's the last I remember. I woke up in this cell, with a sore head. It was bearable until *she* came along."

"Shut up, Conor," Beatrice sniped.

"How did you get here?" Violet asked her.

"She likes Boy…" Conor teased.

"Stop it, Conor!"

"You told me you followed Boy into the tunnel," he continued.

"Because I was looking for you."

"Ignore him, Beatrice," Violet encouraged, wanting to hear the rest of her story.

"I found Boy in the Ghost Estate, after I'd talked to you, Violet." Beatrice sighed. "I asked him about the bike, but he denied it, just like you said. I actually believed him. He's a good actor. Anyway, then I met him in Town later. He said something had happened to Conor, he was stuck and needed my help, so I followed him to the graveyard…"

"You went into a tunnel with a psychopath, and he didn't even have to make you!" Conor laughed.

"Boy's not a psychopath," Violet said crossly.

"And we're not locked in a cell, in an underground tunnel, left to rot," Conor snapped.

"Well, I didn't know he was a psychopath then, did I—" Beatrice replied, but Conor cut across her.

"And the best bit, Violet," he laughed, "is that Beatrice walked into the cell all by herself."

"I didn't!"

"You did. I was just waking up as she came through the gate. I thought for a minute she was coming to rescue me, until I saw Boy close the door behind her. Idiot."

"Leave me alone," Beatrice sobbed.

"So he didn't hurt you at all?" Violet asked.

"As if that matters, Violet. Stop trying to defend him," Conor snarled. "Boy locked us up – what more does he need to do?"

"No, he didn't hurt me," Beatrice replied, "but he said something weird when he was leaving."

"What?"

"Sorry. He said sorry."

"Really?" Violet sat forward a little. "Why would he say that?"

"He's not nice, Violet. We've been here for ages! If Boy was sorry, he'd have opened that gate and let us out!" Conor fumed. "Enough of your questions. What's going on in Town? Is anyone coming to save us?"

"They don't know we're here," Violet responded.

Just then the bulbs in the tunnel outside fizzed to life, and light trickled into the cell.

"Someone's coming," Beatrice gasped, rushing back to hide in the dark corner.

Violet and Conor followed her, and the threesome held their breath.

Footsteps echoed down the flagstone floor. The sound got louder, until a shadow fell across the narrow, arched doorway.

CHAPTER 18

THE RETURN

Boy walked through the doorway, to the iron bars of the cell. Gripping them, he leaned forward as if searching the darkness. Violet pulled further into the corner. She was hiding from the person who was meant to be her best friend.

"Ahem…I…I hope you had a good night's sleep, Conor and Beatrice," Boy stammered, "because it will be your last." He sounded stiff and silly, almost as if he'd stolen his words from a film.

"Please don't hurt us," Beatrice cried out.

"What do you think I've held you here for? Of course I'm going to hurt you. I used to hurt kids all the time in the orphanage. I'm good at it," Boy snarled.

"You never told me that before," Violet said, crawling forward.

Boy's face stiffened as she emerged from the darkness.

"Powick said you were here," he muttered quietly.

"I told her you caught me," Violet replied, staring at him.

She was hoping to catch a glimpse of her old friend in his face. He didn't react.

"Who is that woman, Boy? What's going on? I saw you in the graveyard with her and the monster," she continued.

"How did you find the tunnel?" he whispered, almost to himself.

She was about to tell him about how she'd fallen into the white room, when something stopped her. He wasn't really her best friend any more; she couldn't trust him.

"I...I..."

"What are you two whispering about?" Conor asked, walking out of the darkness. "Are you a spy for him or something, Brown?"

"Shut up, Crooked," Boy barked loudly, "or I'll hurt you first!"

"You wouldn't hurt anyone, Boy," Violet replied.

"I'd hurt you too," he snarled, poking his head through the bars.

She saw it again, just like the night in her garden – a flicker of ice-blue showed at the edge of his black iris.

"Your eye, Boy." She pointed.

He looked away.

"What's going on?" Violet pleaded. "First you tell me you've done nothing wrong, then you tell me you're bad but tell Anna you're good. You saved me from the Child Snatcher that night on my driveway – no matter what you say, I know you did. And you didn't give me or Anna away to the nurse in the graveyard. I don't understand. If you're in trouble, I can help! Please, Boy. No matter what it is, we can figure it out together, just like we did in Perfect."

"Shut up, Violet!"

"I saw you with the black bird, the raven. You were playing with it. Nobody really bad would be that nice to an animal! And I've seen the bird loads lately. Were you there every time it was? Were you following me? Maybe you were protecting me, like that night on my driveway?"

Boy gripped the iron bars again. This time his expression was vicious.

"Don't tell anyone about the bird or I will cripple you. I swear I will," he hissed.

"I…I promise," she stammered, moving quickly back from the bars. This time she really believed him.

At that moment Violet heard footsteps in the tunnel, as if someone was running. Boy looked to the arched entrance.

"He's coming," he whispered.

"Who's coming?" Violet asked.

"LEAVE THOSE CHILDREN ALONE!" someone roared.

Her heart skipped.

Beatrice raced forward, clasping the black iron bars. "Help, help!" she cried.

"I'LL SAVE YOU, CHILDREN!" the person shouted, their footsteps heavy on the stone-flagged floor.

The sound grew louder. Strangely, Boy didn't move.

Moments later, a small, squat figure burst through the archway and attacked Boy. The pair fell to the floor, swapping punches. A set of keys flew across the room, rattling off the iron bars.

"Open the door and get away, children! Wait for me in the tunnel!" the man bellowed.

Conor dived for the keys, pushing them into the lock one by one until it clicked open. He was the first to escape.

"Come on!" Violet called, pulling a petrified Beatrice towards the opened cell door.

She dragged the girl out of their prison and shoved her through the archway, as Boy and the man continued to battle it out on the ground. Conor was waiting anxiously in the tunnel.

"Which way, Violet?" he panted, looking left and right. "It was dark when Boy brought me here. I don't want to run into the monster."

"That man said to wait for him," Beatrice whimpered.

"I don't care what he said. We need to look after ourselves!"

"But he's rescuing us, Conor," Beatrice stammered.

Grunts and crashes filled the passageway. Violet's chest pounded, as Beatrice clung to her elbow.

"Maybe Conor is right – we should just go now," Violet whispered.

Something about their rescuer felt all wrong.

Just then there was a loud groan, and everything immediately went quiet. Moments later the small, squat man walked out through the stone arch, dragging Boy behind him.

Beatrice gasped. Violet felt sick.

"Edward Archer!" Conor exclaimed, stepping in front of the girls. "I knew none of that stuff people said about you was true. You saved us!"

"Stand back, young Crooked. Boy is dangerous."

Edward Archer had saved them? How could this be? Violet backed away towards the shadows, hoping the man hadn't noticed her. She was sure she wasn't exactly Edward's favourite person.

"Young Brown, how did you get here? I wasn't…"

"I caught her last night, and brought her here," Boy interrupted, looking up from the ground.

"Oh I see, young Archer even turned on his best friend!

164

What a pity. I imagine you thought you were comrades, Violet. Now you know why No-Man's-Land was a necessity and not a cruelty," Edward said sternly. "It was to keep people like Boy away from good people like you and your family."

Violet didn't respond. Her hands clenched in tight, shaky fists behind her back. Edward Archer had never thought she was a good person before.

"But you turned everyone in Perfect blind," she stuttered.

"It was for their own good. But you didn't give us time to explain that, what with your rebellion, did you? Let's not go over old ground now. The main thing is you're safe. I'm sure your parents will be relieved. How is dear Eugene?"

Violet shivered.

The last time Eugene Brown and Edward Archer had met, the stout twin hadn't cared how her half-starved father was. If he had been so caring, he might have fed her dad, while keeping him captive to work on the eye plants.

"I never doubted you, Edward," Conor announced, "not once. Perfectionists for ever! Boy deserves whatever he gets for this. I'll make sure Dad sees to it."

"Revenge is a dish best served cold, young Crooked. We shall leave matters of law to the Committee – they can decide what happens to Boy Archer. I hear that's how Perfect is ruled these days, and it's a welcome relief. Myself and George always endeavoured to do the best for our people, but it was a constant worry as to whether we were being fair. Let the people of Perfect decide for themselves, I say." Edward smiled.

"Town," Violet said bluntly. "It's called Town now."

"I'm sorry, Violet dear, of course it is. Town – what a…a…lovely name."

The stout man riffled through his pockets, pulling out a small tub. Then he poured four tiny capsules onto his palm and picked one up.

"These work great for shock," he said, swallowing a green pill.

Then Edward walked forward and handed similar capsules to Conor and Beatrice. The pair quickly swallowed theirs.

Violet shook her head as he tried to hand her one. "No thanks."

"It's for shock, Violet. I promise you need it."

She shook her head again, remembering the yellow pills she'd been given in Perfect. The ones that almost made her fall under the Archers' mind control.

"I'm fine, Mr Archer," she stuttered. "I'm not in shock."

"You are in shock, Violet. Anyone who can go through

what you have been through and say they're fine is quite clearly in shock."

"Take it, Violet," Beatrice urged, her eyes a little glazed. "I feel much better."

"It's good for you," Edward encouraged, leaning threateningly over her.

Reluctantly, Violet picked up the pill and placed it under her tongue.

"Swallow," Edward ordered.

He didn't look away until she'd done as instructed.

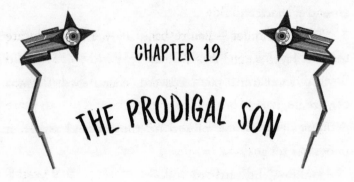

CHAPTER 19

THE PRODIGAL SON

The next thing Violet knew, she was standing in the drizzling rain on the footbridge into No-Man's-Land.

She shook her head, trying to remember how she'd gotten there, but everything between when Edward had rescued them and now was a blur, almost as if there was something in the pills he'd given them.

As Violet rubbed the water from her eyes, a strong anger overcame her, and her mind raced with worry again.

Conor and Beatrice were just ahead of her. Ahead of them, dismounting the bridge into No-Man's-Land, was Edward Archer, dragging Boy roughly by his coat collar.

A bright light flashed repeatedly across the sky on

the far side of the river, dazzling Violet, as a figure danced around Edward and Boy.

"Edward Archer – you're back! How did you locate the missing children? Was William Archer there? How did Boy Archer react to your appearance? Are you ashamed of your nephew? Have you a message you'd like to share with the *Town Tribune*?" Robert Blot shouted excitedly.

What was he doing here?

The newspaper man was about Violet's dad's height, but he was very thin, his face was pencil narrow and dark circles rested under his eyes. Around his neck hung a camera which he was constantly flashing, in his left hand he held a notebook, and a pencil rested behind his right ear.

"What day is it?" Violet asked Robert Blot, as he stopped to take some notes.

"It's Sunday afternoon, Violet," he stated, his tone a little sharp. "Aren't you a lucky girl? Reported missing in the morning, and rescued the very same day. You owe Edward Archer a great deal, darling!"

Violet smiled awkwardly, unsure how to respond, when she noticed a low humming noise. It sounded as if something was taking place up on Edward Street.

"What's going on? What's that noise?"

"People have come out to welcome you all home, Ms Brown!" Robert Blot responded, snapping closed his notebook. "Give me a quote! Tell me, how do you feel about that?"

"Erm…" Violet was annoyed and a little thrown by his request. "But how do people know we're here?"

"I received a tip-off this morning. A letter through my door informed me that Edward Archer had located the missing children hidden in the Ghost Estate, and would be bringing them and their kidnapper to the Town Hall this afternoon. Of course I printed the new revelations and, using my journalistic nose for a story, waited in No-Man's-Land to get an early scoop! You'll give me your story once you settle back, Ms Brown, there'll be a pretty penny in it. 'Good Boy gone bad', 'his best friend speaks openly'." Robert Blot handed her a business card. "What a story. Boy Archer, confirmed kidnapper! Town has gone wild for it already. How was your ordeal, Ms Brown? Were you tortured? How indebted are you to your rescuer?"

"But that can't be right," Violet said, confused. "Who gave you the tip-off?"

Though her head was a muddle, she was sure she hadn't fallen down the tomb until late morning – which would mean they weren't rescued until long after Robert Blot got his tip-off.

The low hum grew louder as they stepped into Rag Lane.

"The tip-off was anonymous. When you're a journalist,

170

you know a good tip-off when you get one. It's an instinct we're born with. Writing is a vocation, you know, stories just find me."

"But don't you want to know who gave you the tip-off? How did they know about the rescue? I'm not sure the times add up. Shouldn't you find that out?"

"Details equal delay," Mr Blot huffed angrily, looking through his camera. "I want to get this shot – the victims led home by their rescuer, to Town's applause. What a front-page winner!"

"Asking questions again, are we, Violet?" Edward Archer hissed.

She hadn't noticed him stop ahead of her, and almost walked into his stout frame. As Robert Blot snapped pictures of Beatrice and Conor walking up Rag Lane, Edward Archer leaned forward, so he was millimetres from Violet's ear.

"You better be careful, young Brown," he whispered. "I'm not the worst of the Archers, am I, Boy?" Edward yanked his nephew backwards.

"No, I think that would be me." Boy glared at Violet as if he hated her.

She looked away, tears prickling her eyes. Edward smirked and pushed Boy forward.

Violet gasped as the group reached Archers' Avenue and turned into Edward Street.

The rain had finally stopped, and a huge crowd had gathered outside the Town Hall. People were packed more than ten deep. Their faces were angry, and they hissed and booed at Boy. A terrifying energy filled the air.

The crowd parted, creating a path to the Town Hall as the group approached.

Violet spotted Iris Archer at the front of the crowd. Macula stood by the old woman, hiding her face behind a navy shawl.

Boldly, Iris stepped out in front of her son, blocking his advance.

"Lovely of you to welcome me home, mother!" Edward Archer spat.

"This is all a lie, Edward – for once, listen!" she urged him.

"Haven't you missed me? At least you're here to witness Town discover your precious William is poison," he said, loudly enough for all to hear.

He grabbed the old woman's bony wrist and pulled her towards him, kissing her cheek. Iris pushed him away and ranted wildly at the crowd.

"Don't believe what you're told by Edward and George. They're a terrible pair. All Edward knows is lies, they're his truth. My grandson is no thief…"

All eyes gravitated towards the old woman, and the crowd swelled around them. Violet was squashed against

Boy, just as Macula snuck forward to speak to her son.

"Where is he?" Boy's mother whispered. "Whatever that nurse told you is not true. She took you from us! I love you, and your father loves you. You have to know that!"

"You'll never find him!" Boy replied, his eyes filled with hatred.

"Enough," Edward barked, spying the pair.

He pulled Boy away from Macula, and continued towards the steps of the Town Hall.

The crowd hissed and booed at Iris.

What was going on? Why was everyone so angry?

Violet spotted Mr Hatchet through the crowd. The man punched a fist in the air, his face contorted. It was odd, she'd hardly ever seen anything but a smile on the butcher's lips until now.

Edward mounted the steps of the Town Hall, pushing Boy ahead of him. Violet followed behind with Beatrice and Conor, as Robert Blot snapped every detail.

A small group of parents huddled by a microphone underneath the canopy of the Town Hall, a little away from them. Violet spotted her mum and dad. Eugene was standing still, looking stiff and stern, as Rose fiddled nervously with the buttons on her jacket.

Next to her mother was a tall red-haired woman holding hands with a much smaller, balding man. They were Beatrice's parents. Patricia Prim looked like her daughter in adult shoes.

Beside the microphone was another couple. Violet recognized Vincent Crooked from the Town Committee meetings. He was tall and "stately", as Rose used to say whenever Mr Crooked's name came into conversation at home. His black hair, flecked with white at the temples, was gelled back. His wife's blonde hair reached just below her ears, framing a small face and a mouse-like nose and mouth.

"Conor!" the woman squealed, as she caught sight of her son.

Conor Crooked swaggered across the stone platform to his parents.

"Mam, shut up, you're so embarrassing!" His whispered tones caught in the microphone standing nearby.

Vincent pulled Conor close, patting his back.

"Good to have you home, son." He nodded, smiling out at the crowd.

A hush fell over everyone as Mr Crooked walked to Edward and pumped his hand.

"You saved our son." The microphone relayed Vincent's words out onto the street. "Let me be the first to welcome you back to Town with open arms."

"It's good to be back." Edward smiled, then he looked

towards the Townsfolk and cleared his throat. "When someone attacks the children of this town, they attack me. Bringing these little ones home is the least I could do."

"But you attacked our children, you locked them away in No-Man's-Land," a man shouted.

An angry hiss filled the air.

Violet tiptoed over to her parents, who both looked more than a little anxious.

"We were worried sick when you disappeared this morning, pet. Who kidnapped you? Is this true, did Edward Archer really save you? For the life of me, I can't believe anything good of that man," her dad whispered, as he wrapped his arms tightly around his daughter.

"Eugene, stop it, just welcome Violet home. Not everything has to be a conspiracy," her mother scolded, elbowing past to give Violet a hug.

"Did I say it was a conspiracy, Rose?" he huffed.

Her parents were still fighting? Violet's blood boiled. Shouldn't they just be happy to see her?

"Stop it!" she snapped, pushing back from her mother's arms.

Just then a loud screech filled the air, grabbing everyone's attention. Edward Archer held the microphone aloft in his blocky hand.

The angry crowd silenced.

"I owe you, my people, an explanation," the Archer twin announced. "I abandoned Perfect, at a time when you most needed my leadership."

"You abandoned the No-Man's-Landers long before that," a woman shouted.

"Yes, I'm afraid it might appear that way, but that was not the case. Regardless of what lies my younger brother William has told you, No-Man's-Land was created for your own good. Perhaps I can explain…"

"Our own good? You locked us up and made our families forget we ever existed," the woman replied. "You stole their imaginations."

"Let the man speak," someone else shouted.

"Myself and George created No-Man's-Land because we grew up with a sick younger brother and it tore our family apart." Edward paused for a moment. "My poor parents worked tirelessly to cure their son and, as his brothers, we helped in that role. We were still trying to fix him when, only a year ago, William stormed our perfectly peaceful town with his army and brought terror to our streets. I disappeared because I knew if I stayed, my brother would imprison me as he has done George, and I would be unable to challenge him.

"You must understand," Edward continued, "William is a tortured man. My mother Iris, though she would deny this tale, moved us here to escape his terrible past. He is what they call 'a Divided Soul', and destruction follows him everywhere."

"A Divided Soul? What nonsense is this? We won't believe your lies this time, Archer," somebody shouted.

"Don't listen to them, Edward, we were waiting for your return. This place has gone to pot. Bring back Perfect!" called someone else.

Angry whispers raced the street. Some No-Man's-Landers tried to protest, only to be hushed by the Perfectionists around them. It seemed Edward was winning favour.

He continued, "When William – a hateful, cruel child – began to show sinister behaviour, Arnold Archer, our loving father, took him to a psychologist. My brother was diagnosed with DSS, Divided Soul Syndrome. It's common in those with different-coloured eyes.

"A Divided Soul has a manic mind, split between good and evil thoughts. William is the perfect example – he could charm you one minute and harm you the next. Of course, our adoring parents always covered up for his actions, until the day William tried to strangle my mother for pocket money. Father then threatened to have him committed for treatment, and was murdered in his sleep that very same night, strangled by my little brother's shoelace."

The crowd gasped.

"Stop it, Edward! You are telling lies – awful lies!" Iris yelled from the crowd. "William did nothing of the sort; you know what your father was like, and what these ridiculous tales have already done to our family."

"Mother, your secret almost cost this town three of its children," Edward replied.

When people began to turn on Iris, Macula wrapped an arm protectively round the older woman and quickly guided her away down Archers' Avenue.

"We created No-Man's-Land to heal William," Edward continued, "and to heal others suffering with similar conditions. We tested the people of Perfect for signs of mental instability and anyone found to be unstable was put into No-Man's-Land for treatment. It was developed as a rehabilitation centre, to protect both those in No-Man's-Land from the stresses of daily life, giving them the time and space to get better, and those in Perfect from any immediate danger due to their family members' ill health. We built No-Man's-Land from a place of love, we built it to fix our brother."

"Danger? How were we a danger to anyone?" Merrill Marx shouted indignantly.

"It's not your fault you're unhinged, Merrill. Yours is one of the many minds we tried to fix." Edward shook his head solemnly. "If only myself and George could have seen out our plans. Town would be thriving – there'd be no robberies or kidnappings, and, people would not be angry. Happiness and community spirit would fill our streets, just like it did when this place was Perfect."

"What about stealing your Perfect people's imaginations? Would that still be happening if you'd seen out your plans, or would everyone now be looking at the world through your eye plants?" Merrill replied.

Edward said softly, "We weren't stealing imaginations, we were testing everyone for madness. Insanity shows itself in the imagination. The eye plants were developed as a security system – just as they are being used now, to protect the No-Man's-Landers from themselves and Perfectionists from the No-Man's-Landers – until such a time as they were healed and ready to come back home."

"Bring back Perfect!" someone shouted.

A similar chorus echoed round the street. Violet grabbed her father's hand.

"They can't really mean that, Dad, can they?" she asked.

Eugene didn't reply.

Edward held up his arms, calling for silence.

"William's cruel nature was passed on to his son, a young boy abandoned by his father. Tell them, Boy."

Edward Archer pushed Boy forward. Violet's friend stared at the microphone, then at the crowd.

"Speak up, Boy," Edward ordered.

179

"Ahem...Dad made me do it." He coughed, stepping quickly back from the mike.

The crowd grumbled and roared terrible things about William.

"Where is William? Did you find him yet, Dad?" Violet anxiously looked around.

Eugene Brown shook his head, not lifting his eyes from Edward.

"How did your father make you do it, Boy? The people need to know. It's their right!" Edward ordered again.

"He, ahem...he coerced me into it, but I didn't take much persuading," Boy mumbled.

Violet pulled on her dad's sleeve.

"What's 'coerced' mean?" she whispered.

"He's saying William forced him into doing it, Violet. This is all very strange."

Violet was now certain something was up. The Boy she knew, the one who was her best friend, did not have a clue what *coerced* meant and would definitely never use it in a sentence.

Maybe Edward was doing something to Boy's mind. Maybe he was making him act this way and say these things? He'd done it to everyone in Perfect before, so why wouldn't he try it again?

Boy continued, furious now. "My father will make all of you suffer. We will steal your Perfect children. The No-

Man's-Landers will take revenge on all of you who forgot they ever existed. Perfectionists will pay!"

"What?" a No-Man's-Lander cried, from the middle of the crowd. "I have nothing to do with any of this. I don't want to take revenge on anyone!"

Pockets of fighting broke out amongst those in the street. Splits were forming and Violet could see No-Man's-Landers slipping out from the crowd to disappear inside their homes.

Though the rain had stopped a while ago, the sky had darkened further, mirroring the mood.

"We need to leave," Rose spluttered, grabbing her daughter's hand.

"Everyone, calm down!" Edward Archer ordered. "I see fear and anger have taken hold in my absence. I hope my reappearance will allow your feelings to settle. Together we can create the place of peace and beauty envisioned by my brother George and I, many moons ago."

The dark clouds rumbled. People reached for their hoods and umbrellas.

"Don't hide your heads today," Edward announced, "let the rains cleanse your worries, wipe away your fears and bring a bright new future."

Suddenly the clouds erupted, releasing a downpour.

Edward walked out from under the canopy of the

Town Hall, throwing his hands skywards. He was drenched within moments.

The crowd followed suit. They removed their hoods and let down their umbrellas. Slowly, laughter filtered through the streets, as though Edward Archer had lifted a great weight from Town.

CHAPTER 20

CLOUD NINE

Violet watched from her place under the canopy of the Town Hall, while Edward Archer stood in the rain, surrounded by happy well-wishers. She pulled on her dad's sleeve, directing his attention, as she noticed Vincent Crooked grab hold of Boy.

"Release George Archer from the clock tower and lock Boy in his place," Vincent ordered a man standing beside him.

"Hold on a minute, Crooked – you can't release George, that's a Committee decision," Violet's dad announced, stepping forward.

"I'm on the Committee, Brown!"

"It's the whole Committee's decision, Vincent. You can't

go off making decisions like this on your own. William is still missing. We haven't even heard his side yet."

"William's side? That man is clearly mad. Didn't you hear a word Edward said?"

"And what about Edward's history? Are you going to just believe him without question, Vincent? William deserves to tell his own story. We need a Committee meeting – this has to be discussed, before any rash decisions are made."

"Maybe you're not fit to sit on the Committee any more, Brown. Maybe we'll discuss that. Your daughter was a No-Man's-Lander, wasn't she? Are you a sympathizer?"

Eugene's face was red and his fists were clenched. Violet had never seen him this angry before; he wasn't the type of person who normally got cross.

"Come on," he said, yanking his daughter away. "We're going home. Town is not the place it used to be."

Violet stumbled behind her dad, out from under the cover of the Town Hall.

The downpour was so heavy she was soaked in minutes and should have been annoyed, but for some strange reason the rain made her smile. The weight of anger she'd been carrying lifted, and Violet found herself laughing.

She spotted her mother a little down the street, swinging round a lamp post.

"Violet, Eugene…isn't life just beautiful?" she cried, laughing as the pair joined her. "I feel euphoric! Have I ever told you how much I love you both?"

Rose was right. Everything was just beautiful. Violet felt light as a feather. All her worries disappeared, her mind was clear and she couldn't understand why she'd ever been so angry.

"I love you too, Mam," she laughed, wrapping round Rose's waist.

"Oh, my two favourite girls," her dad smiled, joining the family hug. His mood had lifted too!

Happily squashed between her parents, Violet looked around the street. Everyone was smiling. All the anger and fear that had hung over Town had somehow disappeared.

As the family walked towards home through the rainy streets full of joyous people, Violet began to wonder if perhaps Edward Archer's reappearance had brought this good mood back to Town. Maybe things would be better with him in charge again. Maybe Edward deserved a second chance?

"What if Edward's return is a good thing?" Rose said, as though plucking the thought straight from Violet's mind.

Eugene Brown kissed his wife's forehead. "I don't entirely agree, but I'm not sure I even care at this moment, Rose. Life is good, and I'm the luckiest man alive!"

Violet's dad whistled to himself as the rains eased and the family turned up their driveway.

Suddenly Madeleine and Anna Nunn stepped out of the surrounding trees, their yellow raincoats like beacons in the grey afternoon light.

"I'm so sorry to surprise you like this." Madeleine hesitated, a wide smile sweeping her face. "It's just… I know I look happy, and I do feel a huge weight has lifted off my shoulders, though I'm not quite sure what that weight was. But I am a little worried for Anna – at least, I know I should be, though I honestly can't bring myself to worry. I know it sounds crazy. This is the only place I could think to come to for help."

"Of course, Madeleine." Rose smiled. "Whatever is the matter, on this amazing evening?"

"Well, Rose, as you all know, Anna was a No-Man's-Lander – but I'm telling you she's not mad. What Edward said is simply not true. If the Archers were indeed testing our imaginations for insanity, then Anna's results must have gotten mixed up with someone else's. There is nothing unhinged about my daughter."

"I know what you mean, Madeleine. Come in." Eugene smiled, opening the door of their home. "I don't believe Edward's tales myself – in fact, I was very angry about it up until a while ago, but our walk home must have done me the world of good. I feel light as a feather. I don't for a minute believe that William is unhinged or any of that stuff about the No-Man's-Landers. I worked with Edward and George, and they are not good men. Though, just as you said, for some reason, I can't quite bring myself to worry about it right now."

"But what about William's syndrome, the Divided Soul stuff?" Rose asked, ringing out her wet hair.

"It's folklore, Rose, utter nonsense. Nothing scientific about it at all. I judge the person I know, not the stories I hear. The William Archer I know is not the person his brother described today, and neither is his son."

"Well, there's no use in worrying about it, Eugene." Rose laughed, kissing him smack on the lips before heading into the kitchen. "I'll turn on the heating to dry us all off."

"Nothing is making much sense." Madeleine's smile was beginning to falter as she sat down at the table. "I mean, Boy kidnapping children and Edward Archer saving them? Really...fact is sometimes stranger than fiction!"

"But Boy didn't kidnap me," Violet replied.

"What exactly happened, pet?" her dad asked. "In all the commotion, I never got to talk to you about it."

"There was mist coming from a tomb in the graveyard," Violet said, "and when I went to look, I fell down a metal pipe into a weird white room, where I think the mist was being made. I escaped, but then the nurse found me in the underground tunnel and made the zombie Child Snatcher take me to where Beatrice and Conor were being held, and…"

Violet's happy mood faded a bit, as she began to dry out in the warmth of their kitchen.

"Zombies, really? Are you feeling alright, pet? You haven't been the same since I found you on the driveway. And now this kidnapping." A slight worry edged Rose's tone, and her smile had faded a little.

"She DID fall through a grave, and we DID see a zombie and a nurse. I was there too. I told Mam about it already!" Anna stomped her foot so the adults would listen.

All eyes turned to Madeleine.

"I thought Anna was making it up; she has a huge imagination," the woman replied sheepishly.

"We were trying to help Boy," Violet continued. "We followed him to the graveyard, hoping we'd find out what was going on."

"Are you ever going to learn?" Rose tutted, sounding angry again. "The last time you followed Boy, you got into a world of trouble in Perfect, and we're not even sure that was worth it now."

"What do you mean, Mam? We saved Perfect!"

"Well, according to Edward, it didn't need saving."

"How could you say that, Rose?" Eugene scowled.

"You were a victim of the Archers' plot. Do you not remember forgetting your own daughter?"

"Oh…I really didn't mean that. I'm a mess right now, my emotions are all over the place. One minute I'm angry, then happy, now I'm angry again. I just don't know any more, Eugene!" Rose buried her face in her hands.

Everyone's earlier happy mood seemed to have taken a quick turn.

"How could you just forget what happened in Perfect so easily?" Eugene fumed. "I certainly haven't forgotten that the Archers kept me captive and half-starved, forcing me to work on their eye plants. It's obvious Edward is up to something again, and I don't understand how those people at the Town Hall today can't see that. It seems like all the Perfectionists believe his story."

"That's not fair, Eugene. You were in your right mind during Perfect," Rose argued, "the majority of us were not! Our imaginations were stolen and we don't have clear memories from that time. Maybe the reason Edward is so easily believed now is because the Perfectionists still don't fully understand what it was the Archer brothers did back then."

Rose looked down at her hands.

"If I could take back that time when I was under the Archers' control, I would. I hate that I forgot you both, my own flesh and blood. I hate that I believed everything

I was told, and didn't question. I hate that I was so easily fooled. It would be easy to blame someone else. Blaming William and the No-Man's-Landers makes sense. It would mean that what I did wasn't wrong."

"It wasn't your fault, Mam." Violet tried to reassure her. "The Archers made you forget us!"

"I'm the same, Rose," Madeleine said, grabbing her hand. "These past few days I've felt so awful – all the shame returned and I was so angry at myself. When Edward said those things at the Town Hall, I wanted to believe him. His words made me feel better. I danced the whole way home!"

Eugene looked at them all. "But Violet's right. How you acted during Perfect wasn't your fault, Rose – or yours, Madeleine. The Archer brothers stole your imaginations."

"But the No-Man's-Landers didn't change, Eugene. They could see the truth when we couldn't. Sometimes it feels like they were stronger than us." Rose looked at her family. "You're both stronger than me."

"But that's not true, Mam." Violet hugged her. "I've been scared and angry too, just like I was the first time I entered the Ghost Estate. Then Edward spoke today, and I felt happy again."

"Me too," Anna said, grabbing Madeleine's hand.

"My mind's been clouded too," Eugene said, shaking

his head. "Again, until Edward spoke earlier. The whole thing is very strange indeed."

"The clouds!" Violet jumped up, as an idea hit her. "Dad, could someone make you feel awful by using the clouds?"

"Do you mean the weather, Violet?" Eugene replied. "Dark days can affect a person's mood, especially long winters without much sunlight…"

"No, not like that, Dad. I mean, could someone put something into the clouds to make you feel bad?"

"I'm not quite sure what you're getting at, pet."

"Well, the mist in the graveyard made me feel horrible – like I did in the Ghost Estate, except a million times worse. The mist was floating into the sky and making clouds. It came from the white room, Dad, the one I fell into…"

"Slow down, Violet," Eugene said, leaning across the table towards her. "Tell me everything about this white room."

Violet started her story again.

She told her dad all about the steam and the cold-air hatch, and the stuff that was sprayed into the room before all the smoke was sucked out through the ceiling. Then she told him about the storage place and the small metal canisters.

"They were marked with the letters OA—" She hadn't

finished her sentence, before Eugene Brown jumped up from the table.

Quickly, her dad grabbed a bucket from under the sink. Everyone followed as he raced outside and placed it in the middle of their gravel yard.

"What are you doing?" Rose asked.

"There's a little drizzle still, we should get just enough rain to test it."

Eugene Brown the scientist had sprung to life. He hurried back inside and grabbed a knife from the kitchen drawer before returning.

"That's my mother's good cutlery," Rose barked.

"Well, it should do a good job then," he said, kneeling down on the soggy lawn.

Violet's dad muttered to himself as he cut round a sod of grass, removing a deep clump of clay from the middle of the lawn.

"Eugene, look at the state of the garden," Rose wailed, following him back inside.

"Can't be helped, Rose, the water deep in this clay will be a little older than the rain that's falling in the bucket."

Violet stood beside her dad in his office. She watched as he placed the clay carefully onto his stainless steel workbench, before reaching for his starched white coat.

"Get the bucket, Violet," her father instructed. "It should have enough rainwater in it by now. If what you described happening in the white room is what I think it is, pet, and the sudden change of mood we all experienced today after Edward spoke is also as I fear, then we should have a different chemical reading from the water in this clay than we will have from the water in that bucket."

"What kind of a reading, Dad?" Violet asked.

"Patience, pet!" he said, using a syringe to carefully extract water from the clay.

Violet raced outside and carried the bucket back into her father's office, leaving it on the floor. Dr Eugene Brown was in full flow. He divided the water gathered into test tubes, and was using all kinds of equipment to investigate his samples.

While Eugene worked, the others returned to the kitchen for some *UniTea*. Violet rested her head on her forearm, her worries returning a little. She stared at the purple and gold packaging adorned with the tagline, "Bringing Town Together". Town definitely didn't feel together right now.

"I knew it," Eugene finally cried, popping his head round the door. "The minute you explained that room to me, Violet, I knew what was going on. You're a genius, pet. Those Archers do love mind manipulation. This has Edward Archer all over it!"

"What do you mean? What's going on, Eugene?" Madeleine asked, standing up.

193

"Come here, I'll show you." He opened the front door and raced outside. "Do you see those big, beautiful clouds?"

"They're not that beautiful, Dad," Violet said, looking skywards.

"Play along with me, pet," he replied excitedly.

"Yes, Eugene – yes, obviously we see them." Rose was growing impatient.

"Well, can anyone remember when the recent weather started in this town of ours?"

"A few days ago, I think," Madeleine replied, impatient now too.

"And what else happened around that time?" Eugene asked earnestly.

"I know, I know," Anna cried, her arm catapulted into the air.

"Yes, Anna?" Eugene nodded like a school teacher.

"Well, all the kids started going missing. I'm sure I would have been a bit scared that someone would kidnap me too anyway, but when it started properly raining, I got really, really, really scared, and really angry too."

"Precisely!" Eugene exclaimed.

"What do you mean by 'precisely', Eugene? Stop being so cryptic," Rose said, fuming.

"Just like Anna said, the weather's making everyone angry and scared, and, as of today, even happy!" Violet's dad replied, racing back to his notes.

194

The others followed and stood around Eugene's workbench, as he threw open his findings and began to explain his discoveries.

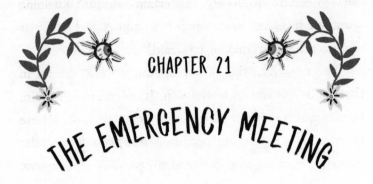

CHAPTER 21

THE EMERGENCY MEETING

"Making clouds is a simple school experiment," Eugene told them. "Hot air – as Violet described streaming out of a pipe in the bottom of the white room – rises to meet cold air pumped in from the hatch at the top of the room. This cools the hot air, which wants to turn back into a liquid but needs help to condense – cue the gas sprayed into the mixture, forming clouds."

"So Edward Archer's making clouds?" Madeleine interrupted, bending closer to eye the notes.

"Yes, Madeleine – well, someone is making clouds, but it does have his signature all over it. I know how those twins think."

"But that doesn't explain our moods, Eugene. How

can clouds make us feel a certain way?" Madeleine questioned again.

"Are the clouds making us afraid?" Anna asked.

"The rain from the clouds is, Anna. The chemical in the clouds falls down in the rain. It seeps into our skin, our clothes, our soil, our water – even our food. These chemicals alter our perception. I read about a similar experiment, years ago, in one of my periodicals," Eugene said, getting excited. "Researchers used a range of toxic gases to control the mind. Depending on the concoction, they could instil fear, hysteria, happiness, anything. I found OA gas in the water sample I took from deep in the soil. It's full name is oxide adrenatonin – it's a delirium used to create fear and fury in individuals. And in the bucket, our recent rain, the water contained nitreous oxitocin. It's a happy, calming chemical with euphoric and relaxing properties."

"But why would the Archers want to make us angry?" Violet asked, confused.

"It's another control mechanism, Violet. Those brothers are forever trying to mould our minds! If you can instil fear in a person, it will build anger. Give them a reason for their fear and you can direct their anger, thereby controlling them," Eugene stated.

"Divide and conquer, a method used to gain or to maintain power," Madeleine rattled off, as if reading from a textbook. "I remember learning about it for a philosophy exam. Who knew that'd ever come in useful?"

"Why would Edward want to divide conkers? Is he going to hit people with them?" Anna questioned.

"No." Madeleine smiled. "It's called divide and conquer, Anna. Edward is using our anger and fear to turn us against each other, the No-Man's-Landers against the Perfectionists. If he can divide us, he can win back Town."

"But why make us feel happy earlier?" Violet asked.

"Oh, Edward's a clever man," her dad replied. "This has all been very carefully stage-managed. I suspect he's behind the robberies and the kidnappings, using them to grow fear in Town. Then he added the rain, building on this fear and anger until he returned into Town as a hero, having rescued our lost children.

"He pointed the blame at William and the No-Man's-Landers, giving us all a reason for our anger. Cue the fresh downpour, this time filled with nitreous oxitocin, and we were all happy and calm again, believing Edward's return made us feel that way. I counted back on the rain showers – I think they're on a cycle, a couple of hours apart each. Edward's return was timed to perfection, to coincide with the last rain shower."

"But I'm starting to feel a bit angry again, Mr Brown," Anna whispered, "and I'm not in the rain now."

"The anger will probably linger for a while, Anna.

We've been exposed to the OA gas for a few days now, and it's worked its way into our bodies. It will take some time of non-exposure to work its way properly back out. The effects of the happy gas, I'm afraid, will be much more fleeting. I'm certain Edward has used it over Town just once, so its force was only really felt when we were directly in the downpour."

Suddenly there was a pounding on the door.

"Who is it?" Rose called, racing into the hallway.

"It's me!" Merrill Marx mumbled through the wood.

Violet's mam opened the door and the toymaker rushed inside.

"They're releasing George! They've swapped him for Boy, who's now locked in the clock tower," he panted, as though he'd run the whole way from Town. "I've heard rumours the Watchers are being let out next!"

"I told Vincent he couldn't do that," Eugene fumed, grabbing his coat. "It's a decision for the Committee to make."

"Crooked has gone ahead and given the order," Merrill continued. "I tried to stop him, but he wouldn't listen. Everyone there was cheering. Trouble's brewing. If they let out the Watchers, we're finished. Crooked's called an emergency Committee meeting, right now. Who knows why, since he's acting like he owns the place! I left to find you and Madeleine."

"Crooked's an idiot. He won't get away with this!" Violet's dad said, striding towards the door.

"No, Eugene, please! Just let things settle. Edward is dangerous." Rose shook her head. "It's getting late, can't we just wait and see what happens in the morning?"

"And let them take over Town? We didn't battle against Perfect, just to have it happen all over again, Rose."

"Please, Eugene, can't we just think about it a bit more? Put together a plan?"

"It's a Committee meeting, Rose. The Archers won't be there, and if they are, they won't try anything in front of everyone else. They'll want to keep up a nice front, at least for a while. They need to build back trust."

Madeleine Nunn turned to her daughter and kissed her forehead. "Stay here, Anna. I'll be back as soon as I can."

"But, Mam, I want to go too…"

"No buts, Anna." Madeleine was firm as she stepped out the door. "I'll be back to get you soon. I promise."

"But what if it's a trap?" Violet insisted.

She remembered when the Archers told her mam that her dad was called to an urgent opticians' conference, just before he disappeared from Perfect.

"Violet," her dad said, bending down to his daughter. "We know what Edward is like now. We won't fall for his tricks again, I promise."

Eugene looked at Rose and kissed her forehead.

"If we don't come back, find Iris and Macula. They might know where William is," he whispered. "And be aware of your feelings, don't get swept away by them."

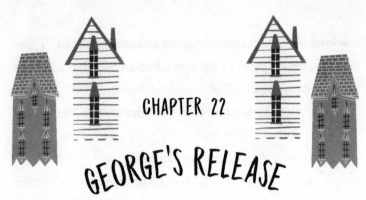

CHAPTER 22

GEORGE'S RELEASE

"Your father will be fine, Violet," Rose stuttered, as she closed the door of their home.

Her mam sounded worried. Violet was worried too. She wished Boy was here, he'd know what to do, but right now he was another worry of hers.

As her mam disappeared back into the kitchen, Violet pulled Anna aside.

"I have to follow them," she whispered. "Dad and the others could be in trouble."

"Then I'm coming too," Anna replied, her eyes wide.

"No, you have to keep Mam busy. Ask her to show you how to bake – she loves all that stuff, since Perfect. Dad always jokes that they gave her back the wrong imagination. If she says anything about me, tell her I was tired and angry, and I've gone to bed and locked my door so you couldn't get in."

"But why do I have to stay behind?" the little girl huffed.

"Sometimes you have to do things you don't like, Anna, because it's good for somebody else," Violet replied, remembering what her mother had told her when they first moved to Perfect.

Anna scrunched up her face and was about to protest again, when Violet turned and sprinted up the stairs. She didn't have time to lose and couldn't waste any of it trying to convince Anna. She locked her bedroom door, raced over to her window and lifted up the bottom pane.

As quietly as possible, Violet eased herself out onto the roof tiles, just as she'd done the night Boy appeared in her garden. Her ankle was still sore from earlier and she tried to ignore the pain as she crept across to the overhanging branch, then clambered towards the tree trunk and finally climbed to the ground, only releasing a breath when her feet touched grass.

Night had almost fallen and it was easy sneaking past the kitchen window. She grabbed her bike and slipped down the driveway, before pedalling towards Edward Street.

The closer Violet got to the Town Hall, the more

people filled the street. Many carried banners announcing their support for the twins.

Violet pulled on her brakes, a little back from the crowd, and got off her bike, resting it against the Brain. Then she pushed her way towards the steps of the Town Hall.

She arrived in time to see George Archer stride out the door of the old building, under the columned stone canopy, to his brother's side. She'd forgotten how strange the twins looked together – one tall and pencil thin, the other short and wide.

The crowd erupted in applause. Violet shuddered.

"Thank you for welcoming my brother so graciously, you truly wonderful people." Edward smiled. "George has something he'd like to say."

The tall twin bent down to speak into the microphone. The crowd held their breath.

"No, I haven't," he grunted.

Violet remembered how George was never one for words. He always scared her more than his twin. At least his brother pretended to be nice.

"It seems prison has stolen his voice," Edward quickly interjected, "but George asked me to impart his sincere and grateful thanks for his compassionate release. Though he was unlawfully imprisoned, he bears no grudges."

"I bear a few grudges," George growled, as Edward snatched the microphone away.

"He wasn't unlawfully imprisoned – the No-Man's-Landers were!" a woman cried.

Violet turned to see who it was, but her view was blocked by a small group who circled the heckler, pushing her aggressively from the gathering.

Town was becoming divided. If things kept going like this, the Archers would be in charge again soon.

Vincent Crooked took the microphone. He seemed to be in charge of the proceedings and thanked everyone for coming out to support George, before dispersing the crowd.

Violet looked around for her dad, spotting him just as he disappeared inside the Town Hall with Merrill and Madeleine following behind him.

She snuck up the steps and crossed the flagstones to the door. Checking no one had noticed her, she slipped inside.

A thick red velvet curtain, acting as a draught excluder, was the perfect hiding place. From there she watched her dad, Madeleine and Merrill climb the steps of the spiral staircase to the Committee meeting room on the second floor. After a few minutes, Vincent Crooked entered the hall and ascended the steps after them.

Violet waited until the coast was clear, then raced upstairs and crept into the public viewing platform; a small windowed area that overlooked the Committee

Room below. It was used so members of the public could attend meetings. Violet had fallen asleep there many times, on the nights her dad made her go.

She was just in position when Mr Crooked stood up behind the wooden lectern.

"What's going on, Crooked?" Eugene asked. "It's not like the others to be late."

There were usually ten Committee members, but, besides Vincent, nobody else was there except Violet's dad, Merrill and Madeleine.

Mr Crooked was about to speak, when the double doors of the room swung open.

"Oh goody, we're all here!" Edward Archer laughed as he walked briskly across the pinewood floor, followed in slow, looping strides by his brother George.

"This is a private Town Committee meeting," Merrill announced, standing. "Nobody else is allowed in here!"

"Oh shut up!" George spat. "This is our town, so it's our meeting."

"It's not your town any more, George, it's run by the people now," Violet's dad replied.

"But you called us to this meeting, Eugene," Edward smiled.

"No I didn't," Violet's dad insisted, looking confused.

"Yes you did, Eugene. You wanted to speak to us about William," Edward said. "Then you just started to attack me. It was completely unprovoked. Of course, Merrill and Madeleine joined in. William turned up too. Vincent tried to pull you all off, but he couldn't. You were simply too strong for him."

"What is going on?" Madeleine asked, also standing now.

"This," George spat, picking up a wooden chair and whacking it across his shoulder.

Violet's heart pounded. Why had George Archer just hit himself?

"This is madness," Merrill protested, as Edward ripped the collar of his own shirt.

Eugene, Madeleine and Merrill stood open-mouthed as George and Edward Archer beat themselves up.

"Of course Vincent, as a witness, will have to report this to the paper." Edward smiled, his left eye now a little puffy and bruised. "How will the story go, Mr Crooked?"

"Oh something like, 'William Archer and friends – in a final, desperate attempt to seek revenge on Perfectionists – stormed the Town Hall, freed Boy, and tried to release the Watchers, to take full control of Town. Edward and George heroically stopped them, though both were left a little bruised by the battle.' I'm sure Robert Blot will word it much better than I can." Vincent smiled.

"No one will fall for that, Edward," Eugene snapped. "The Watchers are your army – why would William or any of us try to free them?"

"The people will believe what they're told, Eugene, they always have. Minds are easy to mould when you know how. I can hear the gossip now... 'Those loonies from No-Man's-Land are causing a lot of trouble these days – with break-ins, robberies, kidnappings – so why wouldn't they try this? They are clearly unhinged, wouldn't you agree? The streets would be much safer without them... Throw them in No-Man's-Land,' they'll be crying, soon enough. We'll have Perfect again in no time."

"What about the trial?" George replied.

"Of course, Georgie, I almost forgot. Democracy is all the rage in Town now. William and you three," Edward pointed, "will be publicly tried for this crime. We'll make sure the crowd's calling for your blood."

"Where is William? What have you done to him?" Merrill asked.

"You need to learn patience, my dear toymaking man. If you'd just left Perfect perfect, you wouldn't be in this predicament."

"No, but we'd be living like rats in your No-Man's-Land, Archer!"

"Soon you'll be envious of the rats, Marx," George spat.

There was a noise outside. George walked across the room to the window. Violet's dad grabbed the broken leg of a chair and swung it at Edward, hitting him smack in the stomach.

"Run, Merrill, Madeleine – now!" Eugene shouted, grabbing his friends as he raced for the door and down the spiral staircase.

Violet scrambled across the viewing platform to follow after them, when Madeleine's cry cut the air.

"Eugene!" she roared, as a loud bang shook the building.

Violet gasped and pulled back into hiding. She gripped the grey carpet and tried to breathe.

There were feet in the stairwell again. The door of the Committee Room opened. Violet shuffled forward and forced herself to look down.

Edward and George stood by the lectern. The stout twin was smiling, the taller wore a grimace. Vincent Crooked stood behind them, white-faced.

Madeleine and Merrill were just inside the main door. Anna's mother trembled as she edged away from a large figure to her right.

Violet gasped.

The Child Snatcher stood just beside the twins. Violet's dad was resting, unconscious, over one of the monster's shoulders, while William Archer was in a similar condition over the other.

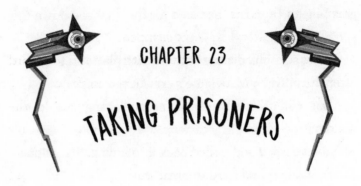

CHAPTER 23

TAKING PRISONERS

"Let that be a lesson to you, Merrill and Madeleine – if you want to stay conscious, don't try to escape," Edward snarled. "Now, I'd like everyone to meet Hugo. He's affectionately known as the Child Snatcher."

So Edward knew about Hugo, Violet realized. Her dad was right – this was proof that he must have been involved in the kidnappings and that the rescue was staged.

"That thing...that thing is a monster." Madeleine struggled with her words.

"It's not all about appearances." Edward smirked. "Let's see what you look like when you've been dead a few years, Madeleine. He's in great condition for a zombie!"

"A zombie?" she exclaimed, looking away.

"What have you done to William?" Merrill interrupted, stepping towards his friend.

"Get back, Marx!" George snapped.

"Hugo's had some fun with our little brother," Edward laughed. "Bring them up to the clock tower, Hugo."

The Child Snatcher grunted and stomped to the Committee-room door, Eugene and William still over his shoulders.

"You too," Edward growled, pushing Madeleine and Merrill after them.

Violet listened. Footsteps climbed the spiral stairs to the clock tower where Boy was being held.

George stared out the window as Vincent Crooked, who'd kept quiet all this time, slipped silently along the wall, heading for the exit. He was looking more than a little nervous. Mr Crooked was almost at the door when it swung open and Edward strode back inside, followed by the Child Snatcher.

"You weren't trying to escape, were you, Crooked? Not chickening out, now you're up to your neck, are you?" The stout twin's smile was evil.

"No...of course not. I was...I was just cleaning up the place," Vincent stammered picking the leg of a chair from the floor.

"Leave that, we'll need photographic evidence of the attack, for Blot's front page."

Vincent Crooked dropped the chair leg and it clattered to the floor. His forehead glistened with sweat. He startled as the door opened again and Boy walked inside.

Violet gasped.

"Is everything okay in the clock tower? They can't get out? The doors are securely locked?" Edward asked.

"Yeah, everything's in order." Her friend nodded.

Violet's head swam. Boy really was working for the Archers!

But why? Maybe she was right, and he was being controlled somehow. Edward said minds were easy to mould. The Archers had to be controlling Boy's mind, otherwise she was sure he'd never turn against his dad or Town.

"Ahem... Can I...can I go now?" Vincent Crooked stuttered, edging closer to the door.

"Patience, my dear man. So you know what you have to do next?"

Conor's dad nodded, his face a little red. "I tell Robert Blot, so the story's in the paper tomorrow."

"Excellent, Vincent." Edward smiled. "You seem nervous, though, my dear fellow. Is something the matter?"

Conor's dad hesitated. "Ahem...the payment... When can I..."

"You're a greedy man, Mr Crooked – selling out your

son and your town." Edward laughed. "You'll be paid when the job is finished. Now go and get Robert Blot, tell him what William and his friends tried here, and make sure he takes lots of pictures! He can call round and photograph our injuries too. We'll be in our emporium."

Vincent nodded and raced out the door, purple-faced.

"We're watching you!" George shouted, as Crooked's footsteps slapped off the spiral stairs and out onto the flagstones below.

Violet ducked down, resting her head on the carpet to gather her thoughts.

So Mr Crooked knew about the Archers' plans from the start. He'd sold out his son and his town for money. The robberies, the kidnappings, the weather, the rescue – everything was a set-up, so the Archer brothers could destroy William and the No-Man's-Landers, and take back Town.

The only part of the puzzle that didn't seem to fit was Boy, but Violet couldn't worry about him right now. She had to stop Edward and George.

Her head hurt. She pushed back up onto her elbows to peer out again.

"Put this on." Edward tossed a dark hooded jacket at Boy. "Take Hugo to the Outskirts, recharge him and pass on word it's all gone to plan."

Boy nodded.

"And don't forget this." Edward threw a tiny red disc at him. It looked like a magnet. "For the time being, you still need to black out the eye plants as you pass. We don't want those things picking you up on the Brain. Once you've sorted Hugo, go straight to the emporium. You'll stay with us there, and we'll sneak you back into the Town Hall the night before the trial. Be careful. We can't risk anyone seeing you from now on – you're meant to be locked in the clock tower."

So that's how Boy was stealing the eye plants, undetected. He was disturbing the signals – just as William had thought – by using a magnet. And the Outskirts. Violet had heard that name before. She rooted through her memories. The nurse, in the graveyard – she'd told Boy to bring the Child Snatcher back there too.

"So the emporium is ours again?" George half-smiled.

"We can return to our home tonight, George. Both William and Brown are in prison, and when people read the papers tomorrow, nobody will dispute us taking back our stolen property!"

"And we can release the Watchers." George fully smiled this time.

"Not yet, my dear brother. If we do that now, we'll lose favour, and people will rise up. We don't have the numbers yet to overpower Town. We need to win back trust, then slowly take full control again. We'll destroy

William, then the No-Man's-Landers. Once they're all locked away, these streets will be ours to play with and we can pick up where we left off."

"And what will you do with William?" Boy asked.

"Why do you care?" George growled.

"I don't, I merely asked a question," her friend replied, a little sheepishly.

"We'll make sure he pays for our suffering – for all of our sufferings," Edward answered, pushing down the light switch and plunging the meeting room into darkness.

"Good," Boy stated.

Violet felt sick to her stomach.

CHAPTER 24

THE WHITE-EYED BOY

Violet waited as Edward, George, Boy and the Child Snatcher headed down the spiral staircase and out the front door. Then she crept from her hiding space on the viewing platform, and raced up the steps to the clock tower.

"Dad?" she called, hoping to hear his voice.

"Violet, is that you?"

"Yes, Dad. Are you okay?"

"What are you doing here? Go, pet, before they see you!"

"But I have to get you out!"

"Just go, Violet. If they catch you here, you're in big trouble. Tell your mother what happened and—"

"Get Anna, please. Make sure she's safe," Madeleine interrupted.

"Is William okay?" asked Violet.

"Yes, he's just hit his head."

"You were right, Dad, it was all a set-up. The robberies and kidnappings, everything. Boy is working with the Archers too. I don't understand it…"

"I know, pet, but you can't worry about that now – just get out of here."

The door handle of the main entrance downstairs rattled. Violet's heart thumped rapidly. Was Crooked back already?

"Go, Violet, before you get caught," Merrill whispered. "You're no use to anyone if you're thrown in here with us. Get help. Tell Iris and Macula. Make sure people know the truth."

"But Robert Blot is going to write the Archers' version of the story. He's going to tell their lies and people will believe him!"

"Not everyone will believe him, Violet. Just get help. Go, pet – now," her dad insisted.

The door handle shook again. Violet looked over the banisters, down the spiralling stairwell. Fear gripped her.

"Dad," she whispered.

"Yes?"

"I love you so much."

"You too, pet – more than you'll ever know. Now go… please!"

She placed her hand on the door, imagining she was hugging her father, then turned and quickly slipped down the stairwell.

The door handle rattled again.

"You're making too much noise. You were much better at this when we lived in No-Man's-Land," someone whispered from the other side of the door.

Violet recognized the voice.

"Shush, I need to concentrate!" someone else replied sharply.

She knew that voice too.

The ornate door knob slowly turned, and the door opened inwards. Two heads poked cautiously through the gap.

"What are you doing here?" Violet whispered.

"Violet!" Anna exclaimed, stumbling backwards in fright.

"We were looking for you." Jack, Boy's friend from the orphanage, was with Anna. He scooted past Violet and checked up the stairs. "What happened?"

"We need to leave," Violet said, ignoring Jack's question. "Vincent Crooked will be back soon, with Robert Blot, to take pictures for the paper. They can't catch us here."

"Why are they taking pictures?" Anna asked.

"Questions later, Anna. Violet said we have to go," Jack replied, grabbing the young girl's arm and running out of the building.

Violet hesitated for a moment, looking back up the winding stairwell to where her dad and the others were held. Then she followed the pair down the steps, out from under the canopy of the Town Hall.

The street was quiet, and it was raining again.

Jack pulled Anna into the doorway of the tea shop for cover, and Violet ducked in after them. She was just catching her breath, when voices reached them from the other side of the Town Hall.

Anna peeped round the deep door frame.

"It's Mr Crooked and the newspaper man," she whispered, pulling back into hiding.

"Don't let them see you," Violet spoke urgently. "Conor's dad is working with the Archers. Town is in big trouble."

"Where is my mam?" Anna asked nervously.

"Madeleine's okay," Violet answered, before stopping to think for a moment. "How did you get here, Anna?"

"I snuck into Town after you," the little girl replied, avoiding Violet's eyes. "I saw you go into the Town Hall and I tried to follow, but the door was locked and I couldn't find Mam's keys. So I waited, and heard terrible noises. I got scared and found Jack, 'cause I knew he'd be able to break in. When we got back here, the Archers and the Child Snatcher were just leaving. Why was Boy with them?"

"Anna, my mam is probably really worried now," said Violet, avoiding the Boy question.

"No, I told her I was tired and wanted to go to sleep, so she put me in the spare room. When you're a kid, adults think you're always tired and they're always trying to make you go to bed, so she definitely believed me. Then I climbed out the window. It was pretty easy, much easier than sneaking out of my house."

"Violet, what did you mean by, 'Town is in big trouble'?" Jack asked.

"The Archers are trying to take back control. They've locked Dad, Merrill, Madeleine and William in the clock tower," Violet replied, before launching into everything that had happened so far that day.

She told Jack about the weather and how her dad had discovered the twins were controlling everyone's feelings. Jack looked a little relieved when Violet explained that the anger and sadness weren't real.

"I've been feeling awful," he said, shaking his head. "And it's the Archers who are making me feel this way?"

Violet nodded before telling them about the Committee meeting and how it was a trick. How the

Archers had attacked themselves.

"Do you mean they actually beat themselves up?" Jack shook his head again, as if trying to take it all in.

"Yeah, it was really creepy." Violet nodded. "They're trying to pretend William and the others attacked them and tried to take over Town for the No-Man's-Landers."

"But the twins are the ones trying to take over Town!" Anna huffed.

"Exactly, Anna. We have to stop them," Violet replied. "They want to bring back Perfect and have all of us locked in No-Man's-Land again."

"But they can't do that." Anna quivered. "I want to be with my family. I don't want to go back to the orphanage!"

"People won't fall for it, Anna – don't worry," Jack reassured the little girl.

"They already have, Jack. Like I told you, the Archers are controlling our emotions and using them against us. They made us all believe that Town was a bad place. Now that Boy is helping the Archers, people will believe every bad thing about William."

"But Boy wouldn't help them," Jack insisted, anger playing round his words.

"I saw him, and he is. But maybe the Archers are controlling him somehow." Violet pulled the photo from her pocket, remembering Nurse Powick.

"This woman has to be involved," she said, pointing to

the picture. "I've seen her with Boy – she's the one who told the Child Snatcher to bring me to the cell. Jack, do you remember her?"

She passed the photo over and watched his face as he studied it.

"I think she worked in the orphanage, that's what the writing on the back says," Violet continued. "Boy wrote on the back too – at least, it looks like his handwriting, but I don't understand what he meant. He just wrote, *Two of me?*"

Jack's face turned slowly white, as if he'd seen a ghost.

"What is it?" Violet whispered.

"I know what Boy meant by 'Two of me'," he replied softly.

Jack's hand was shaking as he passed the picture back to Violet.

"You're scaring me," Anna said, tugging on his sleeve.

"Look at the photo again…really closely," he stressed.

Violet did as directed, unsure what Jack wanted her to see.

"Are you in the picture?" Violet asked, confused.

"No." Jack shook his head and pointed to the back corner of the photo. "Do you recognize anyone there?"

A boy and a girl were huddled together, staring stone-faced at the photographer, and tucked in – almost hidden behind them – was another small figure.

Violet looked closely at the boy shyly peering over the little girl's shoulder. Then she looked to Powick and the boy in her arms.

"Boy's right," Jack whispered. "There are two of them."

CHAPTER 25

MACULA'S SECRET

"I don't understand," Violet said, looking back and forth between the two identical boys in the picture.

"Boy has a twin!" Anna exclaimed excitedly.

"Twins?" Violet shook her head, confused. "But Boy never said anything to me... Did he say anything to you, Jack?"

"No," Jack answered, still staring at the image. "Maybe he didn't know. I don't remember him ever talking about a brother, and I never met one. I was seven when I was taken from my parents, though, and Boy had already been in the orphanage five or six years by then. Maybe his brother was gone before I got there?"

"It says on the back of the picture that Powick was

224

retiring, and she said something about rearing Boy – or, I mean, his brother, I guess – when they were talking in the graveyard. So maybe the nurse took his twin when she left the orphanage?" Violet mumbled, trying to make sense of her thoughts.

She couldn't take her eyes from the image. The two boys were identical except, strangely…

"His brother's eyes are white!" Anna announced, as if reading Violet's mind.

Anna was right, but Violet wouldn't describe his eyes as white exactly. Boy's brother had startling ice-blue eyes, a direct contrast to his twin's almost black ones.

William Archer, their father, had different coloured irises. Violet had noticed it when she first met him, after ducking into his house to avoid the Watchers. She had found it almost impossible not to stare at his eyes, though she'd gotten used to them now. One was dark, almost black, and the other, cold blue, like an icy winter's morning. Edward had even talked about them in his recent speech on the steps of the Town Hall. He'd called William a Divided Soul and used it as a reason to explain his brother's made-up madness.

Violet had always thought Boy's eyes unusual in their darkness, and now, as she looked at his brother's icy pair, she shuddered. It was almost as if William Archer had been split in two.

A memory hit her.

When Boy was in Violet's garden, the night of the first rainstorm, she'd noticed a thin sliver of ice blue rimming his eye. A flicker of the same colour had also edged his black iris when he poked his head through the cell bars, just before Edward staged the rescue.

Nurse Powick was angry with Boy when she'd met him in the graveyard. She'd ordered him to put something back in, in case someone saw him. Violet hadn't thought much about it then, but Boy had fiddled with his eyes for a while.

One Halloween, Violet's mam had worn green trousers, a red top and wrapped lots of red silk scarfs around her head. She'd said she was dressing up as a rose, in honour of her name, and even went as far as wearing red-coloured contact lenses.

Except for their eyes, the infant twins looked identical in the picture, so Violet imagined they still were. If Boy's brother wore dark-coloured contact lenses, no one would be able to tell the difference. They would think he was Boy.

Her heart pounded.

Lately, when Violet believed she was talking to Boy, had she really been talking to his brother? It would explain why she thought Boy was acting weird and talking strange, using big words Violet was sure he didn't know.

It explained too, why Boy didn't have a clue about Lucy's stolen bike or playing with Conor in the Ghost Estate.

The Boy Anna talked to – the one who was acting the same as the Boy Violet knew, the one who hid in Anna's secret place under the stairs in the orphanage, and left the picture of himself and his twin behind – that Boy must be the real one. But where was he now?

Violet looked at the back of the photo again.

Two of me?

Maybe Jack was right, maybe Boy didn't know about his twin either.

A pang of guilt hit her. All along, she'd been angry with him for lying to her. She thought he wasn't her best friend any more. But it was Violet who wasn't being a good friend. She hadn't believed him, when Boy was telling her the truth.

"So it's not Boy, it's his twin helping the Archers?" Anna asked, wide-eyed with excitement.

"I think so," Violet replied, a little red-faced from her memories. "I think he's been pretending to be Boy for a while."

"I knew Boy wasn't bad," Anna said.

Violet explained to Anna and Jack about Boy's eyes the night in her garden, in the cell underground and in the graveyard with Powick.

"I feel awful," Violet said softly.

"Why?" Jack asked, looking straight at her. "This is great news – it means Boy is good."

"But I thought he was lying to me, and I was angry with him," she blurted out.

"We were all angry." Anna hugged Violet. "The Archers made us angry. It wasn't your fault."

"But even before the weather got worse, I didn't believe Boy. I was so confused. I can't imagine how he felt."

"How were you to know he had a twin?" Jack stated bluntly.

Jack was right: how was she to know? But one person at least did know. Violet felt her blood boil.

"Macula knew," she snapped. "Why didn't she tell the truth? Everyone believes Boy is bad, and she could easily fix that."

"Boy said she's been acting strange lately," Jack replied, shaking his head. "Maybe there's something wrong with her?"

"Yeah, Boy told me that too," Violet replied quietly.

The group slipped into silence for a moment.

"Why don't we just ask Macula why she didn't tell anyone about the twins? Maybe she knows where our Boy is now too," Anna suggested. "Mam always tells me if I want to find out something about a person, I should ask that person. She said in Perfect she just believed the stories she was told about other people, without ever finding out if they were true or not. She said she'd never do that again, because it's not a nice thing to do."

Jack smiled, and rubbed the little girl's head.

"Anna's right – we should ask Macula. If we could find Boy, we could prove the Archers are telling lies. Macula might know where he is, or at least know something about his twin that might help us find Boy," he said.

"But what if Macula doesn't want anyone to know about him?" Violet asked nervously. "If she didn't tell Boy he had a brother, then maybe she didn't tell anyone else."

"Well, her secret's out now." Jack shrugged.

"You're right, Jack," Violet said, before stepping from the doorway.

"Where are you going?" Anna looked worried.

"To talk to Macula."

Anna jumped with excitement as the threesome slipped from the cover of the tea shop. Violet didn't know if this was the best idea she'd ever had, but they needed to find Boy, and Macula might be the only one able to help them. The whole of Town was quiet as they passed through the rain, down Forgotten Road, across Market Yard and into Wickham Terrace.

Jack's fist shook as he took a deep breath and raised it to knock on the door of 135 Wickham Terrace, Boy's home. It was clear the rain was still affecting everyone but, equipped with new knowledge, they were much better able to handle it now.

Violet and Anna stood beside Jack, filling the doorway.

Since their first meeting in the Ghost Estate, Violet had always been fascinated by Macula.

Boy's mam was beautiful – one of the most beautiful people Violet had ever met. Her long black hair had once swept down to the floor, but now rested just off her shoulders. Her eyes, green like grass in summer, shone from her clear, pale skin. People were in awe when they saw Macula and, when she spoke, Violet's dad said she'd stop a room.

Macula was smart too; she always seemed to know what she was talking about, though not in an annoying way, like Beatrice. Macula's brain could fit everything she'd ever seen inside it, Boy told Violet one day. He was explaining how his mam could name all the elements in the periodic table, when his dad couldn't, even though he was the scientist.

Macula was also an artist – she had painted all the pictures that once hung from the walls of her room in the Ghost Estate, the ones that looked like freedom. Her pictures always seemed alive, as if the things in them could get up and walk off the canvas.

The door creaked open and Macula peered out, bringing Violet's thoughts back to the present.

"What are you three doing here at this time of night?" she asked, stepping back to let them inside.

Boy's house had no hall, and they walked directly into the warm kitchen. A large cream stove heated the room.

"Erm…" Jack looked awkwardly at Violet as he stepped inside.

"Ah, we…erm…we came to talk to you," Violet answered.

Boy's house was nothing like it had been when Violet was first there. William lived alone then, and everything had been piled up and covered in dust.

Macula loved colour. Every door and room was a different bright shade. Boy's bedroom was yellow with an orange door, and the kitchen they were standing in was purple with a lime-green entrance.

"What did you want to talk to me about?" she asked, looking at the three children curiously.

Violet searched her brains for a way to phrase the question. Her dad always told her to think before she spoke.

"Does Boy have a twin brother?" Anna blurted out.

Violet threw her hand over the little girl's mouth.

Macula's cheeks flushed, and her eyes dropped to the floor. Violet's heartbeat quickened.

"Is that what you've come to ask me?" the woman replied after a moment, her tone even.

Anna nodded.

Violet's head spun – she couldn't grasp a single thought.

"It seems the others have lost their words?" Macula said, leaning against the wooden kitchen table.

"Ahem, we...we hadn't meant to ask you that way," Violet stammered.

"But you had meant to ask me?"

Violet nodded.

"I think you'd all better sit down." Macula sighed.

CHAPTER 26

A CONCERNED CITIZEN

Anna sat down beside Macula at the kitchen table, while Jack and Violet sat opposite. Boy's mam didn't speak for a while. She looked broken, weak, just like Boy had described.

"Tell me how you know about the twins," she said.

Violet looked at Jack, then slowly took the picture from her pocket, passing it over to Macula.

"We found this in the orphanage. I think Boy left it there – he'd been hiding out under the stairs."

"In our secret place," Anna interrupted.

"How long ago was he in your secret place, Anna?" Macula asked keenly. "Do you know where he is now?"

"No." Jack shook his head. "We came here because we thought you might."

Macula looked down at the picture, and thumbed the paper.

"No." She sighed. "I've been trying to find him, but so far my search has been fruitless."

Macula's voice finally broke as she looked at the image.

"My son. I've haven't seen many pictures of Boy at this age. I missed so much of his life!"

"His brother is there too." Anna leaned over the photo and pointed him out. "That's how we found out about the twins."

"Oh." Macula cupped her mouth and took a sharp breath. "Why wasn't I able to protect them? I let them both down."

"No you didn't," Violet said. "Boy loves you, and Mam said what you did giving up Boy – or, I mean, giving up both of them – was brave. She said you gave him – them – away to protect them, and that's the hardest thing any mam could ever do."

A tear raced down Macula's cheek.

"Thank you," she sighed, squeezing Violet's hand. "I don't deserve praise. I tried to protect my boys, but it didn't work out as I thought it would. Tom suffered."

"Tom?" Violet asked. "Is that his name?"

Macula nodded.

"Why didn't you tell anyone about him?" Anna asked bluntly.

Violet threw Anna a sharp look.

"It's okay, Violet," Macula replied. "I wanted to, Anna. But the first time I met Boy again I was in shock – everything took place so quickly that night. When he didn't mention a brother, I wondered if maybe something bad had happened to his twin. The first private moment I had with William, I told him everything, and we've been searching for Tom ever since.

"I didn't want to tell Boy straight away. The fact that he never talked about Tom made me worry, and so I wanted to wait until we knew more. Then I got a letter from Priscilla Powick, the woman who took my other son, and we decided not to tell Boy at all until we found Tom. We thought it might be too painful for him. Though I have tried to keep things normal for Boy, the search for his brother has engulfed me. Until now, that is. Now I search for *both* my sons."

"Priscilla Powick!" Violet darted forward, pointing to the nurse in the picture. "She's called Nurse Powick. Is she the woman who took him?"

Boy's mam looked back down at the image, and her cheeks burned red.

"I never met her, but you're telling me this woman is Priscilla Powick?"

"Yes. Well, I think she must be the same woman," Violet answered. "Her name is Powick and she worked in the orphanage. I saw her with Tom in the graveyard, but I thought he was Boy then and she talked about rearing him or something."

"So she is mixed up in all of this? Have you met her, Violet?" Macula asked, her voice barely even.

"Yes, in the tunnel underground. She got the Child Snatcher to put me in prison."

Macula looked confused, so Violet launched into her story about suspecting Boy to be bad, and following him to the graveyard before falling down the pipe into the white room. About the nurse catching her and throwing her in a cell with Conor and Beatrice. Then she told her about Tom, who she thought was Boy, mock fighting with Edward, as he pretended to rescue them.

"So Edward is behind everything?" Macula said, her cheeks flushed. "I knew it. I knew he had to be, somehow. All those lies he spun. All those lies about William – it just makes me sick. The whole Town believes him."

"Edward's making the Town believe him," Anna stated. "He's using the clouds."

"What?" Macula looked confused again.

Violet launched into the rest of her story about the weather, and what had just happened in the Town Hall.

"So they have William too? I knew he didn't run away.

236

He would never do that to us." Macula was angry now. "Why do those brothers insist on destroying my family? They won't get away with it – not this time."

Macula stood up and paced the floor, just as was her husband's habit. Boy used to do it too – it helped him get ideas, he'd said. Violet tried not to think about him, as everyone in the room slipped into an uncomfortable silence.

Then Boy's mother sat back down. Her brow furrowed.

"I don't think Tom is a bad child – he can't be, it's not in his blood," she said. "Did you speak to him, Violet? I think this woman must be making him do bad things. Do you think she loves him? Do you think she treats him like a son?"

"She, erm…" Violet wasn't sure how to respond. "She didn't really talk to him like she loved him."

"She didn't seem to really like him at all, if you ask me," Anna stated.

"If I thought she took care of him, if I thought he had a family that loved him – even if they weren't his real family – I would be okay with that. All I want for my children is for them to be happy. But his actions…they are not the actions of someone who is happy, of someone who is loved." Macula had tears in her eyes. "If I ever meet that women, I'll…I'll…"

She stood up and paced the floor again.

"Maybe if I could talk to Tom, I could tell him he has a real family who love him. Maybe he'd even help us then. You said he's staying in the emporium with George and Edward?"

"I don't think you should go to him," Violet said anxiously. "We can't let the Archers know that we know any of this, and we can't trust Tom."

Macula looked down at her hands.

"I know he's your son," Violet continued, afraid she'd upset her, "and I don't think he's bad either, not really anyway…" She hesitated for a moment. "Tom didn't kidnap me when he was supposed to – the nurse told him off for that. And in the graveyard, he saw me and Anna hiding and he didn't give us away. He could have, easily. He has a bird too, it's his pet. I don't think someone who cares for animals could be bad."

"Thank you, Violet." Macula half-smiled. "It's nice to hear those things about him. Maybe you're right, but maybe we can't trust him just now."

"Can we see the letter from Nurse Powick?" Violet asked, feeling braver. "Maybe there's something in it that might help us find her. We know she's working with the Archers, so if we find her, then maybe we'll find Boy."

Boy's mother hesitated before walking to a pale-blue painted cupboard on the far side of the room. She pulled out a pile of letters from the drawer, tied neatly together by brown twine. Then she sat back down and undid the bundle.

A letter fell open on the table in front of Violet. Curious, she leaned forward and started to read it.

Dear Boys,
I dreamed about you again last night,
you were so happy. I truly hope I'm somehow
seeing what you see, and that you are both
strong and well...

"You can't read that, Violet!" Anna said sternly. "It's not your letter."

Violet blushed, and folded the piece of paper back up.

"It's okay, Anna." Macula smiled. "Violet's seen some of these notes before."

"I thought it was strange that they all started with 'Dear Boys'," Violet whispered, remembering. "There were piles of them in your room in the estate. There's a letter there still – I found it when we were looking for Conor."

"There is? I must have dropped it when I was leaving," Macula answered. "I've written thousands, all to my boys."

"I thought you meant William and Boy," Violet replied.

"I kept William in my heart and round my neck." Boy's mam thumbed a beautiful gold locket inset with green stones, just as she had done when she'd first met Violet in the Ghost Estate. It was the locket William had given her. The same one that, when Violet mentioned it, persuaded him to join the fight against Perfect again.

"Found it!" she cried a short while later. "Priscilla Powick wrote to me a little while after Perfect fell and I returned to this house to live with William and Boy. I'm not sure there is anything in here to help, though, Violet. She just goes on with the same nonsense Edward spouted from the steps of the Town Hall today."

Boy's mother opened the pristine pink paper.

"I can't bear to look at that woman's words again. Would one of you mind?" She handed the letter across the table.

Violet took it and began to read aloud.

Dear Mrs Macula Archer,
I'm writing to you as a concerned citizen.
    I've recently discovered that your son, Boy, is the heir of William Archer, a renowned Divided Soul. As you will well know, Boy has a twin brother and, through no ill-gotten means, I own his other half. For your references, I called him Tom.
    It is a much known fact that if a Divided Soul,

such as your husband, has twin offspring, the curse of the Divided Soul is split in half and each twin reaps separate otherworldly powers of good and evil. In short, one twin will be bad and the other good.

Tom, as you know, has white-blue eyes. He is an angelic child and his gift clearly governs all that is good. However, this of course means that Boy, the twin in your possession, has powers to master all that is dark and evil.

I'm writing, as a concerned individual, to warn you that soon Boy will be coming of age, and I'm sure is already showing signs of the curse. Watch out for dark acts or he might just terminate you in your sleep.

Yours with the warmest of wishes and regards,
Priscilla Powick

PS Early signs of the curse may include dabbling in thievery, lying, running away, etc.

"What a weird letter," Violet remarked.

Macula nodded. "I know. I thought so too. I just wish I knew why she took my son. Though, she is quite obviously mad."

"Maybe she wanted a baby," Anna said, "and she liked Tom, so she took him for herself. But she didn't talk to him like she liked him, did she, Violet? There's a boy in my class and his mother never talks to him like she likes him, either. Mam said she's just a very busy mammy and that makes her cross, so maybe the nurse is just very busy?"

"Maybe, Anna." Macula's face lightened as she pulled the little girl onto her knee and wrapped her tight.

"Will we get my mam back?" Anna whispered, her voice cracking a little.

"In no time, Anna, I promise." Macula kissed the top of the blonde girl's head.

"But why would Powick write all that about Boy and the Divided Soul stuff?" Violet asked. "Dad says it's only folklore, and not true."

"All I can think is, for some reason, that woman wanted to turn me against my own son. It worked a little – when Boy's name was first connected to the kidnappings, I did wonder if it was all true, somehow. My mind was a muddle. I will feel forever guilty about that."

"Edward talked about the Divided Soul thing at the Town Hall," Jack piped up.

"Yes, and he told a story of how William murdered his own father. I heard it," Macula replied angrily. "It was all lies, of course. Because Priscilla talked about the Divided Soul in her letter too, I thought there had to be a link between herself and Edward, and now you're telling me there is—"

"But how did the nurse meet Edward, and why would she help the Archers?" Violet interrupted.

"Maybe Edward found out about Boy's twin, somehow, and thought he'd be good for their plans to get back Perfect," Anna said, getting excited again. "So he found the nurse and asked her if they could borrow Tom?"

"Something like that had crossed my mind, Anna." Macula leaned her chin on the little girl's head. "I suspect she's probably being paid."

"But what exactly is a Divided Soul?" Jack asked, looking a little confused. "I never heard of it until today."

"I have heard of it," Macula almost whispered. "Only once before."

The woman fell silent and the three children waited for her to speak again.

"Other than William, I haven't told anyone else this story. I think I tried to forget about it – the whole thing still gives me chills. It happened years ago, when I was living in Perfect. The Archers had made me believe William had died about eight months previously. I'd just had the twins a short while. I kept my pregnancy a secret from everybody except Iris, who helped me. If Edward and George found out about them, I knew they'd go after my boys, just like they did my husband.

"Late one night, a man called at the door. He seemed friendly, and said he was lost and needed to use a phone to ring his family. I put him off and tried to close the door, but he pushed past me and came inside. Then he demanded to see my twins."

Violet gasped. "How did he know about them?"

"He said he'd been watching me closely." Macula's face was white. "I was petrified. I'd never seen this man before, and all I could think of was how to protect my sons. The boys were asleep in their cot in the sitting room. I was afraid he'd harm them, but he just stared, smiling strangely. It terrified me. He said he knew they were children of a Divided Soul and that he suspected they were special, but that it would be apparent soon. He said he'd keep my secret safe, but would visit again. Then he left."

"What did you do?" Anna asked, her eyes wide.

"I knew at this stage what the Archers were up to with Perfect. I'd found the round glasses in their shop and discovered their secret No-Man's-Land, so I'd been planning on leaving the boys at the orphanage anyway. I was delaying it, as I couldn't bring myself to let them go. But after this man's visit, I wrapped up the boys and snuck into No-Man's-Land late that very night. I left them at the door with the glasses and my note, and watched, hidden, as they were taken in.

"It was the hardest thing I've ever done. The next morning I gave myself up to the Archer brothers. I didn't tell Iris or even say goodbye. I thought she'd be safest if she knew nothing. I've never heard of a Divided Soul since, until Priscilla Powick's letter and then from Edward today."

"Who was the man?" Violet asked.

"I don't know anything about him, Violet, and I don't care to know. He wasn't a nice individual." Macula closed her eyes.

"Why do Edward and George hate William so much?" Anna asked innocently. "I don't like my sister sometimes, but I'd never act like they do."

"I never understood why they hated him, but Iris says they've been the same since childhood." Macula sighed, shaking her head.

"Iris told me it's because she protected William when he was young, and the twins thought that she loved him more than them," Violet replied. "She never told me why she had to protect William, though."

"She wouldn't tell me either, Violet. I have asked, but she skirts round the question. That woman's a well of secrets. I'm not sure we'll ever figure Iris Archer out."

"Would Iris be able to help us find Boy?" Jack asked.

"She doesn't know any more than I do. She helped me when I tried to question Tom today, as Edward paraded him through Town pretending he was Boy."

"I heard you," Violet remembered. "Tom said something like 'You'll never find him'. That means he must know where Boy is. Both Powick and Edward told

Tom, at different times, to go back to a place called the Outskirts. Maybe that's where they have Boy?"

"I've never even heard of the Outskirts before," Macula replied.

"I think you get there by going through a tomb in the graveyard," Anna said excitedly. "We saw it open up and Boy – I mean Tom – walked down steps into the ground. Remember, Violet?"

"Yes." Violet nodded. "We tried to open it again after they'd all disappeared, but we couldn't."

"It's possible. There are lots of those tunnels all over Town," Macula said. "I remember playing with William in the one beneath the Archers' Emporium when we were kids. Iris owned the shop back then, and whenever she was working we'd pretend we were looking for hidden treasure. We tried to find more tunnels, but we never did, though there are rumours that many more tunnels exist."

"Let's go there now then," Jack said, jumping up.

"Don't you listen, Jack? We don't know how to open it," Anna stated.

"We'll figure it out. It's the only idea we have so far."

"Jack's right." Violet stood up too. "We're wasting time talking."

"Okay," Macula said. "I'm coming with you."

"But kids are way better at sneaking around than adults. Adults are slow," Anna replied.

"I won't let you go off on your own in the middle of the night." Macula shook her head. "A mother's instincts are to protect. I won't slow you down. Just let me change my clothes."

Violet looked at Jack and Anna as Boy's mam left the room.

"I don't think Macula should come. What if we meet the nurse?" she whispered. "You saw how Macula was when she talked about Powick. We can't risk something going wrong. If anything happens, the Archers will know that we know their plans, and then we may never find Boy."

"I agree with Violet," Jack said, looking straight at Anna.

"Why are you looking at me?" the little girl protested.

"Because you have to distract her while we sneak out."

"Why do I always have to stay behind?" Anna half-cried.

"Because you're the best at it. Just say you need to go to the toilet, like you used to do to the nurses in the orphanage."

"Yeah, but that only worked when I was small, Jack. I can go to the toilet by myself now!"

"Please, Anna, you'll think of something," Violet said, looking anxiously back at the door. "For Boy. He really needs your help."

"Okay." Anna sighed heavily. "But next time I'm coming with you."

The little girl turned and walked out of the room in a huff, as Jack and Violet slipped from the house and disappeared out into the dead of night.

CHAPTER 27

UP

Following behind Jack to the pillars of the Ghost Estate, Violet shivered, unsure if it was the cold or the effects of the falling rain which made her teeth chatter.

"We have to be careful going through here," she whispered. "Tom could be about. Watch out for a black raven, it might mean he's near."

"I am being careful," Jack snapped, glaring back at her while he passed through the entrance.

"Don't snap at me," Violet replied angrily, as they slipped round the green.

Jack stopped for a moment at the bottom of the hill leading up to the graveyard.

"I'm sorry." He sighed, curling his fingers into tight,

shaking fists. "I know it's the rain, but I feel like I'm about to explode."

"It's...it's okay," Violet stuttered, fighting her own thoughts. "I feel it too, Jack. Just keep reminding yourself it's not real. When we get down into the tomb, out of the rain, it should be easier."

He nodded and, without uttering another word, the pair climbed the hill and pushed through the creaking turnstile into the graveyard.

"Look, Jack," Violet whispered, pointing to a stream of thick white vapour billowing from a grave a short distance away. "That's the tomb I fell into, the one with the pipe that leads to the white room. The mist blows up into the sky and forms the mind-controlling clouds. See?"

Jack nodded. "Is that where the passage we're looking for is too?" he asked.

"No." Violet shook her head as she snuck up the weed-ridden path, finding her way by memory.

Gingerly she passed by broken crosses and overgrown graves in the darkness, until she stopped beside the tomb she'd seen Tom and the others disappear into.

"The tunnel to the Outskirts has got to be in here," she said, looking back at Jack. "We just need to figure out how to open it."

The tomb looked like a large rectangular stone box. The pair walked around it searching for clues. Violet was bent down studying its surface, when Jack laughed.

She looked up nervously – laughter didn't sound right in the graveyard.

"Jack, where are you?" she whispered, unable to see him.

"Here!" he said, popping up from the other side of the tomb.

Violet gasped and stumbled back.

"Don't do that, Jack!" she snapped.

"Come here, look at this," he said, ducking back down.

Violet picked herself off the ground and walked around to the other side. Jack was sitting on his heels and seemed to be reading a poem carved into the stone tomb.

"O FORTUNE, CRUELLEST OF
HEAVENLY POWERS,
WHY MAKE SUCH GAME OF THIS
CRUEL LIFE OF OURS?"
Quintus Horatius Flaccus

"What a name," Violet mocked. "I'd kill Mam and Dad if they called me anything like Horatius Flaccus!"

"It's Horace," Jack replied, "he was a Roman poet."

"Horace?" Violet joked. "That's even worse. Anyway, how do you know that, Jack, are you a brainbox or something?"

"There were lots of old books in the orphanage, and I read them all. I really like his writing."

Jack was so different to Boy.

"Oh right," Violet replied, unsure how to respond. "Does he write adventure stories? I love a good adventure."

"He was a Roman poet, Violet," Jack answered, a little impatiently.

"Well, I love poems too," she said sternly, annoyed at Jack's tone. "He must be good, 'powers' and 'ours' rhyme – not all poets are good enough to make poems rhyme, you know."

"Anyway," Jack said, ignoring Violet's response, "look at the word 'game'. It's different to the others. All the rest of the words are carved into the stone, but game is sticking out. I think maybe if I—"

Jack pushed gently on the word as he spoke. There was a faint click, and the small rectangle of stone holding the letters G, A, M and E, moved backwards into the tomb wall.

The air was filled with a familiar scraping noise. Violet and Jack watched, open-mouthed, as the front panel of the rectangular tomb moved down, revealing steps leading into the ground.

"That's amazing," Jack said, standing up.

"I hope no one heard that noise," Violet whispered.

"We really don't want them to know we're coming."

Jack took a deep breath. "I guess we better go in?" He looked nervously at Violet.

She nodded, and the pair began to descend the steps together. A shiver of fear raced along Violet's spine. Her mam always told her it was bad luck to walk on someone's grave – she wondered what Rose would say about walking into one.

Jack stopped, halfway down the steps. His fingers rested on a small rectangular piece of stone jutting in from the wall of the tomb. It had to be the piece that contained the word *GAME* on the outside. He pushed it again, there was a click, and the strange scraping sound filled the air once more. The narrow front panel of the grave rose up from the ground and the passageway was plunged gradually into complete and utter darkness.

"We didn't bring a light." Violet panicked, as she wobbled unsteadily down the remaining steps onto flat ground.

"Just wait a little bit for your eyes to adjust," Jack whispered. "We weren't allowed lights at night in the orphanage dorms, but I could still read. I got used to the dark."

After a few minutes, just as Jack had said, her sight cleared enough to make out their surroundings.

The walls of the tunnel were brown and uneven, like roughly-cut dirt. The floor was covered in worn flagstones, and a string of unlit light bulbs hung above their heads. It seemed very familiar.

"Straight ahead?" she whispered.

"Doesn't appear to be any other way," Jack replied from just behind her. His breath was heavy, and she could tell he was nervous as they moved quietly along the passage. When they grew more accustomed to the dark, their pace picked up.

They'd been walking a short while when Violet saw a room to her left and she ducked quickly inside. The stone space was stacked with boxes and a huge propeller spun round high in the opposite wall.

"This is where they store the gas," she whispered excitedly. "I was caught by the nurse just outside this room. The cell that Conor and Beatrice were kept in is not far from here."

"Come on, Violet," Jack said, pulling her back, "we can't waste time."

Quickly, they continued onwards and were just nearing the room with the prison cell when the light bulbs hanging along the tunnel flickered and lit up.

Violet panicked and grabbed Jack's arm. Racing forward, the pair ducked into the only hiding place available – through the archway and black-iron gate, into the darkest corner of the tiny cell.

Violet held her breath.

Footsteps echoed, coming towards them. The sound grew louder until someone was almost outside the arch. Violet tensed, ready to spring when the person passed by.

After a few minutes, the place plunged back into darkness. The pair waited for a while before shakily slipping out of the cell and returning to the tunnel.

"I wonder who that was," Violet whispered.

Jack shook his head and put a finger to his lips. "Be quiet, they could still be about."

They continued forward and soon a breeze whipped Violet's hair. She was sure they were nearing the outside, when she hit a dead end.

This couldn't be it – where was the breeze coming from? Violet threw her head back and looked skywards.

"Jack." She grabbed his jumper, pointing upwards.

A shaft stretched vertically above them, as though reaching for the heavens. The walls were curved and laid in stone and a small circular opening framed the distant night sky. She could just see the edge of a large white moon.

"It looks like we're at the bottom of a dry well," Jack gasped.

Violet's heart pounded – that's exactly what it looked like.

"But how…how do we get out?" she stuttered.

All of a sudden, Violet felt trapped. Her chest

tightened and the tiniest of sounds convinced her someone was coming. The pair paced back and forward across the small space, looking for a ladder or a rope or something to help them get up to the outside.

"The quote on the tomb said life is a game. We had to push on the word *GAME* to get into the tunnel. So maybe this is another game of sorts," Jack mumbled.

"Like a puzzle?" Violet asked. "I'm not very good at those."

"Well, I was the orphanage puzzle master," he boasted, searching the walls.

Maybe Jack was right, maybe it was some sort of a game. She traced her hands over the roughly-cut stone, hoping to find some sort of a hidden lever or button that might help them escape.

After a while, feeling panicked and tired, Violet slid down the curved wall onto the stone floor to gather her thoughts. Something caught her eye.

She scrambled onto her hands and knees, and crawled forward. Engraved into the top left corner of the flagstone beneath her was a small carved *W*. She looked at the stone beside it and rubbed away dirt to reveal an *X*, also in the left corner.

Violet continued across the rest of the floor, wiping away bits of debris to uncover more hidden letters. Each of the lettered stones gave way slightly under her weight.

"It's an alphabet, Jack," she whispered. "It's an alphabet floor. Each of the stones has a letter on it, see? You can press them down like buttons."

Jack scrambled onto his knees beside Violet.

"I bet we need to spell something out," he said excitedly.

He reached for the G, then the *A*, the *M* and finally the *E*. Nothing happened.

"I thought since we used the word game to get in, it might be the same word to get out," he whispered disappointedly.

"What about 'Archer'?" Violet said, spelling it out on the floor.

"No, Violet," Jack replied, before she'd even finished. "The Archers didn't make this tunnel. These passageways have to be ancient."

"Then what did that quote say exactly, the one on the tomb we used to get into the tunnel? Can you remember?" she asked breathlessly.

"Something about life being a cruel game. Maybe spell 'life' or 'cruel'?" Jack tried both, but neither worked.

"What about that poet's name? The ridiculous one?" Violet was flustered now.

"Q, u, i, n, t, u, s, H, o, r, a, t, i, u, s, F, l, a, c, c, u, s," Jack spelled, but nothing happened. "I'll try 'Horace'," he said a little later, but, again, there wasn't a stir.

The pair spent what felt like hours racking their brains for words, until finally Violet sat back against the wall, defeated.

"Maybe the floor's got nothing to do with getting out of here." She sighed. "Maybe we have to do something else, like climb out?"

"I don't think so!" Jack craned his head back to look up at the circular piece of sky which was just beginning to lighten as dawn approached. "The floor has to have been built this way for a reason."

"I feel like giving up." Then it hit her. It couldn't be that simple, could it?

Violet crawled across the stones until she found U, and put some pressure on the paving. Then she searched out P and pressed it.

The floor shook a little, then moved swiftly up the walls of the well like a lift, towards the outside.

"Up," Violet whispered, relieved. "Maybe I should be crowned puzzle master!"

CHAPTER 28

EYE SPY

Violet and Jack were propelled up into the open air. When the platform stopped, the pair jumped off and quickly hid behind a huge twisted tree. The tree was growing beside a lane that wound behind them, disappearing into a forest some distance away. There wasn't a single cloud in the sky.

Directly across the lane from their hiding spot was a cottage thatched in straw, like the homes in history books. Its rough walls were painted white and the window sills and door a bright yellow. A yellow, wooden fence edged an elaborate rose garden to the front and side of the house.

On the other side of Violet and Jack's hiding spot was a large ploughed field, and across the field were two stone stables with yellow-painted doors.

Perched on the edge of the lane where they crouched was a road sign. It was covered in dirt. Jack pulled himself up beside the sign and rubbed away the years of green gunge to reveal raised black letters beneath.

THE OUTSKIRTS

"I knew it," Violet said, reading the worn wording. "This is the place Edward and the nurse talked about. Boy has to be here somewhere."

"And if he is, the nurse probably is too," Jack whispered. "So we have to be quiet."

"Let's check out the stables first then." Violet pointed across the field. "It might be easier to look there – someone might be asleep in the house."

Jack nodded and the pair kept low and to the edges of the ploughed field, trying to keep out of sight of the cottage. They moved quickly towards the stables, their pace only slowed a little by the thick brown mud.

A small cement footpath led up to the stables, and Violet stepped onto it, ahead of Jack.

"In here," she said, ducking inside the first yellow door.

The stable was dark and, like in the tunnel, it took a moment for Violet's eyes to adjust.

Though she hadn't been in many stables, she knew they were normally filled with straw or animals, or some mixture of the two. But straight in front of Violet, fixed to the far wall in a line, were three small screens. In the middle of the stable was a black leather chair, facing the screens. To the right of the chair was a small table with a neat black box resting on top of it.

"What is this place?" Violet whispered.

Jack shrugged and walked towards the screens. Violet followed, stopping at the chair. She sat down and inspected the box on the table beside her.

In the middle of the box was a small joystick, and behind the stick were three green buttons.

"It looks like some sort of control box, Jack," she said. "Maybe it's a remote for the TVs?"

"There are names on the buttons," Jack pointed out, walking back towards her.

Violet bent forward for a closer look. Jack was right – small clear stickers rested over each button. The first sticker read *Denis*, the second *Hugo* and the third *Denise*.

"Hugo!" she whispered excitedly. "That's the Child Snatcher's name."

The pair looked at the button, then back at each other.

"What do you think the buttons are for?" Violet asked slowly.

"I don't know." Jack shrugged, looking nervous.

"Will I press it?"

"What if it's an alarm or something, and it lets the Archers know we're here?"

"But what if it's a camera or something, to show us where Hugo is? Maybe he's in the same place as Boy."

"Okay, just for a second though – then turn it straight back off," Jack warned.

Violet nodded and her hand shook as she pressed down on the green button bearing Hugo's name.

The middle TV on the back wall turned on. An image filled the screen. Violet's heart pounded and her finger shook as it was poised over the green button, ready to slam back down.

The TV showed the inside of a stable that looked exactly like the one they were in. The picture on the screen moved from the door across the stable until Violet and Jack were looking at the side view of a man strapped to a stone wall. It was like something from a scary film.

"What are we watching?" she stuttered nervously. She didn't lift her eyes from the screen. "Will I turn it off, Jack?"

A long, slow groan filled the air. It sounded close by. Violet's skin broke out in goose pimples, as her left hand gripped the arm of the leather chair.

"What is it, Jack?" she said again, looking round this time.

Jack had disappeared. Violet's chest tightened, then suddenly he reappeared on the TV screen in front of her.

His face was as white as a Perfect bed sheet.

"Violet," he whispered.

The sound didn't seem to come from the screen but from somewhere nearby.

Her goose pimples grew.

"Violet, you need to come in here," Jack hissed.

"Where are you?" she asked, talking to the air.

"I'm in the stable next door."

Her mouth dry, Violet slipped outside and in through the second yellow door. Jack was standing in the middle of the stable. In front of him was Hugo.

The Child Snatcher was strapped to the stone wall by some sort of a harness, and either side of him were two other monsters, also tied to the wall.

Violet grabbed Jack's arm, as a wobble rocked her legs and her stomach churned. She closed her eyes in case she was dreaming, and steadied her breath, before slowly opening them again.

The three monsters were still there in front of her. They were standing upright, their feet firmly on the floor. The black harnesses sat over their shoulders, securing them to the stone wall. They looked as though they were about to take a trip on a roller coaster. Two of the bodies had bowed heads, as if asleep, but Hugo, the third figure, was awake, and staring at Jack.

The Child Snatcher grunted and squirmed, pushing

against his harness as if he was trying to release himself.

"The green button, Jack. I...I must have switched Hugo on!" Violet stammered, dashing back next door.

She stabbed the button bearing the Child Snatcher's name, and the TV went blank.

"He's gone back to sleep," Jack called weakly.

Violet breathed a moment's relief, before heading back to the stable.

Jack was standing frozen in front of the Child Snatcher.

"What are these things?" he asked, breathless. "They're not...they're not human!"

Violet had forgotten he had never seen Hugo properly before.

"I'm not really sure," she replied, joining him. "They seem part-human, part-machine. Hugo has some kind of a metal outer-skeleton – I think it helps him move." She pointed to the steel bars that traced his arms and legs. "And his skin is patched up with bits of weird fur."

"So the buttons next door switch these monsters on and off?" Jack whispered, moving closer to examine Hugo.

"And...and I could see you on the screen, Jack, as if I was looking at you through Hugo's eyes," Violet stuttered.

"His eyes are the eye plants," Jack whispered, now only millimetres from Hugo's half-eaten away nose. "So maybe that's how you saw me on the screen next door.

Hugo's eye plants must be connected to the TV somehow."

"Maybe they work like the Brain in Town," Violet said excitedly. "William told us the eye plants in the beds around Town send out signals of what they're seeing and the Brain converts them back to pictures – he called them electric magnets or something. That's why they worked perfectly as a security system – until Tom started stealing them."

"Electromagnetic signals," Jack said, nodding. "We learned about them in school. It's how our real eyes send messages through the optic nerve to our brains."

"You really are a brainbox!" Violet shook her head. "I know we learned a bit about eyes in school, but Mrs Moody is so boring I could barely keep mine open."

"I like learning," Jack stated, still inspecting Hugo.

He really was so different to Boy.

"You mentioned Edward said something about charging Hugo up," he continued, walking around the Child Snatcher. "Maybe these bodies run on some kind of battery power?"

"But Edward told Madeleine that Hugo was dead. He's a zombie," Violet replied, wide-eyed.

"I'm not sure zombies exist, except in books. All these bars and wires, they look mechanical. Maybe he's some sort of robotic zombie..."

Jack kept to his exploring, as Violet went to check out the other two bodies.

Denise and Denis looked similar to Hugo. Both were traced in stitches, and strange furry patches covered various parts of their bodies.

The male, Denis, smelled just like Hugo. His skin was a ghostly pale mixed with yellow and purple bruising, and a large pink furry patch was sewn over his left cheek.

Denise appeared to be a female, though it was hard to tell. Her hair was long and straggly. Large chunks were missing from her greenish scalp, replaced by what looked like blonde doll's hair.

A faint beeping sound caught Violet's ears. She was drawn to a monitor screwed to the wall by Denise's left shoulder. The monitor's small screen was filled with flashing numbers, and a quick blue line zipped up and down across it, just like a heart machine in hospital. Beneath the monitor was a black box, again screwed to the wall. Red and black cables ran from it to a similar box dug into Denise's upper arm.

"It's a battery," Jack said from behind her. "All three of the zombies have them. They look kind of like the ones in cars."

"So you were right, they do run off batteries," Violet whispered. "Look, Jack." She pointed up to the top-left corner of Denise's monitor, where a battery symbol blinked slowly. "It says eighty-five per cent. She must be almost fully charged."

"I didn't notice that," Jack said, stepping forward again for a look.

Violet moved back towards the door.

"We should go," she said, eager to get away from the monsters. "We need to find Boy and we don't want to be here when these things are fully charged."

Jack looked around and nodded.

"That's fine by me," he said, as he crossed the stable and out the yellow door.

"What about the cottage?" Violet pointed when they were both on the concrete path outside.

"Like you said, there could be somebody asleep in there," Jack replied. "It looks like a home."

"We'll just have to be quiet then," Violet whispered, leading the way.

CHAPTER 29

POWICK'S PASSIONS

Violet pushed open the small yellow gate and stepped onto the red-brick path that led to the door of the thatched cottage.

"Let's just check in the windows first – we might be able to see if there's someone inside," Jack said, behind her.

"Okay, I'll look in the front two windows, and you go around the back. Meet here again in a few minutes."

Jack nodded and disappeared, as Violet snuck forward and gingerly peered in the two front windows. Both were covered in a thin veil of white lace. She couldn't see clearly, but there didn't appear to be any movement inside and she didn't hear any either.

She crept back and was already standing at the front door when Jack returned.

"Someone is snoring in one of the rooms," he panted, "but other than that, I heard nothing else. There's a caravan attached to the back of the cottage too, Violet, like some sort of strange extension."

"Do you think Boy is in there?" she asked.

"I tried to check it out," he whispered, "but the door's locked. I think we can get into it through the house though. But we have to be really quiet – we don't want to wake up whoever is snoring."

Violet gently turned the doorknob.

"It's open," she mouthed, slipping inside.

They were standing in a cream-painted hallway. Warm flickers of light soaked out into the narrow space from a room on the right, highlighting the burned-red and black tiles that chequered the floor. A stained-glass light-fitting hung from the low ceiling. It looked like something from a church.

There was another room a little further down on the left, and straight ahead at the end of the short hallway was a step leading up to shiny metal double-doors, like the ones in hospital operating rooms. The doors looked really out of place in the rest of the cosy space.

"They must lead to the caravan," Jack mouthed.

Violet wasn't listening, as she stepped into the room

on the right. It was painted pale-blue, and wooden beams lined the ceiling. A cream stove set in the middle of the far wall warmed the space. Sitting in a semicircle around the stove was an unusual gathering of teddy bears and dolls. Just inside the door, which was propped open, was a low wooden table, the legs of which appeared to have been sawn short. The table was set with doll-sized cutlery, as if ready for breakfast, and plastic food sat on miniature plates, untouched.

"This place gives me the creeps," Jack whispered, stepping back out into the hallway.

Violet trembled as she quickly followed behind him, eager to get away from the strange space. Her friend stopped outside the next room.

"This is where the person was snoring," he whispered softly, before creeping inside.

Violet followed him as quietly as she could.

This room was pink with soft blue, ice-cream-cone patterned curtains. The dark wooden floor was filled with rows of tiny beds, covered in miniature matching yellow duvets and pillow sets. All the beds were occupied with either teddy bears or dolls, though the bears were in the majority. Oddly, each of the toys seemed to be damaged in some way. One ragged bear had a bandage round his arm, a doll a few beds from him was bald and wore a bandage round her head, while a stuffed rabbit lay flat on its back, connected to a tiny drip. It looked like some kind of weird toy hospital.

A loud snort rose from the far corner of the room, and Violet's heart jumped.

She followed the sound and her eyes fell across a human-sized single bed, squashed against the far wall. A navy cape hung on a hook by the end of the bed, and Nurse Powick was soundly asleep under a large yellow duvet, a replica of the miniature sets that adorned the beds by Violet's feet.

Violet pulled on Jack's arm and gestured out to the hall with her eyes.

"We better go," she whispered, when they were both standing back in the hallway. "I don't think Boy's here."

Jack shook his head. "I want to get into the caravan. I've a feeling about it," he insisted.

He moved forward, towards the silver operating-room doors. Violet nervously followed behind. Each step she took, she imagined Powick watching her, and had to turn around to check the nurse hadn't woken up.

Jack pushed open one of the doors, and freezing air licked Violet's skin. She shivered uncontrollably as she stepped round the cold metal.

They were now standing on a white-tiled floor in a stainless-steel walled room – a complete contrast to the rest of the cottage. Shiny steel workbenches ran around the edges of the space, their surfaces covered in lots of sharp metal instruments, like on a dentist's table.

Small round magnets dotted the metal-clad walls, securing hundreds of drawings and images to its surface. Violet stepped closer for a look. Some of the pages looked to be torn from books and were of men in white coats sewing together the badly-wounded limbs of soldiers on the battlefield; others were detailed illustrations of the human body, showing every muscle.

Violet stepped back slowly, shaking her head, and knocked against something behind her. She turned around quickly and struggled not to scream.

Lying flat on a long, steel table beside her was a body. Its clothes were ratty and torn, its hair caked and matted in dirt, and its half-eaten grey and yellow skin was patched together with blue-coloured fur in places. Resting on a smaller steel table beside the figure was a set of sewing needles, a blue teddy bear who was missing a leg, and two potted eye-plants. On the floor, under the bigger table, were a load of welded steel bars and a pile of electrical wires.

The body looked like a half-finished version of Hugo, and Violet shuddered as she stepped away from it.

"Is that nurse really making these zombie-monsters?" Jack whispered. "It's crazy, Violet!"

"I think so," she replied. "She told Tom that Hugo was her creation, and look at all of this."

"But what does she want with them?" he asked in disbelief.

"I…I don't know, Jack," Violet stuttered. "Let's just go. I don't like it here!"

"Go that way." Jack pointed to the far side of the room and another set of double hospital-doors. "I think that's the way to the caravan."

Eager to get out of the room, Violet shoved open the cold steel doors and rushed through.

She was now standing on a threadbare orange carpet, in a small space crammed right up to the low ceiling with cardboard boxes.

"We must be in the caravan now," Jack said, elbowing through the pile-up.

One of the boxes fell down from its perch, and a load of teddy bears toppled out. Violet bent down and picked up a purple bear.

"Do you think Powick is using the teddies' fur to patch up her zombies?" she asked, holding tight to her new furry friend. "There's a blue bear in that room, and the monster in there is covered in blue patches."

"I don't really want to think about it, Violet," Jack said, manoeuvring his way towards the exit.

He was just fiddling with the white plastic door lock, when Violet heard something.

"Shush," she whispered. "Listen!"

Her heart pounded, and Jack stood still.

"I don't hear anything," he said. "We need to get out of here, Violet."

"No, listen," she insisted.

Then she heard it again. A dull thud, followed by a low mumble.

Jack stopped what he was doing and looked up. Another thud rattled the space, and the mumbling grew more frantic. Suddenly a cardboard box at the back of the caravan jumped into the air.

"There," Violet said, pushing her way towards the sound.

The box was resting on a bench seat. She threw the cardboard aside and lifted up the top to reveal storage space beneath. A tartan blanket was wrapped round a large, wriggling bundle. Violet pulled it away.

"Boy!" she gasped.

CHAPTER 30

THE DECEIT

Boy's face was even paler than usual. His dark eyes were ringed in deep-purple circles, as if he badly needed some sleep, and his cheeks looked a little sunken too.

Violet pulled the yellow tea towel, being used as a gag, from his mouth.

"Y-you found me, you f-found me!" Boy stuttered, stumbling, as he tried to climb up from the storage space.

"Hang on, your legs are tied." Violet grabbed his arm to stop him moving, as she leaned over and undid the knot of rope wound round Boy's ankles.

Jack then helped to lift him out of the cramped space.

"My legs are numb," Boy muttered, struggling to stand.

The pair grabbed their friend and helped him shuffle him through the tight space towards the door.

"How…how…?"

"We have to get out of here. We'll tell you everything when we get back to Town," Jack insisted, when Boy tried to ask questions.

"Hold on," Violet rushed back and quickly wrapped a pile of teddies in the tartan blanket.

She pushed the large bundle into the storage space, closed the lid and put the box back on top of the seat.

"In case Nurse Powick comes looking," she explained, smiling at Boy. He half-smiled back, and they fell into an awkward silence. Violet's cheeks flushed a little as Jack gently opened the caravan door and the trio eased down the metal steps outside.

"It's so good to be in the air! I thought I was going to suffocate in there. My broth…that boy," Boy said, as he hobbled behind the caravan, "gave me water and let me out to the toilet, but he hasn't been here in hours. How did you find me?"

"Violet heard Edward and Nurse Powick talking about the Outskirts, and she thought you might be here," Jack replied.

"We found your pic—"

"Edward?" Boy interrupted, surprised. "What's he got to do with this?"

"So you haven't seen him?" Violet asked.

Boy didn't answer.

"So you don't know everything that's happened?" Jack continued. "Well, Edward's back. But we'll tell you later – we have to get out of here first. That nurse could wake up at any time."

"The nurse? Is she the crazy woman with the navy cloak-thing, who's working with the boy pretending to be me?" Boy asked.

Jack nodded.

"Tom's your brother, Boy," Violet said softly.

"I don't have a brother," he replied, his tone sharp.

Violet's cheeks grew hot. Boy was annoyed with her.

She stayed silent, watching the rising sun as the three passed quietly across Powick's back garden. They were almost rounding the side of the small house, when a door banged.

The nurse emerged from the front of the cottage, carrying a woven basket and some garden clippers. She walked to a large bed of roses, and whistled as she began to cut some flowers off, placing them in her basket.

Violet, Jack and Boy stood frozen. If the nurse turned round, they were all caught.

Boy pointed silently back to where they had come from, and the others nodded. Then they all turned and raced for cover. Jack was much quicker than the other two and had already made it round the caravan when Violet tripped over a stone and stumbled forward onto the grass. Pain seared through her damaged ankle.

"What do we have here? Is some nasty little creature interrupting my morning routine?" a voice cackled behind them.

Boy stopped just ahead of Violet. He waited for a moment, then turned and walked back to Violet's side, placing a foot solidly on her back.

"Stop falling over, you lazy girl," he snarled above her.

Violet froze, forgetting her throbbing foot. What was going on?

"Edward told me to bring her here," he called, pointing to the caravan. "I was going to put her in there."

"Is that the Brown girl?" the nurse asked, walking towards them.

Violet kept her head down, staring at the grass, her whole body tense.

"Yeah, it's her. Edward said she was giving him trouble again, just like in Perfect. He's sick of her already."

"That's strange, I thought he wasn't going to do anything drastic until after he destroyed William. Let me take a look at you," the nurse said, grabbing Violet by the hair and yanking her head back, so Violet was looking straight up the woman's dark, hairy nostrils.

She could almost taste the nurse's stinking breath.

"How could a little mite cause so much trouble? I know what I'd like to do to you," Powick growled, pushing Violet's head roughly back down, so she was almost eating the grass. "You're right, put her in the caravan. Edward can decide what he wants to do with this one. Maybe she'll be a plaything for Hugo!"

Boy nodded and pulled Violet up from the ground.

"Hold on," Powick called, as the pair rounded the back of the caravan.

Violet stiffened.

"Yeah?" Boy replied. His voice was even, not nervous at all.

"Bring me a box of bears – Hugo needs some patching up this morning. I warned you about mistreating him, you little swine. If you weren't so precious to the boss and his plans, I'd use you as spare parts – save my poor little teddies the torture. My hospital is full to capacity already."

Boy nodded quickly, then continued on, dragging Violet – a little too roughly – up the steps of the caravan.

Jack was hidden inside behind a load of boxes, peering out the window.

"She's gone back into the house," he whispered, looking round.

"Give her a minute before we go again," Boy said, picking up a box.

"What are you doing?" Violet asked.

"She told me to get her teddy bears. Don't you think she'd be a little suspicious if I didn't turn up with them, Violet?" His tone was cutting.

"Fine," Violet said. "If you want to be angry with me, then be angry – see if I care. I only came the whole way to the Outskirts and risked my life to save you!"

"Save me? If you'd believed me in the first place, I wouldn't be here, and neither would you!" Boy fumed.

"Hey, stop it," Jack said, placing himself between the two of them. "I don't care who's to blame for anything – I just want to get out of here without being caught by that woman or one of her monsters."

"It's his fault."

"Oh, very mature, Violet," Boy sniped.

"Stop!" Jack snapped again, glaring at Boy. "Give the nurse the box, then get to the twisted tree. You'll see it just across the road from the cottage. We'll meet you there."

Boy nodded, a little red-faced. Then he slipped down the metal steps and across the neat garden, disappearing round the side of the whitewashed cottage.

Violet and Jack sprinted for a gap between the roses, jumped the wooden fence and crossed the road to the twisted tree, crouching down behind it.

A few nervous minutes passed, then Boy appeared round the side of the house, heading straight for them.

A thought hit Violet, one she didn't want to have.

What if it was a trick and this boy wasn't her friend? What if he was Tom after all?

Her heart pounded as she tried to shake the thought from her head. She couldn't doubt him again, could she?

As Boy neared them, Jack grabbed her hand, jumped out from hiding and raced to the well.

"Here." He beckoned to Boy.

Their friend sped up and jumped onto the stone platform beside them.

Violet muttered to herself, trying to think quickly. "Up, we used up to get up, so…so…down, DOWN!" she gasped.

She plunged her hands onto the D, then O, W and finally the N, and breathed a sigh of relief as the platform shifted beneath them, moving back down the well shaft. The Outskirts began to disappear, as the children were carried into the earth.

CHAPTER 31

THE TRIBUNE'S TRIBUTE

The platform came to an abrupt halt at the bottom of the shaft, and Jack was the first to stand up, pulling Boy with him. Violet scrambled to her feet behind them. The three then sprinted through the tunnel, past the cell where Conor, Beatrice and Violet had been imprisoned, then past the canister room, until they reached the steps leading up to the graveyard.

Boy was leaning against the wall now as if feeling a little weak. Violet imagined he hadn't eaten for a while.

Jack raced up the steps and felt around in the darkness. Suddenly everything shook, and the front stone of the tomb moved into the ground, allowing the morning light to trickle down the tunnel.

It was still raining outside – heavier now – even though the sky had been cloudless in the Outskirts.

Violet sprinted up the steps after Jack, then turned to see if Boy needed a hand. He looked away as he climbed up, ignoring her offer. Jack closed the tomb and no one spoke as they moved steadily down the hill and through the estate. When they mounted the footbridge, Violet stopped for a moment.

"Do you hear that?" she said, a little breathless.

"What?" Jack asked, looking back at her.

"It sounds like there's something going on in Town." She was sure she could hear people shouting.

"Let's just get to Macula's," Jack said.

The three snuck over the bridge and turned left onto Wickham Terrace, continuing until they reached number 135. Boy knocked on the door, but nobody answered. He tried the handle and it was locked.

"Wait here," he said, disappearing round the side of his house.

A few moments later, the door opened.

"Mam always leaves a spare key out the back. She's not here!"

"We should find her," Violet said, walking inside.

Boy ignored her again, as he rooted through the kitchen cupboards looking for food. Violet and Jack sat down at the table. An emergency edition of the *Town Tribune* had been delivered and was sitting in front of them. Robert Blot had obviously been very busy working right through the night. Violet stopped dead when she saw the headline.

TRIAL OF THE CENTURY
WILLIAM ARCHER TO PAY A PERFECT PRICE
FOR HIS PERILOUS PERFORMANCE

The article, which was full of lies, went into detail about how William, Boy, Eugene, Madeleine and Merrill were to be publicly tried on the steps of the Town Hall at nine the following morning. Violet tried not to panic; they only had a day to save her dad and everybody else.

She turned the page.

FAMILY LIES: ARCHER TWINS SAVE TOWN FROM
BROTHER WILLIAM'S WRATH

This story went into great detail about William's plot to take revenge on the Perfectionists, and how his plans to take over Town for himself and the clinically crazy No-Man's-Landers, were thwarted by his heroic brothers.

NUNN TOO SOON, BROWN BEATEN BACK, MARX HIS CARDS and *A MAN DIVIDED* were other headlines that dotted the pages. Again and again, the articles were filled with lies. Robert Blot was clearly having fun.

Violet felt sick. If the Perfectionists in Town believed the *Tribune*, then anyone who had been a No-Man's-Lander was in big trouble.

"Edward might be right – he could get Perfect back in no time," Violet said, holding up the paper.

"What do you mean?" Jack asked, his mouth full. He'd joined Boy in the scavenge for food.

"They've set a date for the trial – it's tomorrow morning. The paper is full of the Archers' lies!"

Boy walked over and pulled the *Tribune* off Violet.

"What is going on?" he asked, scanning the pages. "The paper says Dad tried to take over Town?"

"Never believe what you read, Boy." Violet half-smiled.

"It's not funny, Violet. How could you joke?" he said, munching on a sandwich.

Violet fell quiet as Jack explained what had happened in Town since Boy had been captured.

"I think we need to go see Iris," she interrupted, when Jack had almost reached the end of the story. "Macula will probably be there too."

"But we need to save Dad first," Boy said.

"My dad's locked up there with him too." Violet raised her voice.

"It's not a competition, Violet!"

"What is up with you two?" Jack snapped. "You're friends – so act like it!"

285

"Friends believe you when you tell them things, Jack!" Boy avoided looking at Violet.

"Well, it's hard to believe your friend when he has an identical twin brother who's pretending to be him," Violet fumed.

"It wasn't hard for Jack, was it?" Boy replied.

Jack turned his back on the pair and pretended to be searching in a kitchen cupboard.

"Well, he didn't have Tom telling him lies all the time, did he?" Violet's face was bright red with anger. "Maybe you're not even the real Boy. How would I know?"

She stopped, as rage flooded her veins. She shouldn't have said that. Boy's face dropped. He looked down at his hands.

"Maybe I'm not," he whispered. "Maybe I'm not anyone any more." He sounded hurt, and mixed up.

"We should go to Iris's now," Jack said quickly.

Boy and Violet looked away from each other and nodded in unison at Jack, both eager to break the tension.

"You should put on a hat or something," Violet mumbled at Boy. "Just in case someone sees you. Everyone's so angry, I don't think it's safe, especially with what the paper's saying."

Boy got up and left the table without a word. Violet could hear his feet on the stairs. A few moments later, he was back in the kitchen, his clothes changed, and he was now wearing a hat and a hoodie.

Violet stood up from the table, a little lighter inside. At least Boy had listened to her.

"Let's go then," she said, opening the front door on the miserably wet morning.

The three friends quickly headed through Market Yard, towards Forgotten Road. People were gathered in whispering groups. An awful, angry energy played on the air.

Violet kept her head low and repeated to herself, over and over, that what she was feeling was simply the weather.

They were near the top of Rag Lane when a huge crash rang through the morning streets and somebody yelled: "NO-MAN'S-LANDERS, OUT!"

Boy raced ahead, following the sound. Violet chased after him, leaving Jack, as he questioned an ex-orphan they'd just met about what was going on.

"Stop, please!" she panted, reaching Boy's side. "We have to go to Iris's. You can't be seen out here. Everyone in Town is angry with you right now."

"They're not angry with me, Violet," he replied, stopping at the top of Archers' Avenue.

Suddenly the dark clouds seemed to explode, and the morning rains turned torrential.

"I know they're angry at Tom, but they don't know

that! Everyone thinks they're angry at you and your dad," she called through the maddening weather.

Another crash rang round Town. Boy darted down Edward Street, towards the sound. Violet followed. They stopped short of a small group standing laughing outside Merrill Marx's toyshop.

All Merrill's windows were smashed and giant black letters were sprayed across his bright-green door.

GO BACK TO NO-MAN'S-LAND, MARX!

Violet turned and glared at a woman who was laughing nearby.

"Why would you do that? It's not funny!"

"You're a sympathizer! I knew I recognized you, you're that Brown girl. Your mother is a Perfectionist, isn't she? No matter, you're obviously on the other side. Your lot are causing no end of trouble around here. The No-Man's-Landers need to find their own place to live and leave us in peace, like we used to be. Perfect was beautiful once, now look at the state of this Town!"

"Perfect was controlled by the Archers," Violet replied angrily. "They brainwashed you. How could you want to go back to that?"

"I don't remember feeling like this back then. We're under constant threat from those No-Man's-Landers. If it's not our property, it's our children – they take whatever they can get their dirty hands on. They're lunatics! They were put in No-Man's-Land to get better, you know, and now look how they repay the Archer brothers' generosity. They deserve to be locked up again!"

The woman was shaking angrily as she finished her speech.

Thunder boomed overhead, and the downpour increased.

"We need to get inside. It's not safe out here!" Jack puffed, catching up with them.

Boy's face was almost purple with rage.

"We need to get to Iris's, quickly," Violet insisted, looking at Jack.

The pair grabbed their friend's arms, and led him swiftly through the hostile streets.

CHAPTER 32

A GOOD PAIN

"Violet! Have you found my grandson?" Iris exclaimed, as she opened her front door.

Violet beckoned Jack and Boy forward, and followed them into the house. Once safely inside, Boy took down his hood and removed his hat.

"Oh, thank heavens." Iris hugged Boy for what felt like ages, then pulled back to properly see her grandson. "You look pasty, my lovely. Come in, come in. I'll make you something to round those hollow cheeks."

The old woman ushered them down the hall to the kitchen. Macula, Rose and Anna stood up from the table as they entered the warm room. Rose rushed round to hug her daughter as Macula and Anna welcomed Boy and Jack.

"You gave me such a fright, pet," Rose stuttered.

"I'm fine, Mam," Violet replied.

She watched as Boy pushed back from his mother's embrace, choosing to hug Anna first. Macula's face dropped as he gave his mam a quick nod and sat down to the table.

The room slipped into an awkward silence.

"What happened to you, Boy?" Macula asked softly, breaking the quiet.

"Tom took me."

"We found him in the Outskirts, Mac—" Violet tried to explain.

"I can speak for myself," Boy snapped.

Everything stopped. The room fell utterly still.

Boy's face turned red. Then he stood up and raced from the table, banging the kitchen door behind him. Macula tried to follow, but Iris grabbed her arm.

"No," she said, shaking her head, "give him time."

Boy's mother sat back down in silence.

"Tell us what happened?" Iris encouraged, as she finished making sandwiches.

Violet's mind was caught up with worrying about Boy. Jack began to tell their story and as she tuned in and out of snippets, Iris nudged her.

"Take this to Boy," the old woman whispered, passing her a sandwich she'd just prepared. "He could do with his best friend right now."

"But he doesn't like me at the moment," Violet whispered back.

"He's just pretending. It's a little thing called pride, Violet. Take this to him, you'll both be fine."

Violet got up from the table and was walking towards the door, when Macula grabbed her elbow.

"Tell him I'm sorry," Boy's mam whispered. Her eyes were sad.

Violet nodded, and went out into the hallway.

Boy was sitting on the bottom stair, his head in his hands. Violet walked round the banisters and stopped in front of him.

"Can I sit down?" She coughed awkwardly.

"Free country," he huffed.

A surge of rage raced through her, but she held her composure as she sat down beside him.

"Ask me," Boy urged.

"Ask you what?" Violet asked.

"Something that proves I'm me. I know you won't believe me until you do. Go on!"

"I do believe you, Boy. I know it's you."

"No, you don't – don't lie. Ask me. Now!" He was angry, much angrier than Violet had ever seen him.

"Okay…erm, where did we first meet?"

"In your bedroom, after I gave you the glasses. Though, technically it kind of wasn't. It was in the Archers' shop, when you were getting your first specs and I was being chased by the Watchers."

"See? I knew it was you." Violet smirked, though secretly she felt guilty for doubting him earlier.

"This time, maybe."

They slipped into an uneasy silence.

"I'm really sorry," Violet whispered, after a few minutes.

Boy played with the strings of his hoodie.

"I was just so confused and angry. I was sure I saw you with Conor, and you said it wasn't you. I didn't know what to believe. I mean, how could I have known you had a twin brother?"

"How could you think I'd do anything like that?" Boy replied. There was pain in his voice. "How could you think I'd kidnap Conor or Beatrice, or anyone, Violet?"

"I don't know," she replied quietly. "I saw you – or who I thought was you – and strange things were happening around Town. Nothing made sense."

"But you're meant to know me, Violet. At least, I thought you did…" Boy's voice faded.

"You weren't telling me anything – I tried to ask you questions, but you said nothing was wrong!"

"I told you to trust me."

"Yes, without giving me any reason to!"

Tears streamed down Violet's face, though she'd willed

them not to. She looked away. The clock ticked over the fireplace in the sitting room, and noise from the street outside filtered in.

The kitchen door opened, and Macula stepped into the hall.

"I heard you two fighting..." she said, looking a little uneasy.

"We weren't," her son answered.

"You were, and I am truly sorry for being the cause of that."

"Why didn't you tell me I had a brother?" Boy asked, not looking up from his feet. "The first I knew about him was that photograph."

"I wanted to tell you – so many times, Boy – but I thought I was protecting you. I wanted to find out what happened to Tom, first, before I told you anything. I know now that was a mistake."

"Would you stop trying to protect me?" Boy responded. "I protected myself for twelve years!"

His mother's head dropped, and Violet could feel the sting of Boy's words.

"I know," Macula whispered. There were tears in her eyes. "I'm so sorry, son."

"Tom –" Boy winced as if the word caused him pain – "how can he be my brother, when he's trying to hurt everyone and make people believe I'm bad? How can I be related to him? He even turned my best friend against me."

"No, please, Boy – I wasn't against you. I was worried about you," Violet corrected. "Please don't think that I hated you. I wanted to help you, that's all."

"I don't believe your brother has had a nice life, Boy." Macula's voice was steady. "I did the wrong thing giving you both up."

"Maybe," Boy said under his breath.

"I'll leave you be," his mam said, nodding gently at her son.

She stepped away down the hall.

"Mam," Boy said, when her hand was on the kitchen door.

"Yes, son?"

"You didn't do the wrong thing."

"I love you, son," Macula replied. A sad smile played on her lips as she pushed open the door and disappeared inside.

The pair sat in silence for a while more, as Violet racked her brain for something to say. She was about to stand up and leave, when Boy spoke again.

"Thanks for finding me," he said quietly.

"Jack helped," Violet answered, unsure of what else to say.

"I probably would have found you a lot quicker,

though." Boy half-smiled. "I was starved by the time you got there."

"Well, you needed to lose some weight," Violet joked tentatively.

Boy hit her shoulder, and her opposite elbow banged against the banister.

"Hey, what was that for?"

"For taking too long to rescue me," he joked.

Violet grabbed her elbow – it throbbed a little, but it was a good pain. A pain that meant she might just be getting her old friend back.

CHAPTER 33

THE WITNESS

Violet pushed open the kitchen door and walked in, followed a little sheepishly by Boy. Rose, Macula, Iris, Jack and Anna were deep in conversation, and they all pretended not to notice the pair slip back inside.

Iris caught Violet's eye and winked, as Violet sat down at the table beside her mam.

"Here," the old woman said, putting a sandwich down in front of Violet and another in front of Boy, "get those into you."

Boy smiled up at his grandmother. Iris squeezed his shoulders.

"But why have a trial at all?" Jack asked, staring down at the *Tribune* on the table. "Surely the twins could just release the Watchers and take over Town? I don't understand."

"Edward told George they need to win back people's trust before releasing the Watchers," Violet replied, remembering. "The Watchers were horrible – I don't think people have forgotten that and I think he's worried the Perfectionists won't believe all his crazy lies if he releases them too soon."

"He wants to avoid a battle like the one we had in Perfect, I suspect." Iris shook her head. "He knows, even with the might of the Watchers, if the Perfectionists and No-Man's-Landers remain united, they won't be stopped. He's trying to divide us, and it's working."

"Divide and conquer," Rose muttered, remembering Madeleine's words.

"Those two sons of mine have a madness in them, an evil streak – just like their father. I expect the humiliation of Perfect has added extra venom to their hearts," the old woman continued. "They are power-hungry creatures, who want to control everything. They will relish destroying William all the more because they're using his own son Tom to do it. Poor young thing."

"I won't feel sorry for Tom," Boy stated bluntly. "He's pretending to be me, and doing terrible things in my name."

"But he's your brother," Anna replied, wide-eyed.

298

"I don't want a brother! Can we not talk about him? I need to figure a way to get Dad out, so we can leave this place."

"I don't think having a brother is a choice," Anna said, looking a little confused.

"And what then, Boy?" Iris interrupted, sounding stern. "Let Edward and George take back Town, and create Perfect part two?"

"I don't care about Town any more. Nobody here cares about me or Dad. If they did, they wouldn't hate us so easily."

"That's not true, Boy, they don't hate you," Violet pleaded. "The Archers have made people sad and afraid, and made them think all of that is because of you, William and the No-Man's-Landers. They've given them someone to blame for their pain. That's all."

"Well, I'm sick of being the person to blame. Let this place fall apart. I just want to get Dad and Mam, and leave."

"Thanks," Violet huffed, looking away.

"Yeah thanks," Anna sobbed. "You said you'd always be my friend, but now you're leaving."

"It was a bit of a waste risking our lives for you then, wasn't it?" Jack replied drily.

"You don't mean what you say, Boy," Macula said quietly, looking him in the eyes. "I know you're hurt, son

299

– but this is a good place, full of good people. You know that too."

Boy dropped his head and continued eating his sandwich.

"We can save William and our friends, and still save Town," Macula continued. "You've all done it before. Why can't we do it again? Together we can beat Edward and George!"

"But how, Macula?" Rose looked anxiously at the woman. "Maybe Boy is right. Maybe we should all just leave, and give George and Edward what they want. It's not as if people's imaginations are gone any more – they have the ability to think for themselves, and they seem to be choosing those horrible men."

"No, they don't have the ability to think for themselves, Mam," Violet corrected, sitting forward. "Like Dad said, fear can take over a person's mind and make them do strange things."

"But we can stop the rain," Anna said excitedly. "All we have to do is block up the pipe! Won't that stop the fear? Maybe people's heads will feel better then?"

"That's brilliant, Anna. But if we block the pipe, the rain will stop and the Archers will know we're on to them. We need the clouds to be there still, but maybe we could put something else into them, to relax people a bit – like the laughing gas. There must be more of it in the canister room." Violet was thinking fast.

Iris nodded. "Yes, we can certainly do as Edward and George have, and change how people feel – but the key is to change how they think. That will prove a little more difficult."

Boy looked up, suddenly paying attention.

"What if I tell them the truth?" Boy said quietly. "Won't it change how they think, if they know the truth?"

"The truth?" Rose laughed bitterly. "Nobody listens to that any more."

"Boy's right though," Violet said, remembering her dad's words. "If you tell the truth, you'll never be wrong. We wanted to find Boy so we could help him by showing people he had a twin. If somehow we could still do that, show Boy and Tom together, then Boy can tell the truth."

"But how would people know who is who, Violet?" her mother asked. "Wouldn't that confuse everyone even more?"

"Everyone trusts the Archer brothers. What if *they* told the truth?" Anna shrugged.

"Edward and George will never do that, Anna." Jack smiled, patting her head.

"Anna might be on to something," Macula said, thoughtfully. "We could trick them into telling the truth, and play their confession on the Brain. Wouldn't it be lovely if my husband's latest invention were to trip his brothers up?"

"The Brain...yes, brilliant, Macula!" Violet exclaimed. "What if we get them to admit the truth in front of a bed of eye plants? Then people would see it on the Brain!"

"But how do we get my sons to do that?" Iris asked. "It could be a little tricky to orchestrate."

"Hugo!" Jack jumped up. "Hugo's eyes are made of eye plants. What if we somehow get the Archers to tell the truth, and Hugo is there to witness it? They won't be suspicious of him!"

"That thing's eyes are eye plants? I knew there was something strange about them." Boy shuddered.

"Yes." Violet nodded. "His eyes are connected to a screen in the stables near Nurse Powick's cottage. I could see everything Hugo was seeing on the screen."

"If we can tune all the screens in the Brain into the electromagnetic frequency of Hugo's eyes and have him witness the Archers telling the truth, we could roll up the sides of the Brain and play it on all the screens. Then all we'd need is someone to see it," Boy replied, sitting forward.

Violet smiled, jumping up from her seat. "What if everyone saw it?"

"Of course, the trial," Macula said excitedly. "Everyone will be outside the Town Hall for the trial. If we can somehow trick the Archers into telling someone their real plans, and Hugo is there to witness it, we can play it on the Brain for the whole of Town to see. We'll turn William's humiliation into Edward and George's defeat!"

"The trial of the century!" Iris laughed.

"I might just stay around for that." Boy smiled.

CHAPTER 34

THE SWAP

Macula had been home and raided William's toolbox, and now Boy was busy fiddling with a signal transmitter at Iris's kitchen table. Violet was sitting beside him, in front of a piece of paper, trying to recall the details of the white room – the one that created the clouds. She felt a little better, having caught a few hours' sleep before the next stage of their plan, tonight.

"All those hours watching Dad paid off." Boy smiled as he fiddled with the small black box in his hands. "Now all we need to do is go back to the Outskirts tonight, and attach this new transmitter to Hugo's eyes while he's recharging. It'll be tuned into all the receivers in the Brain, and every screen will show whatever Hugo is seeing!"

"And I thought Jack was the intelligent one," Violet joked.

"He is, isn't he? He was always reading in the orphanage. He's got an encyclopedia for a head." Boy looked back down at the transmitter.

The sound of trouble outside swept through the house, making Violet nervous.

Jack had gone to tell some ex-orphans their plans, as they'd need their help tomorrow at the trial. Rose, Iris, Anna and Macula had gone to the Brain. Boy had given them the code for the transmitter he was going to fix to Hugo's eyes. They were inputting the code into every single screen.

"How did Tom catch you?" Violet asked Boy. She'd wanted to know for ages.

He stayed silent for a minute.

"I was hiding in the orphanage, because everyone was blaming me for things I didn't do," he said eventually. "Madeleine wanted to talk to me about the kidnappings. They had a picture of me stealing the eye plants, and I knew nobody would believe it if I said it wasn't me. I was confused too. I mean, who was it? Anyway, someone knocked on the side of the stairs. I thought it was Anna—"

"Was it Tom?" Violet interrupted.

Boy nodded.

305

"What did you think? Were you scared? It must have been weird, looking at yourself."

"It was weird, but at that point I already had an idea that he existed. There were lots of boxes of photos from the orphanage under the stairs, and I'd been looking through them. I found the one with the two of us in it, and something made sense. It was almost as if I knew already, deep down."

"Did you talk to him?"

"Not really – he talked mainly. He started saying weird things – like how he was the chosen one, or something. He said that Mam and Dad didn't think he was good enough for our family, so they gave him away, but that he'd show them."

"What did he mean?"

"I don't know. He talked about this Divided Soul thing too, as if he believed it…then I tried to climb out from under the stairs and saw Hugo. I think he hit me on the head, because the next thing I remember is the cramped space and the darkness."

A knock on the front door made Violet jump. Boy quickly hid as she walked over to open it.

"Jack!" she said, relieved, as he strode in, soaking wet.

"They're tearing down shop signs and writing stuff about No-Man's-Landers all over the walls," he panted. "The rain is heavy, even heavier than earlier. I felt awful.

I had to keep reminding myself about the clouds and it not being real. Did you sort the transmitter?"

"Yes." Boy nodded, stepping out from behind the door. He held up the little black box. "We just have to wire this to Hugo's eyes and, if the others have done their part right, the Brain should be able to see whatever Hugo does."

"But people are really angry right now." Jack shook his head. "Will they even look at the Brain, or take in what's happening? It's crazy outside."

"When we add the happy gas to the rain, it should stop people being so angry," Violet answered. "Remember how relaxed and happy people were when Edward spoke that day? If we can make them that way again, they'll be calm enough to take it all in."

"Something's been playing on my mind though," Jack said with a frown. "I know the people waiting outside the Town Hall for the trial to start will be able to see what's happening in the Committee Room on the screens of the Brain. But how will they hear it – even if we do manage to trick George and Edward into telling the truth?"

Boy and Violet both dropped what they were doing and looked at their friend. They'd got carried away with the plan so much that they never stopped to think about something this simple.

Jack was right! Everyone outside would see the

Archers' confession through Hugo's eyes, but if they couldn't hear it, then all of this plotting was pointless.

Violet's throat tightened.

The front door of Iris's home opened again, and Boy raced to his hiding spot. Violet peered out from the kitchen, relieved, as Macula, Iris, Rose and Anna shuffled inside.

"Oh, it's awful out there. This is never going to work – we're doomed. Doomed, Violet," her mother cried, as Boy returned to his place at the table.

"Mam, that's just the rain getting to you, remember. It's all going to be okay," Violet replied, though she was becoming a little doubtful herself.

"Getting the nitreous oxitocin into those clouds is crucial to everything, though," Iris panted. "People need to be calmer, before they'll listen to reason. It's chaotic out there."

"We've recoded all the receivers, Boy." Macula smiled. "I found these in the Brain too. I thought they might be useful?"

Macula held up a pair of walkie-talkies; the ones Violet and Boy had used to speak to William, the night they discovered the missing eye plants.

"I thought when you've attached the transmitter to Hugo's eyes, you could let me know with one of these, and then I can check it's working properly in the Brain."

"Good idea, Mam!" Boy said, trying to sound enthusiastic. "But we have another problem—"

"I'm not sure we do, any more," Jack interrupted.

Everyone watched as Jack walked forward, took a walkie-talkie from Macula and started fiddling with the buttons.

"Do you have an old radio, Iris?"

"Yes…" Boy's grandmother answered, her brow furrowed. "Why?"

"While we were all worried about how the people outside the Town Hall would see what was happening inside the Committee Room, we forgot something. How will everyone hear the Archers' confession? If they can see it but not hear it, then our plan won't work. But now, we can use these…"

"The walkie-talkies. Of course!" Iris muttered. "You're a genius, Jack! They work on a frequency. So if we can tune my radio into the frequency of the walkie-talkie, then the radio should be able to broadcast whatever the walkie-talkie is hearing. Am I right?"

"Exactly," Jack replied triumphantly. "If someone can hold the walkie-talkie in the Committee Room, we will be able to hear what's happening!"

"But how do we tune the radio into the walkie-talkie?" Violet asked, wishing that they had her dad or William with them right now.

"I think I can do it, it's simple enough," Jack said confidently. "There were lots of old technical books on radio systems and frequencies in the orphanage. I read them loads of times."

"Really?" Violet asked, wondering why anyone would put themselves through that.

"We didn't have much to read in the orphanage," Jack said, shrugging, by way of explanation.

"I can help too, Jack," Iris replied. "Radio systems were a hobby of mine in my heyday. In fact, I was quite the inventor. I'll see what I can do, while you're in the Outskirts."

"Great," Boy said, putting the black transmitter safely in his pocket. "Are we ready to go then?"

Violet looked at Boy and Jack.

"We've done this before, we can do it again," she said bravely.

Macula pulled her son close, wrapped him in her arms and kissed the top of his head.

"Be safe, please," she whispered. "I love you."

Boy blushed and Violet was about to tease him, when she thought better of it – they were only just back on good terms.

Then Jack, Violet and Boy grabbed their coats and headed for the front door. Iris, Macula, Rose and Anna followed them out into the hallway. Rose paced nervously around the small space.

"Now you will be careful, Violet, won't you?" she said, cupping her daughter's face. "I really shouldn't let you go alone. I mean, what kind of a mother am I?"

"A brave one, Rose," Iris answered, easing her away from her daughter.

"I'll be grand, Mam. I promise." Violet smiled. "The last time, you didn't have a clue what was happening, and I had to face the Watchers then. This is easy compared to them."

Jack opened the door and stepped outside into the driving rain.

"Right, let's go," he said.

"Oh, don't forget this!" Macula ran out the door and put one of the walkie-talkies into Boy's hand. "I'll be waiting for your call."

❄   ❄   ❄

Everything was still as Violet, Boy and Jack took shelter behind the twisted tree in the Outskirts. The moonlight fell gently across the ploughed field and reflected off the stable roof.

The lights were on in Nurse Powick's cottage, and the thatched home looked picture-perfect as the glowing windows warmed the night. Violet imagined the nurse sitting down by the stove to feed her dolls and teddies. The only sign that anything was wrong was the lump in Violet's throat.

She pointed to the stables.

"Hugo's over there," she whispered.

Boy nodded. Silently, the three children slipped along the edges of the field until they reached the yellow stable-door and crept inside.

Boy gasped as he spotted Hugo, Denise and Denis strapped to the back wall, their heads bowed as if asleep.

Violet walked forward to check the battery symbols on each of the monster's monitors. They were all at ninety per cent.

Boy and Jack got to work on Hugo. They were unwiring his current transmitter, the one that linked to the TV screen in the first stable, and attaching Boy's new one, that now linked to all the screens in the Brain.

As Violet kept lookout, she noticed how Boy and Jack were finding it difficult to reach up to the back of the monster's head.

"I'll get you something to stand on," she whispered, remembering the black leather chair.

She slipped next door.

The leather chair was exactly where it had been before, parked beside the small table that held the black box with the three green buttons.

Violet grabbed the seat, but one of its wheels was stuck between two cobblestones and wouldn't budge. Roughly, she jerked it to the side, accidentally knocking against the table as she dislodged it.

She was just manoeuvring the large leather seat through the doorway into the second stable, when she heard a commotion.

Hugo's eyes were open. How had he woken up? He was still strapped to the wall, but his hands were wrapped firmly round Jack's neck. Boy kicked frantically at the Child Snatcher, trying to free his friend.

Overcome by panic, Violet raced at the monster, hitting him smack in the stomach. Hugo didn't flinch. They didn't have much time; Jack was turning blue. Boy grabbed the creature's hands and tried to prise them off, even biting down into Hugo's rotten skin.

Suddenly Violet had a thought. Tom looked like Boy... and the Child Snatcher listened to Tom.

"Tom, control Hugo!" she ordered, staring hard at Boy.

Boy stopped what he was doing and caught her eye. Something registered.

"Hugo! Stop," he commanded. "Put Jack down."

Hugo looked at Boy, then back at Jack in his hands. Slowly he released his grip, dropped Jack to the floor and grunted. Violet grabbed the leg of Jack's trousers and, with Boy's help, pulled him away from the monster.

"Jack...are you okay?" they both cried, gently slapping him on the cheek.

Their friend moaned and began to come round.

"Boy, do something!" Violet pointed urgently at Hugo. The Child Snatcher was trying to wriggle from his harness.

"Stop, Hugo. We're just trying to fix your eyes, that's all. It's nothing to worry about," Boy ordered.

"What happened? How did he wake up?" Violet looked at Boy as the monster stopped struggling.

"I don't know," he replied. "You went to get something to stand on, and then Hugo's eyes opened and he came alive."

"So you didn't do anything weird with the transmitter, or something?"

Boy shook his head, confused. "We weren't even near him when his eyes opened."

"Oh no...the table! I hit against it when I was moving the chair. I must have accidentally switched Hugo on," Violet said, jumping up.

She sprinted next door and plunged down the green button bearing Hugo's name.

When she walked back into the zombies' stable, the Child Snatcher was asleep. Boy was still sitting on the floor beside Jack, who was lying down, breathing heavily.

"I'm sorry," she apologized, joining them on the cobbles.

"It's okay, Violet," Boy replied. "At least Jack's alright, and now we know how to get Hugo to come with us to Town. I'll just order him!"

"I think there might have been an easier way to figure that out," Jack spluttered, pushing himself upright.

"Right, back to work!" Boy said, after a few minutes.

He stood up and walked over to the Child Snatcher. Using the chair, he was much quicker at wiring the new transmitter to Hugo's eyes, and didn't even need Jack's help.

"Finished!" Boy smiled widely, jumping back down a little later.

"Brilliant. That means we can go then?" Jack wobbled as he tried to stand up.

"Don't forget we have to call Macula, to check if she can see what Hugo is seeing, right now," Violet said. "I'll turn him on when I'm putting back the chair."

"I almost forgot about that," Boy said, taking the walkie-talkie his mother had given him earlier from his trouser pocket.

Violet wheeled the chair next door and put it back beside the table. Then she switched Hugo on and sat down for a moment to steady herself. The image of Jack's neck in the monster's grip still frightened her.

She was getting up to leave, when a voice that wasn't Jack's or Boy's floated in from the stable beside her. Could it be Macula? She listened harder.

"Tom, I'm talking to you!" the muffled voice filtered through the stone wall.

Macula would never call Boy Tom. Violet shivered. She took a deep breath, and pressed Denis's green button on the table beside her. She needed to turn him on so she could see what was happening next door.

The left-hand screen on the wall in front of Violet came to life. Boy and Jack stood in the middle of the stable, facing the door, and in front of them was Nurse Powick.

CHAPTER 35

THE UNWANTED GUEST

"What are you doing in here, Tom?" Powick's muffled voice snarled through the stone wall. "I thought you were going to the Town Hall tonight, to be ready for the morning. And who is this with you?"

Violet was frozen to the spot, as she watched the nurse on screen.

"I…erm," Boy said, looking across at his friend. "I, erm… Edward asked me to come and fix Hugo. He hasn't been seeing straight lately. His eyes are a little fuzzy."

"Fuzzy?" Powick said, marching past the boys, right up to the Child Snatcher, so Violet could only see the side of the nurse's face. "There's nothing wrong with his eyes, unless it's those faulty eye plants again. The eyes Brown developed are just not good enough for the job at all. Anyway, it's strange timing for Edward to be sending you here now, on the cusp of his big day. Who is this with you?"

Powick turned around, so Violet could only see her back on Denis's screen now. She was facing Boy and Jack.

"Answer me, Tom."

"He's erm, Jack… He's good with technical stuff, like this. Edward said he didn't have time to fix Hugo, because of the trial tomorrow, so he told me to bring Jack for… erm, for help."

"That man is self-obsessed. What is it he wants to achieve tomorrow? Revenge on his brother? Petty, in the scheme of things. Let him have his fun, I say. He'll see the bigger picture soon enough, though, won't he, Tom?" She laughed.

Boy laughed too. It was obvious to Violet that he felt awkward, and she was sure Powick would notice. The nurse would never fall for Boy's story.

"So are you finished here, then?" she asked.

"Erm, yes, I think he is." Boy looked over at Jack.

Jack shrugged and half-smiled.

"Bit funny Edward not asking me to look at Hugo's eyes, isn't? Since Hugo and the others are my creations. Don't you think?"

Boy shifted uneasily.

"So how did you fix Hugo's eyes then, lad?" Nurse Powick asked, as she walked over to Jack, leaning right in.

She was facing Denis again, and Violet could see her wild eyes.

Violet tensed. She had to do something. Powick couldn't find out everything, or their plans would be ruined. The nurse was millimetres from Jack's face, staring into his eyes.

"I...I just...I rewired them," Jack stuttered.

"Oh really?" She laughed again. "And how is it Mr Edward Archer asked a boy like you to do that? You're an orphan, aren't ya, son? You've the smell of a lost sheep!"

Out of the far corner of the screen, Violet could see Hugo. She remembered noticing a red button just below his battery pack with the word RELEASE on it. It had to be the button to free the monster from his harness.

She had an idea. She turned off Denis and quietly snuck into the stable next door. Powick had her back to her, and was still intimidating Jack.

She signalled silently at Boy, pointing to herself and then Hugo. Boy nodded as though he understood.

Her heart thumped loudly. She tiptoed behind Powick, round the edge of the stable to Hugo, and pushed her hand onto the red *RELEASE* button.

The monster's harness clanked loudly as it flew upwards over his head, freeing Hugo from his restraints.

"Call him!" Violet shouted, as the Child Snatcher stepped away from the wall.

"Hugo, attack!" Boy roared, pointing at Powick.

The nurse stood back and laughed, as Hugo lumbered towards her.

"He's my creation. Hugo won't attack me – would you, Hugo? Hugo...?"

The Child Snatcher groaned and lifted his hands up as he trudged towards Powick. The nurse's face changed. She turned and started to run frantically towards the door, just as Jack tackled her to the ground.

Within moments, Hugo was upon his creator. He grabbed the woman by the collar of her navy cloak, hoisting her into the air.

"I'm your mother, your creator! Please, Hugo, please," the woman spluttered.

"You might have made him, but Tom's his friend," Violet said, relieved, as Powick was caught firmly in the Child Snatcher's grasp. "Maybe you should treat your creations better next time!"

"What do we do now?" Jack asked.

"Bring her back here," a raspy voice echoed through the stable.

Everyone scanned the room, unsure where the voice had come from.

"It's me – Macula. The walkie-talkie is in your hand,

Boy. You'll be happy to know Hugo's transmitter is working. Bring Powick back here. OVER!"

"Boy?" Powick laughed. "How did you get out of the caravan, you miserable swine? Did your friends come and save you? Rather sweet, if a little silly. You'll see soon."

"But what if someone notices she's missing? OVER," Boy asked his mam, ignoring Powick.

"And believe me, they will notice," the nurse growled.

"They won't," Macula insisted. "Nobody will be looking for that woman, tonight. The Archers are too busy preparing for tomorrow, as I'm sure Tom is too. Just come straight back, and bring her with you. I'll meet you at Iris's. OVER."

"Okay," Boy said, slipping the walkie-talkie into his pocket. "Let's go back to Town. We can figure out what to do then."

Boy ordered Hugo to carry the nurse. The Child Snatcher threw Powick over his shoulder as they left the zombies' stable and made their way across the ploughed field towards the well-shaft.

"So you're Tom's brother," Powick said, as she hung halfway down Hugo's back. "Are you really going to listen to that fool of a mother? She left you in the orphanage, all that time. I felt so bad for Tom, I simply had to take him under my wing. I would have taken you too, but I could only afford to feed one mouth…"

"Is that because you were already feeding all those toys in your house? Plastic food must be expensive!" Jack mocked.

"Toys? How dare you," Powick spat, irate. "Those are my babies – the babies you orphans destroyed! Children should be locked up, not seen and not heard. That's my motto!"

"At least we're real," Jack replied angrily.

"Real?" Powick laughed. "How does a child with no parents even exist? You're all the discarded, unwanted ones. Your families may have pretended they wanted you back, but look at your pathetic little Town now, falling apart at the seams. The Perfectionists don't want No-Man's-Landers, they never did!"

"Boy, can you get Hugo to shut her up?" Jack snapped.

Boy ordered Hugo to stop Powick speaking. Slowly, the Child Snatcher made a fist and thumped her, knocking her out.

"I'm beginning to like Hugo," Violet said, smiling, as she climbed onto the well platform.

She waited for the others to come aboard, then pressed D, O, W, N, and the stone floor returned to the tunnel.

CHAPTER 36

THE BEST MEDICINE

The group walked back along the tunnel until they reached the storage room filled with boxes of gas canisters. Boy ordered the Child Snatcher to stay put at the arched entrance. Powick was still out cold over his shoulder. Then the three children ducked inside.

"This is where the Archers store their OA gas, the stuff that makes us angry." Violet pointed to a stack of cardboard boxes marked with *OA* in giant red letters. "We need to look for boxes marked nitreous oxitocin or maybe NO. Dad said that's the happy gas. It has to be here somewhere too."

Boy, Jack and Violet began quickly searching the small room. Violet rummaged through stacks of boxes, but every one she touched was marked with the same letters, *OA*.

"Here," Boy called from across the room.

He was ducked down, rummaging in a cardboard box, and pulled out a canister marked *NO*.

"Brilliant," Violet exclaimed. "Spray a little to check."

Boy pushed on the nozzle, and Violet could just about see the clear mist dart across the dark room. Although she could tell he was trying to keep serious, Boy's face lit up, he smiled and then began to giggle.

Violet felt a little of the gas tickle her nose, and she began to giggle too.

"How many boxes are there?" Jack asked.

"Maybe five or six." Boy laughed. "And there's about twenty canisters in each box."

"I'm sure that should be enough," Violet replied, feeling very happy. "Now all we need to do is get that gas into the white room, so it gets mixed into the clouds and rained down over Town!"

"But won't the angry gas still be in the clouds too?" Boy asked. "I mean, we don't know how to stop the spray the Archers are already using."

"Yeah, but if we put enough in, then hopefully the happy gas will overpower the OA. It has to at least have some effect. People should be a lot more relaxed than they are right now, and that's all we need them to be, so they can stop and listen!"

"And how will we get the gas into the room?" Jack asked, keen to get moving.

Violet turned and pointed to the turbine she'd escaped through before.

"That propeller creates the cold air that passes along a short pipe into the white room, where it helps make clouds. If every time the blades stop moving, we put our arms through the propeller and spray the happy gas into the pipe, it should end up in the white room."

"And become part of the clouds."

"Exactly, Jack." Violet smiled. "I'm glad someone here has brains!"

"What's that supposed to mean?" Boy laughed.

"Nothing," Violet teased, grabbing a canister.

"We can use these to reach up to the pipe," Boy said, carrying over a few wooden crates and placing them against the wall under the propeller.

Then Violet climbed on top of the crates and waited for the propeller blade to stop spinning. Once it had wound to a halt, she stuck her arm through the blades into the pipe, pressed the nozzle of the can and sprayed it into the pipe. She was laughing so much by the time the can was empty, she almost fell off her perch.

Boy mounted more crates, covered his mouth with his

sleeve and, before the propeller began to move again, pushed the can inside the pipe and released its contents. Jack did the same.

They continued at a good pace, until a while later four boxes of nitreous oxitocin had been emptied into the pipe, and Boy, Violet and Jack were rolling about in hysterics on the stone floor.

"I can't...I can't...I can't breathe," Violet choked.

"Neither can I..." Boy gasped as he tried to pull himself up against the wall, beaming wildly.

"I think...I can't think..." She burst out laughing once more.

Slowly, Violet managed to pull herself onto her knees and pick up a canister beside her, before trying to scale the crates again. She was laughing so much she stumbled into a stack of OA boxes, sending their canisters clattering across the floor.

"We need to get out...out...out of this room," Jack laughed, using his elbows to drag himself towards the arched doorway where Hugo still stood obediently.

Violet followed Jack, stumbling through stacks of boxes as she passed, while Boy crawled, in convulsions, behind the pair.

"This is tak...taking too...too long," Jack cried, trying to speak between the laughter.

"You're...you're right," Boy giggled. "We need to get

Hugo…ba…back and into…into the Town…Town Hall…
before morning."

Jack pulled himself up to sitting.

"You…you two…go on," he insisted. "I'll keep spraying."

"But what…what…if…if you die laughing?" Violet
tried to keep serious.

All three broke out into hysterics once more.

"At least it'll make…make…a change from anger,"
Jack replied, gasping for air. "Make sure Iris tunes the
radio… She…she has to tune the ra-radio!"

"You go back…Jack, you need to help," Boy giggled. "I
can…can…stay and do the gas…"

Jack shook his head, breathless.

"I'll stay…" Violet chuckled, trying to control herself.

"No…no…I couldn't…couldn't…tune anything… now,
anyway," Jack insisted. "Can't…concen…concentrate!"

"Okay…don't be…be long." Boy smiled, pulling Violet
from the dirty floor. "Hugo…follow."

Violet's stomach hurt from laughing and she struggled
along the tunnel to the exit, giggling uncontrollably as she
watched the tomb open into the graveyard.

She wobbled up the steps and collapsed onto the gravel
path. Even the mist couldn't dull her mood. Boy crawled
out and stopped just behind her, catching his breath.

"We have to be serious, Boy," she mused, looking up at
the cloudy night sky.

"I know," he giggled, "but I just can't control myself."

The rain had stopped, the clouds had parted a little and Violet could see some stars. It was the first time she'd seen them over Town in ages.

"Look, Boy!" She smiled, pointing upwards. The laughing gas made her feel lighter and more carefree than she'd been in a long time.

"I haven't seen stars like that for a while," he replied. "Do you remember how clear the nights were when Town was Perfect?"

Violet was silent, thinking, then she turned to look at her friend.

"Do you think we did the wrong thing bringing down Perfect?"

"No, why would you say that?"

"Because everyone seemed happier then – well, at least, the Perfectionists were. Maybe the No-Man's-Landers and Perfectionists aren't meant to be friends? Maybe they are too different."

"Violet." Boy sighed. "There's no such thing as Perfectionists and No-Man's-Landers. There's just people. That's what Dad says."

Violet had really missed Boy. He always knew how to make her feel better.

"Anyway" – he smiled, giggling again – "we better get going. I...I can't look up at Hugo's nose hair any longer!"

Taken with the stars, Violet hadn't really noticed Hugo standing over them, Powick still lying unconscious across his bony shoulder.

The Child Snatcher's large nostrils did look a little like spaceships, hovering above their heads. Violet looked back at the stars and exploded in laughter.

CHAPTER 37

A SIMPLE TRUTH

The rain had stopped pouring in Town as Violet, Boy and Hugo, still carrying Nurse Powick, made their way back to Iris's house.

Boy knocked on the door.

"Oh goodness! Come in, come in," Iris said, moving backwards as Hugo stomped inside.

Macula stood open-mouthed as the Child Snatcher stopped still in the hallway. "He's, ahem, he's…"

"He's a zombie." Violet smiled. "Hugo's not the nicest to look at, but he's really useful."

"Well…we've been expecting visitors," Macula said, quickly grabbing a pile of rope from the bottom of the stairs. "So I went out and found this. Help me tie her up, Boy."

Boy and his mother wound the worn rope round Powick's wrists and ankles. Then Macula stood back to survey their work.

"Not a bad job," she said, dusting off her hands. "Now put her under the stairs."

On Boy's orders, the Child Snatcher picked up the tightly-bound nurse and deposited her in the closet under Iris Archer's stairs. Then Macula closed the door and bolted it.

"Hugo will stand watch until morning, when we have to bring him to the Town Hall," Boy said, yawning.

"Where's Jack?" Iris asked, as she beckoned them into the kitchen.

"He's just putting the last of the happy gas into the white room. Hopefully the morning rain will make everyone feel a little more relaxed." Violet looked out the window. "It's stopped again now. What if it doesn't start again until after the trial?"

"I've been thinking about the rain showers," Iris answered. "It appears to me the clouds are on a cycle. It seems to take a few hours for them to build back up again after a downpour. By my rough calculations, I think our next batch of rain is probably due just before the trial."

"I forgot! Dad said that too," Violet replied, feeling relieved.

"Iris has been busy while you were away." Macula smiled.

"Yes, my old brain just needed a new challenge. I got our sound solution working too," the old woman said, excitedly running over to a wooden radio sitting on the kitchen counter.

"Do you want me to demonstrate again?" Macula asked, looking inspired.

Iris Archer nodded enthusiastically, and Boy's mother took a walkie-talkie from the kitchen table and slipped from the room.

Violet could hear her tread up the wooden stairs, then stop on the landing above. Iris looked at the pair, smiled, and turned on the radio.

"*Testing, testing, one, two, three,*" Boy's mother's voice rang out across the kitchen, as if she were standing in the room beside them.

"Now, when Edward and George confess their sins, all of Town will hear as well as see them!" Iris said, clapping her hands together, and looking both pleased and proud as she turned off the radio.

"That's brilliant, Gran." Boy smiled.

"There's life in this old scientific dog yet," Iris said, as Macula walked back into the kitchen. "Now, who's hungry?"

Iris poured out two bowls of soup and served it up with some thick, crusty bread.

"Get this into you, you have to be starving."

"Where's Mam and Anna?" Violet asked.

"They're sleeping, pet, getting ready for the morning. You must both be exhausted too."

Violet nodded, only just realizing how tired her body felt. She was just finishing her soup, and finding it hard to keep her eyes open, when there was a thud on the door.

Boy hid in the kitchen, as Iris walked slowly out into the hall.

"Who is it?" she called.

Someone laughed on the other side of the door.

"Open it, Granny!" Boy said, sprinting out to join her.

Violet followed and watched as Iris unlocked the door then rushed out into the Avenue.

"Give me a hand," the old woman called over her shoulder.

Violet raced outside. Jack was lying on the cobbled street, laughing so hard he couldn't stand up or even catch his breath.

Iris dashed back into the house, then returned to the street, holding a paper bag.

"Breathe into this," she ordered.

Jack held the bag to his mouth and exploded with laughter once more.

Boy, Violet and Macula lifted their hysterical friend inside, and down the hall, sitting him on a chair in the kitchen. Macula held the bag over his mouth and he gradually calmed enough to breathe properly through it. When Boy's mam finally removed the paper bag, Jack giggled for another while before collapsing forward onto the table, exhausted.

"You all need some sleep," Iris said, looking at Jack. "Or none of you will be of any use tomorrow. I'll wake you in a few hours."

Iris handed Violet a blanket, and without a word she walked down the hall, past Hugo, who was still guarding the cupboard under the stairs, and collapsed onto the sitting-room couch.

It took moments for sleep to find her.

❋　　❋　　❋

Violet woke to Boy's whispered tones in the hallway.

She crawled up off the couch and looked out the sitting-room window. It was still dark, but she could no longer see the stars. The sky was gearing up for yet another downpour, and Violet hoped this one would ease a little of the tension that hung over Town.

The whisperings continued in the hallway. Boy and Iris were speaking quietly outside the sitting-room door.

"What's happening?" Violet asked, poking her head out.

Boy turned and looked at his friend.

"We were just talking about the plan," he whispered.

"Come into the kitchen," Iris said. "We don't want to wake the whole house."

Violet had just slipped out of the sitting room, when she heard a noise and looked up. Anna was descending the stairs, followed by Macula and Rose, who both looked like they needed a few more hours in bed.

"We're already awake, Iris," Macula said, stepping into the hallway. "I don't think anyone has slept much."

Everyone shuffled past Hugo, who was still staring at the door under the stairs, and wearily took their seats round the kitchen table.

Rose was the first to speak.

"My daughter is forever making me proud," she said, looking over at Violet. "I heard you were great again last night, pet – as were you, Boy and Jack."

"Morning," Jack croaked, climbing out from under the table. "I was so tired I grabbed some blankets and crawled into the first spot I found! Did you get the radio working?"

Iris nodded. "Loud and clear."

Rose smiled, and waited for Jack to take a place at the table before continuing.

"I know I've been a bit of a nervous wreck lately, what with all this weather playing havoc, but I think I've gotten a handle on it now and I want to be of help and make my daughter proud. I wasn't much use in Perfect, but I won't sit on the sidelines this time."

"I am proud of you, Mam," Violet said, grabbing her mother's hand.

"You are strong, Rose. All of us women are strong, so very strong – never forget that," Macula stated. "And as for children – they are capable beyond anyone's belief. This is the second time we're learning that lesson. Now, let's go over the plan for today. We must be precise if we're to win against the Archer brothers."

"Right," Boy said seriously. "We lure Edward and George into the Committee Room in the Town Hall, just before the trial begins. We then trick them into telling the truth about their plans, so that Town's people can witness it with their own eyes, through the screens of the Brain."

"Hugo's transmitter is working perfectly, Boy." Macula nodded at her son. "I checked the screens in the Brain again, after everyone went to bed a few hours ago. Each one had a perfect view of the door under Iris's stairs. Hugo hasn't stopped looking at it since he got here. When we place him in the Committee Room, everyone outside will see what our Child Snatcher sees. I met one of the ex-orphans while I was out too. Tom and the Archers were spotted going into the Town Hall during the night. The twins then came back out without him. I expect Tom's been put in a cell, in preparation for the trial."

"My sons are sticklers for details, as are we," Iris said, holding up one of the walkie-talkies. "Macula will have this handset in the Committee Room, and everything that happens in there will be broadcast live via my radio outside."

"We better get going. It'll be getting light soon," Violet said, glancing out the window.

Everyone nodded, then Macula Archer cleared her throat and stood up.

"I want to thank you all before we go," she said seriously. Macula reached across and took Boy's hand in hers. "William is the wordy one, but in his absence I'll give it a try. I want to thank you for sticking by my family through these troubled times. You have all consistently dared to question and to stand up against the popular tide of opinion, in order to find truth. We are so deeply grateful.

"Each of you at this table is filled with heart and passion beyond anything I've ever witnessed, and I feel so lucky to call you my neighbours. Let's show those Archer brothers that they can fill us with fear and bring madness to our streets, but we will not be divided. There is no 'them' and 'us'. We are men and women and children and husbands and wives and No-Man's-Landers and Perfectionists. We are all these labels and we are none. We are simply people, and we fight for that simple truth."

Rose grabbed Violet's hand and squeezed it. The energy in the room had suddenly come alive.

CHAPTER 38

BEARING WITNESS

An odd band of hooded people, united by a single goal, snuck through the streets of Town in the early morning. Most of the angry Townspeople were home in bed, but some lone troublemakers still wandered the streets, awaiting William's trial.

Violet, Rose, Jack and Anna stopped at different corners of the Town Hall to keep watch as Boy picked the lock. He was much better at it than Jack. Like a loyal dog, Hugo remained obediently by his side.

Macula beckoned Violet over as she waited a little away from the door, for Boy to open it.

"This is where we split up. I owe you and Jack a personal thanks, Violet. Though you did sneak away on me, it was the right thing to do. You saved Boy, and I am eternally grateful. Now let's save the others and Town. Take this," Macula said, handing her the second walkie-talkie. "Use it to let me know if anything goes wrong out here."

"I will," Violet replied seriously.

"Got it," Boy whispered, as the lock clicked and the door to the Town Hall opened.

Macula turned to walk away, then hesitated.

"Tom's not a bad child, Violet. I hope someday, when all this is over, you will help me help Boy to see that."

Violet nodded – though she wasn't fully sure how she felt about Tom, she trusted Macula. Then Boy's mam and Iris silently waved their goodbyes, before slipping inside.

Boy looked straight at his friend. "I'll see you after."

"What if our plan doesn't work?" Violet asked, only willing to air her doubts to him.

"It will, Violet."

"But that doesn't answer my question!"

"Your question is stupid," Boy teased.

"You're stupid," Violet huffed, half-smiling.

"We'll figure it out," Boy said, serious again. "We're a good team, Violet. If this doesn't work, we'll just figure it out."

"Do you really think we're a good team?"

"Sometimes," Boy joked, before disappearing inside, followed closely by the Child Snatcher.

❁   ❁   ❁

Rose was pacing up and down the street outside, when Violet reached the Brain. Jack was there too, holding Iris's radio.

Violet opened the lock of the Brain's main door and stepped inside the small space, the other two in tow.

The screens were bright and her eyes had to adjust before being able to look directly at them. Every single TV showed the same image: a bird's-eye view of the Committee Room in the Town Hall.

"Hugo's in place already." Rose smiled, trying her best to seem relaxed.

"Everything okay out there? OVER," Macula's muffled voice came across the radio.

Violet clicked the button on the side of her walkie-talkie and was about to respond, when Rose poked her head over her daughter's shoulder.

"Everything is perfect, Macula!" she whispered.

"I'll leave this here," Jack said, as he placed the wooden radio on a high stool William used whenever he watched the screens for a long time. "If you need help, just call me. I'll be over by the front steps of the Town Hall, ready to direct people your way."

"I told you I'd make you proud, Violet," Rose said, as Jack left the small space, "and that's what I'm going to do. We'll make your dad proud too."

In all the planning, Violet hadn't thought about her dad in a little while. Now the same feeling of dread played round her stomach. She hoped he was okay, locked up in the clock tower.

✳ ✳ ✳

Gradually, the crowds began to build. Rose and Violet took it in turns to poke their heads outside for a look.

"There's a lot of people out there now. Robert Blot has set up on the steps of the Town Hall too, and he's with Vincent Crooked. It looks like they'll both be running the show," Rose said, ducking quickly back inside as nine o'clock approached. "It seems like the whole of Town is here in force. They're still angry, though – like your father said, that OA gas is everywhere now. We're probably even drinking it in our water! When are those other rains ever going to fall?"

Violet glanced at one of the screens. Hugo was still in the viewing platform, looking down on the Meeting Room. Violet imagined Boy and Macula waiting nervously beside him. Iris was in his eyeline now – the old woman was in place, marching backwards and forwards across the Committee Room.

There was a crackle from the radio, and Macula's voice whispered through their small space once more.

A loud screech rang out on the air and Robert Blot's

voice boomed around the street.

"Welcome to the trial of the century, where William Archer stands accused of heinous, horrifying crimes," the man announced extravagantly.

Everyone erupted – it wasn't exactly a happy sound. The crowd was tense.

"I'm just going onto the street for a quick look, Mam," Violet whispered.

"Be careful, pet," Rose said, glued to the TV screen, watching Iris Archer standing as though frozen in the middle of the Committee Room.

Violet partially opened the door of the Brain. Everyone was looking at the Town Hall, so she covered her head with her hood, and slipped out unnoticed. She pushed her way through the crowd until she had a good vantage point of the proceedings.

Robert Blot, the newspaper man, stood under the canopy of the Town Hall, beside a microphone and two large speakers. Behind him was a large printed poster of William Archer's face, under the words *TRIAL OF THE CENTURY*. A big round red sticker reading *Exclusive insights brought to you everyday by the Town Tribune* was half-covering William's right eye.

To Robert Blot's left-hand side sat Vincent Crooked and the remaining members of the Town Committee, most of them Perfectionists.

"And here they are, the men who will save us!" Mr Blot announced, turning to face down Edward Street, in the direction of the Archers' Emporium.

Edward and George strode up the road triumphantly, as people yelled their names. The crowds parted, giving the two men a clear run to the Town Hall. The crowd roared wildly again as the Archers climbed the steps to join Robert Blot.

Vincent Crooked then stood up from his seat to shake both Edward's and George's hands. He looked nervous.

The microphone screeched again when Edward grabbed the mouthpiece.

"Thank you all for coming out on this both sad and glorious day. Sad because we will see our brother, William Archer, a man who many believed was great, tried for the most awful crimes – including the kidnapping of our beautiful children."

The people exploded in anger. "Bring back Perfect, No-Man's-Landers out!" a woman roared beside Violet, starting a chant.

"And glorious," Edward continued, holding his hands up for silence, "because this could be the beginning of making our once-great town a perfect place to live again!"

The cheer this time was immense, and Violet felt an awful energy grow amongst the crowd.

She turned and pushed her way through the sea of bodies, back to the Brain, checking quickly before disappearing inside.

"You okay, pet?" Rose asked, looking up from the screens.

"Yes, Mam, but it's awful out there. We need the rain soon or they'll all be too angry to hear or see anything!"

Robert Blot's voice echoed around the Brain again. "Vincent Crooked will now bring out the accused."

The cheers were even louder.

Violet looked back at the TV screens. Just as they had planned, Iris Archer was starting to cause a fuss. She seemed to be calling out names and throwing her arms in the air as she stomped around the Committee Room.

"Can you see this? OVER!" Macula's voice crackled across the radio. In the background Violet could hear Iris calling out for Edward and George.

"Yes. OVER," Violet whispered, as she kept her eyes peeled on the screens. Just as they'd hoped, Vincent Crooked walked into the Committee Room, and began talking to Iris.

The radio crackled again.

"She's telling Vincent that she needs to talk to Edward and George. OVER," Macula's voice sizzled across the airwaves.

Violet watched as Vincent Crooked left the meeting

room, looking flustered. She gripped the sides of the screen in front of her. Her heart was pounding in her ears.

"There's just a slight delay in proceedings," Robert Blot announced over the microphone. "I've been told Edward and George need to go inside for a few moments. No doubt their brutal brother is causing even more trouble."

The crowd began to boo.

A few minutes later, Violet watched as Edward and George strode into the Committee Room. The stouter twin looked livid. He grabbed his mother's shoulders and shook her. She wrestled away and seemed to be shouting something at him, then, clearly frustrated, the taller twin disappeared from the room.

"George has gone to get William and Tom, OVER." Macula's voice was very faint.

Violet held her breath.

The door of the Committee Room flew open, and William was pushed across the floor towards his mother. Iris rushed to her son's side, as Tom walked in with George.

"This is it. We'll get the truth. Get ready to broadcast. OVER!" Macula's voice crackled.

"Now," Violet said, looking at her mother.

Violet and Rose raced to either side of the Brain. Quickly, Violet unlocked the roller-door on her side, pushing it up to reveal the screens beneath. Then she helped her mam, who was struggling to open her lock.

"What's going on?" a woman nearby barked. "Why are George and Edward on those screens? Is this some kind of a trick?"

"You'll understand soon," Violet replied, running over to turn up the radio.

"I've tried that, Violet." Her mother looked frantic. "You can't hear the sound over the crowd."

"What?" Violet tried not to panic.

She looked at the screens again. Macula, Boy and Hugo were now in the Committee Room. Macula and Boy were confronting the Archer brothers, but no one could hear a thing.

Jack, Anna and the orphans were trying to get the crowds to look at the screens, but people were angry and roared at them to stop disrupting the trial.

Then the skies burst open, and the rains hailed down around them.

Almost immediately, faces began to soften a little, and some smiles appeared on those gathered nearby. The change wasn't as obvious as the day Edward returned with Town's kidnapped children, but the plan seemed to be working and the crowd calmed enough for Jack, Anna and the other ex-orphans to guide them towards the screens.

"Would you take a look at this – there's two of them, two Boys!" someone shouted. "What's going on?"

The crowd swarmed forward and surrounded the Brain.

"What's going on?" someone else shouted. "I can't hear anything. Why are there two Boys?"

"Nobody can hear anything," Jack panted, reaching Violet's side. "Turn up the radio or our chance is gone!"

"I have turned it up," she panicked. "It's the crowd – they're too loud!"

At that moment Rose appeared, pushing her way through the masses, and pulling Robert Blot behind her.

"Now, Mr Blot, I've always admired your newspaper – you believe in proper reporting," Violet's mother said, charming him.

"Well thank you, Ms...?"

"Rose Brown is my name. I'm an avid fan of yours... avid," Violet's mam lied, as she grabbed Robert Blot by the ear and pulled him down to the radio. "Listen to this and watch those screens," she ordered.

"But Edward... What? He's just told everyone in that room that...that he made it all up, the rescue...everything. Boy has a twin? What is going on here?" the newspaper man spluttered, looking up at Rose.

"Exactly." She nodded. "Those Archer brothers are not here for the good of their so-called citizens! Don't you think you should be the first to break a story like this?"

347

"This is outrageous. I don't like being played for a fool." Robert Blot grabbed the radio and elbowed his way back through the crowd. The newspaper man mounted the steps of the Town Hall and brought the radio right up to the mouthpiece of the microphone.

"And that's the end of it, mother!" Edward Archer's voice rang out into the crowd from the two large speakers resting beside Robert Blot. "Now myself, George, William and his son are heading outside to start this trial. And if any of you, including you, Macula, try to stop us again, you'll pay for it when the Watchers are released. Now, our people await."

Violet looked at Jack in despair. "Oh no. They've finished," she cried.

"It can't be over, we can't...we can't go back to Perfect, Violet. I can't go back to No-Man's-Land," Anna bawled, running over to pull on Violet's jumper.

"It's not over, Anna," she announced, thinking fast. "You and Jack, keep the crowd watching the Brain. I'll get the Archers talking again!"

Violet pushed through the crowd, raced up the steps under the canopy and sprinted through the Town Hall door, and up the spiral staircase two steps at a time, before bursting into the meeting room just as Edward and George were making their way out.

"Young Brown!" Edward exclaimed, as Violet almost

collided with his round stomach. "Have you come to join our fun? Well, I'm afraid you're a little late!"

"I know what you're up to," she shouted. The words spilled from her mouth before she even had time to think. "You're lying to everyone in Town, Edward. William didn't do any of the things you said he did. *You* did them all, along with Boy's twin brother."

Edward stood just in front of her, smiling. Tom was standing beside him. Behind them, George was holding William firmly. Hugo stood in the corner of the room, watching with the others.

"We've just gone through all this, Violet. I'm growing weary. Get out of the way," Edward growled.

She needed to get him talking properly.

"You have the wrong twin. That's Boy, and he'll never lie for you!" Violet shouted the first thing that sprung into her mind, then pointed directly at Tom, as she stood her ground between Edward and the door.

"No I'm not," Tom cried, as George reached out with his spare hand and grabbed his collar.

"You trying to trick us?" the taller twin grumbled, shaking him hard.

"She's right. I'm Tom," Boy exclaimed, stepping forward. "He's pretending to be me!"

The crowd gasped again.

Tom swung his head round to glare at his brother.

"You can't steal my family and then steal my name as well," he spat.

"Boy didn't steal your family, Tom," Macula said softly, searching her son's face. "Myself and your dad have been searching for you, ever since Perfect fell. The nurse – she took you away and told lies about your real family. Please don't believe her lies. We love you so much, son."

"No! You're the one lying," Tom roared, bursting with anger.

"ENOUGH!" Edward cried. He strode forward and grabbed Violet by her pigtail. "Not another sound, or I'll wring her little neck!"

Everyone froze.

Violet tried to wriggle and kick her way free from his grasp, but she couldn't.

"Let her go, Edward. It's me you want – you don't need to get others involved in this," William pleaded.

"Oh shut up, brother, your heroism is insufferable. Now, whichever one of you is the real Boy, step forward, or I promise I will terminate your best friend!" Edward roared. "I have lost but a morsel of my patience."

Horrified cries rang round the crowd outside, strangely mixed with what sounded like laughter. Boy moved, and Violet glared at him, willing him not to step forward any further. She needed just a little more time.

"You planned the robberies around Town and got Tom,

Boy's twin, to kidnap Conor and Beatrice, pretending he was Boy," she shouted. She had to lure Edward into admitting the truth while they still had an audience. "You poisoned the rain, controlling how we all felt. And then you pretended to be a hero, saving the kidnapped children before telling everyone that William and the No-Man's-Landers did it for revenge. You're trying to turn the Perfectionists against the No-Man's-Landers, so you can get back Perfect. So you can control everyone again."

"Oh, you've figured it out. Very clever, Violet Brown, but it's a little too late, I'm afraid." Edward Archer moved his free hand round her neck and began to squeeze.

"Stop it, Edward," William shouted, struggling to get away from George. "Leave her out of this!"

Violet's lungs burned as she tried to suck in air. The crowd had gone silent outside.

"I'm...I am Tom!" Boy's twin squirmed away from George and removed his contact lenses, revealing ice-blue eyes.

A gasp rushed in from outside.

"Perfect," the stout twin replied, tossing Violet aside.

She crashed onto the Committee Room floor. Violet had almost forgotten her injury from the white room, until her foot seared again in pain. Macula, Iris and Boy rushed forward to help her.

"I knew we should have released the Watchers,

351

Edward. Beating that lot into submission would be a lot easier than these silly games," George spat impatiently, as he dragged William towards the door. "This is another one of your stupid ideas!"

"I told you already, we can't release the Watchers yet. We need to gain the trust of those fools outside, otherwise we face another battle like Perfect, and you know how that turned out!" Edward shouted. "For once, use your thick head to think, George. It's true, the Townspeople have mush for brains, but for now, they still have brains. We can't feed them any old rubbish just yet. They have to believe us and like us! Now smile when we face those idiots outside – try a little charm, George."

A crash rang through the air outside, rattling the windows in the Town Hall.

"He's put too much of that stuff in the rain this time. The people sound like they're going completely crazy. I can't tell if they're laughing or crying. We've made them wait too long." George tutted.

"Well, let's get going then," Edward snapped, pulling Tom with him as he opened the door. "The sooner William is found gui..."

Jovial voices filtered inside from the bottom of the spiral staircase, as though the Town Hall was packing up with people. Edward stopped and retreated, confused as the door flew open.

352

"You've messed with the wrong person this time." Rose Brown laughed as she threw herself at the stout twin.

Edward stumbled to the side and Violet watched from the floor as Boy, Iris and Macula raced over and helped her mother wrestle Edward.

Hordes of Town people now barged into the Committee Room, filling up the space.

Robert Blot flashed his camera wildly, while Edward and George were restrained by a mob of half-laughing, half-crying Townsfolk.

Iris and Macula had their arms round William, their heads buried in his chest. He was hugging them both tightly.

"You did it, Violet! Everyone in Town heard. They heard the Archers tell the truth!" Jack laughed, sliding down onto the floor beside her.

Violet lay back, breathing heavily, as relief flooded her body.

Well-wishers bent down to tap her shoulders in congratulations, but she barely registered them. Her heartbeat slowed properly for the first time in ages, and she closed her eyes.

They'd done it again, except this time they'd saved Town.

A feeling formed deep in her belly. She giggled quietly

at first, and the sensation grew until she was heartily laughing out loud. The mood was contagious and the whole room exploded in uncontrollable laughter.

CHAPTER 39

A MOTHER'S LOVE

The throbbing in her foot had eased, and Violet was just playing with the thought of getting up from the floor, when someone tugged on her sleeve.

"I looked for him, but he's not here. Neither of them are, and I saw her in the crowd." Anna Nunn was standing above her, sounding panic-stricken.

"What are you talking about, Anna?" Violet asked, easing onto her elbows.

"The nurse, Powick! I saw her outside, and she came in here with the crowd. Now Boy is gone. I checked everywhere and I can't find him – and Tom is gone, and Hugo. I think she's taken them!"

Violet jumped to her feet and raced to the window.

She quickly scanned the streets outside. Most people were still congregating around the Town Hall, gathered in groups, talking. Violet's eyes fell on Hugo's huge frame as he stomped behind Powick and Tom, who was now wearing a hat. In the Child Snatcher's arms was a hooded figure.

"Boy!" Violet gasped, recognizing the clothes.

"I got Jack!" Anna shouted, pulling him across the Committee Room to her side.

"They have Boy," Violet said urgently. "Nurse Powick and Tom – they have Boy! Hugo is carrying him. They're on Rag Lane, heading towards Forgotten Road."

She looked around for William or Macula, or anyone who could help, but the room was still packed tightly and she couldn't spot them in the crowd.

"Anna, get help," she said, already running towards the door with Jack in tow. "I bet they're heading for the Outskirts. We'll try to stop them."

Violet pushed her way through the people, down the stairs and outside. As the crowd thinned, Jack raced ahead, and Violet's legs were on fire as she tried to keep up with him. They sprinted down Edward Street, onto Archers' Avenue and Rag Lane, turning left onto Forgotten Road.

There was no sign of Hugo, Powick or the two boys.

Violet and Jack then turned down the first laneway

that led to Market Yard, and spotted Powick and her posse just passing by the Rag Tree.

"I'll try to stop them here, and you race around and cut off Wickham Terrace, Jack."

"What's the plan?" he asked quickly.

Violet shook her head. "I don't have one," she said, "but we'll figure it out."

The new rain was making everything seem a lot less scary.

Jack nodded, before sneaking out into the market and turning left, to skirt quietly around the edges.

Violet waited until he was out of sight. Then she stepped from the shadows.

"Stop!" she cried, her voice cutting across the air.

Tom and Nurse Powick pivoted on the spot. Hugo stopped dead near the Rag Tree and turned. Boy was limp in his arms.

"Oh – for a minute, I thought I'd something to worry about. Now I know why Edward always referred to you as a thorn in his side, Violet Brown. However, you're only a child. What can you really do to stop me?" The nurse laughed.

"Tom," Violet pleaded, "please, Tom. Boy is your brother. Please don't hurt him! Everything Powick told you about your family is lies."

"How do you know what she's told me?" Tom asked,

not looking at the nurse.

"Tom, don't even answer her," Powick said dismissively, turning back around.

"Macula loves you, so does William. They're your family!"

"How would you know anything?" Tom snapped.

"I know Macula put you and Boy in the orphanage to protect you from your uncles," Violet said urgently. "She knew they hated William and if they found out he'd had children, you wouldn't be safe. She found out what they were doing in Perfect, and about No-Man's-Land, and thought you'd be safe there. She wrote you both letters every day, hundreds of letters. I've seen them, she'll show you the letters. She thought of you every second of every day."

Tom hesitated.

"She's lying!" Powick snapped, facing Violet again. "Your mother never loved you. I was the only one who took pity on your poor soul. I saved you. I reared you. You owe me everything, Tom!"

"That's not true, Priscilla," someone shouted.

Violet turned around. Macula was standing at the bottom of the laneway behind her.

"Thou shall not bear false witness against your neighbour; it's one of the ten commandments, Macula. Do look it up! I don't lie," the nurse snapped.

Macula strode across the marketplace. Tom's face softened a little as he watched his mother walk towards him.

"Why did you take my son?" Macula demanded.

"Which one?" Powick laughed, gesturing round to Boy in Hugo's arms. "I have both of them now, you know."

"Boy will never be yours, and Tom...you may have reared him, but he is my child. You are a *good* boy, Tom. She is not your family. Come back to us, please..."

Powick laughed. "You seem to have forgotten you gave them both up, now you're all high and mighty, Macula. How does it feel to give away your own flesh and blood?"

Macula ignored Powick, all the time looking at Tom.

"You left them on the doorstep of the orphanage, with nothing but a glasses box as company. You're a fool to ask me why I took your son!" Powick spat. "What kind of a mother are you?"

"I did it for you, to protect you. It is the hardest thing I've ever done. I thought about both of you every day. I wrote to you every day. I love you, Tom. I love you so deeply, son. A mother's love is strong, I know you feel it too," Macula said. She took a step towards him, with her arms outstretched.

Tom mirrored her movement, stepping forward too.

"Don't go near that woman. You're my son, Tom," the nurse said, dragging him back. "After all these years of neglect, Macula thinks she can have you, just like that! I told you, she loves your brother more – don't go listening to her lies, now…"

"Enough," Macula fumed. She strode towards them until she was just in front of Tom and Powick, under the barren branches of the Rag Tree. "You will give me back both my sons, and then you will leave us alone. If you go now, without any more trouble, we won't follow you. Edward and George have been caught. Your game is up."

"Oh, Mummy's come out fighting." Powick laughed. "Edward and George are only a distraction, dearest – there are much bigger fish than those two in these oceans!"

Macula reached for Tom.

"Enough," the nurse roared, "don't take another step!"

"Stop, please, she'll hurt you," Tom begged his mother. There were tears in his ice-blue eyes.

Macula smiled, and opened her arms.

"Don't be scared, Tom," she soothed. "I'm bringing you home, son!"

"No you're not!" Powick cried.

The nurse grabbed Macula viciously by the front of her coat, and threw her roughly to the side. Boy's mam stumbled backward and fell, knocking her head hard against the side of the Rag Tree.

"Macula!" Violet cried, racing to her side.

"I told you not to move, you silly woman." The nurse laughed.

Powick grabbed Tom's hand as he stood, stunned, above his mother.

"Don't get sentimental on me now," she warned, pulling him away towards Wickham Terrace. Hugo, with Boy still in his arms, followed behind obediently.

William and Merrill broke out into the yard, followed by Anna.

"I got more help!" The little girl smiled, running towards them.

"Macula," William whispered, kneeling down by his wife's side. "What's happened? What has that woman done?"

"Macula hit her head on the Rag Tree," Violet said. There was blood on her hands.

Macula opened her eyes, her breathing laboured. "I told him, William... I told Tom we love him..."

"That's great, Macula. Stay awake, now. Tell me more about Tom?" William encouraged her, lifting his wife into his arms.

"We have to get her to a doctor's, quickly, Merrill," William whispered, as the toymaker stepped in to help, and the pair made their way carefully towards Forgotten Road.

"Where's Boy?" Anna asked, looking around.

After Macula's accident, Violet had momentarily forgotten Boy. Hugo still had him!

Feeling calm and relaxed, given the circumstances, she climbed up from the ground and was about to chase after Powick, when Jack came towards them across Market Yard. He was half-carrying, half-dragging a semi-conscious Boy.

"What happened? How did you get him back?" Violet smiled, surprised.

"I'm not sure," Jack panted. "I tried to stop them all going over the footbridge. The nurse laughed at me and pushed by. She had gone on when Tom whispered to the Child Snatcher to give me Boy. It was weird. Hugo just handed him over and continued on. I didn't have to do anything."

"What did the nurse say?" Violet asked, confused.

"Nothing." Jack shook his head, disbelieving. "She was a good bit ahead and still hadn't noticed by the time I turned up Wickham Terrace… I'm sure Tom will get in trouble. He said something strange though…"

"What?" Anna was wide-eyed.

"He said, 'Tell Mam, I do feel it sometimes.'"

"Feel what?" Anna asked, shaking her head.

"I don't know…" Jack shrugged.

Violet smiled. She had an idea what Tom meant and she couldn't wait to tell Macula, when she got better.

They stopped for a while in the middle of Market Yard, enjoying their new-found feelings of relief. Each filled the other in on any missed details of their adventure, while Boy slowly came round to join the conversation.

"We've done it again." Anna smiled excitedly. "I'm only seven and I've already helped save Town twice!"

"We have?" Boy slurred.

Violet and Jack burst out laughing as they lifted their still-groggy friend from the ground, and climbed under a shoulder each. Then the foursome made their way towards the lane onto Forgotten Road. The rain still drizzled down around them, bringing a lightness to their step.

They neared Rag Lane, and Violet began to notice people acting strangely. Instead of the earlier smiles and congratulations from those they met in Market Yard, now no one seemed to want to meet her eye.

"What's going on?" she whispered. "Nobody will look at me."

"Me neither. Maybe they're embarrassed." Boy coughed, able to walk on his own now. "The people in Town did go a little nuts!"

"Maybe." Violet shrugged. "But we all went nuts."

"You were always nuts, Violet." Boy laughed, as they turned onto Archers' Avenue and then Edward Street.

Anna and Jack joined in the laughter and Violet was just about to respond, when she spotted a crowd gathered ahead, by the steps of the Town Hall. They were all looking at something on the ground. Everyone was silent.

She saw her parents in the middle of the congregation.

"Mam, Dad!" Violet exclaimed, running towards them.

The pair broke quickly from the group and made their way towards her.

"Oh, pet," her dad said, burying his head in her shoulder as she jumped into his arms.

He was crying. She'd never seen her dad cry before, not even after all the awful things that had happened to him in Perfect.

"Come this way," Rose said, grabbing Boy by the arm. "Let's go to Iris's."

"But…but we won. We have Town back, don't we? I know Powick and Tom got away, but we can go to the Outskirts and catch them. The Archers are caught, aren't they, and it's half-happy rain. Why are you all so sad?" Violet mumbled, confused, her heart thumping a little stronger.

Boy looked at the crowd, then back at Violet, as Rose tried to restrain him from moving further.

"What's going on?" Violet asked again.

Over her dad's shoulder, she could see Madeleine and Iris, solemn in the crowd. Aided by Merrill, they were helping William Archer to his feet.

Panic rose in Violet's chest. She turned round to look at Boy.

He seemed confused as his dad, red-eyed, strode out from the middle of the crowd towards him.

"I'm so sorry, Boy," William sobbed, wrapping his son in his arms.

"Mam? Dad?" Violet looked back at her parents. "But it's happy rain. Please don't be sad. What's happening?"

"Some feelings are too strong to be controlled, pet," her dad replied.

Rose cupped her daughter's face, and moved so close they were nose to nose.

"Macula's gone, Violet," she whispered. "She's gone to the stars."

CHAPTER 40

THE RAVEN

The approaching summer skies were hazy blue as Violet and her dad headed up Splendid Road on the way to that evening's Committee meeting. Rose had gone to her new music class, so Violet, still not allowed to stay at home alone, was made to go to the Town Hall with her dad.

The birds were singing in the evening sun, and she felt happy as she looked at the huge bunch of colourful flowers in her hands. They were from her mam.

Town felt nice these days – calm and normal and nice.

"Are you looking forward to the summer holidays, pet?" Eugene asked.

"I think so, Dad. No more Mrs Moody for months!"

"Oh that sounds great!" he laughed.

"Did they find anything in the Outskirts yet?" Violet asked, a little nervously.

"No, pet, still nothing." Eugene shook his head. "That's what we'll be talking about again tonight. Madeleine is adamant the whole place is empty – the cottage, the stables, everything. Hugo's transmitter was disconnected from the Brain and there was no sign of him or those other monsters anywhere either."

"They were zombies, Dad – you saw Hugo!"

"They were some sort of mechanical construction, Violet, I saw that much. There's no such things as zombies, pet."

"But what about that road, Dad, the one that went past Powick's cottage? Did they try down there? Maybe they're hiding in the forest."

Sometimes, Violet toyed with the idea of going back to the Outskirts to explore for herself. She knew kids would do a much better job than adults, but she wouldn't do it without Boy, and he wasn't ready to go back there yet.

"They checked everywhere, there was nothing, pet." Her dad sighed. "But Madeleine assured the rest of the Committee they'd keep looking. I told you, they did find your white room a few days ago. Madeleine is going to fill us in more on that tonight. Robert Blot was like an excited child over the finding, though he can't report on it now he's taken Vincent's place on the Committee. What a piece of genius on the Archers' part, though, making clouds like that."

"Dad," Violet corrected, "you can't call the Archers genius, that's just wrong!"

"I'm only admiring their intellect, Violet, that's all."

"What's that?"

"Their brains, pet."

"Oh, Boy told me William's got all the eye plants blooming again. He said it took his dad a while to be able to even think about planting them, but now they're back and watching again," she said excitedly. "We probably don't need to use the Brain, though, because both Edward and George are locked up."

"Better safe than sorry, Violet," Eugene said, waving at Mr Hatchet, who was just closing up his butcher's shop for the night. "And it's helping William – he finds work helps keep his mind off things."

Violet stopped opposite the road up to her school. "I promised Mam I'd drop these off, Dad," she said, holding up the bunch of flowers.

"Okay, pet, I better head on, before I'm late. I'll be checking the viewing platform to make sure you're there though, Violet. So don't delay. I know how much you love these meetings!" he joked.

The setting sun hung low, making the road look yellow

as she walked up the hill, past her school, until the low wall and small wooden gate came into view.

Violet hadn't realized there was a graveyard in Town, having had no need to visit it before. Now, as she looked at the flowers in her hand, part of her wished she still didn't have to know about the place.

This graveyard was nothing like the one in the Ghost Estate, though. There were no crumbling stone tombs with names like Quintus Horatius Flaccus engraved on their sides, or towering grey monuments broken and cracked with age.

The graves here were all marked with simple wooden crosses, and covered in colourful wild flowers. Wild flowers also ran all along the inside of the low stone wall that surrounded it. And, as it was almost summer, the evening was filled with birdsong and the sound of hovering bees as they busily buzzed for food. There were wooden benches dotted around too, and sometimes people just sat there reading. Her mam said they were keeping their loved ones company.

Violet had just opened the latch on the wooden gate, when she looked up and spotted Boy sitting cross-legged at his mam's graveside ahead, almost like he was chatting to Macula.

"Hey," she called, walking towards him. "Are you trying to avoid the Committee meeting too?"

Boy jumped up and stumbled backwards. Violet would have laughed, had she not caught the fear in his ice-blue eyes.

She stopped still on the pebble-stone path. Her heart was thumping.

"Your mam would love that you came, Tom," she said softly.

"Violet!" a voice called behind her.

She turned quickly to see the real Boy approach the low stone wall of the graveyard. "I saw your dad on the way to the meeting, he said you were here."

She swung back around, but Tom was gone.

"They're nice." Boy smiled, glancing down at the flowers as he reached her side.

He didn't seem to have noticed his brother.

"You okay, Violet? You look like you've seen a ghost!"

"Not funny, Boy," she said, trying to discreetly look round the graveyard.

She didn't mention Tom. Boy wasn't willing to talk about him. He blamed his brother for everything that had happened. Sometimes, Violet tried to convince her best friend that it wasn't Tom's fault; she knew Macula would want that, but Boy never listened.

The pair stopped at Macula's graveside, and Violet bent down, placing Rose's flowers amongst the array of giant daisies William had planted.

"Do you think she's around? Mam, I mean..." Boy asked.

"I don't know," Violet said, standing up. "Maybe... My mam believes that stuff, anyway. She sees signs everywhere. She says it means Macula's watching out for all of us."

"Yeah, I think so too." Boy smiled. He seemed happy, happier than she'd seen him in a while. "I keep seeing butterflies everywhere. Dad says they're Mam. And..."

He stopped speaking, and looked down at the grave.

"And what?" Violet encouraged.

"It's nothing."

"You can't kind of tell me something, and then stop!"

"Well, I think Mam follows me sometimes."

"Follows you? What do you mean?"

"I don't know, really. You'll think I'm crazy, but this bird has been following me for a while now. I see it everywhere, especially if I'm lonely, like it's watching out for me. I told Dad, and he said it was Mam."

"What kind of a bird?" Violet asked, goose pimples prickling her skin.

"Look, there it is again!" Boy beamed, pointing.

A coal-black raven was perched on the arm of a bench by the wall, its shiny coat gleaming greens and blues in the evening sun.

Violet's breath caught. What with everything, she'd never mentioned Tom's bird to Boy.

"Maybe," she said, turning to walk back down the path. "But don't you think Macula would be a robin or an owl, or something pretty instead?"

Boy shook his head. "No. She'd be something smart and mysterious and strong. She'd be something magical. I know she'd be a raven."

THE END. FOR NOW...

ACKNOWLEDGEMENTS

I didn't write an acknowledgement for *A Place Called Perfect*. It was forgotten amongst the moments of madness during the lead up to publication. Anne, my editor, asked if I wanted to include one this time round and, though there are still many moments of madness, there are equally as many people I wish to thank:

Firstly, everyone that helped on my self-publishing journey before *Perfect* found its home with Usborne. The teachers, librarians, booksellers and children of Kilkenny proudly promoted a local writer and I was overwhelmed by the support received from my home town.

Then there's Josephine Hayes and Lauren Gardner. Jo found *Perfect* and Lauren nurtured it and *Trouble*. Both played a huge part on my road to becoming a published author and my tentative first steps in this industry. I would have sunk pretty quickly without them.

Having dreamed of publication, meeting Anne Finnis was daunting. My nerves were wasted energy. She was warm and welcoming, immediately putting me at ease. As an added bonus Anne possesses the super-human ability to turn my gibberish into readable books and can hold many the serious conversation about the exact mechanics of a walking zombie. I am forever grateful to her as both an editor and friend.

Everyone at Usborne for taking me on a trip in their hot-air balloon. Sarah, Stevie, Jacob, Katarina, Kath and Tilda are just a few names that set my emails alight and add excitement to my inbox.

Karl James Mountford and Katharine Millichope for making both *Perfect* and *Trouble* objects of beauty. Luckily people do judge books by their covers.

The booksellers, teachers and librarians who took *Perfect* to their hearts. I've been on a whistle-stop tour through the north of Ireland meeting booksellers in love with stories and words. I've interacted online with teachers devoted to their students' learning and talked to librarians who get genuine joy when a child reads their suggestion. These people are filled with passion for their work. Theirs is not a job, it's a vocation.

Children – they know they're far more intelligent than us adults. I sweat over plot points aware that if I make a mistake it will be spotted. They twirl on the spot until they get dizzy or go on treasure-seeking adventures. Children know how to have fun, they're the life and soul of every party and I'm so flattered they're reading my stories.

I've needed quite a bit of propping up this year. *Trouble* was born in a storm and all below steadied the ship:

My friends – girls, I hope you remember what I look like when I crawl out from behind this laptop!

My writing group – the most talented people I know. Two of us have struck it lucky so far – who's next?

My multitude of relatives for rallying round – I will forever remember our sing-song at the campfire last August. How the saddest of moments can be the sweetest of times.

Mam, the original dreamer – you believed in me before I could chew my own food. If I told you I wanted to be an astronaut you'd have hounded NASA. You're the perfect balance of strength and kindness. Without you, Mam, none of this would exist.

Willie, Emer, Monica, Donal, Carmel, Mick and Bernie – I couldn't have come up with a better crew if I'd written you myself. The finest bunch of No-Man's-Landers I've ever met.

The Heffernans – even though I didn't take your name you still took me in, silver spoon and all. Your kindness and caring never stops.

To Robbie, Jo and Tinker – my life. Nothing I can type will ever be enough. We have all the best adventures. Thanks for finding me.

And finally, Dad – it was always going to be your name on the dedication, I just never imagined you wouldn't read it. You gave each of us every bit of your enormous heart, your conviction made us believe that we were something to believe in. Because of you I want Jo to grow up with confidence and feel intensely loved. That way she can do anything.

Just like Rose, I see your signs. You're still a man of magic.

Thank you for everything. Love, Hel.

FIND OUT HOW ALL THE
TROUBLE BEGAN IN

More praise for

A PLACE CALLED PERFECT

Winner of the *Redbridge Children's Book Award, North East Book Award 2018* and *Hillingdon Primary Book of the Year.*

"Your heart is in your mouth and you're knee deep
in adventure."
M.G. Leonard

"The perfect choice if you're looking for a brilliantly spooky,
wildly imaginative story."
Ruzaika, The Regal Critiques blog

"An unusual, creepy story."
Primary Times

"My new favourite. This is honestly the greatest book I have
ever read. I adore the characters, plot twists, action, and all
round brilliant adventures."
Molly

"Amazing. I love this book so much! I couldn't put it down
and even afterwards I read it again."
Katy

EDWARD AND GEORGE ARCHER
ARE IN PRISON.

NURSE POWICK AND HER GRUESOME
ZOMBIES HAVE DISAPPEARED.

BUT SOMEONE HAS PLANS TO BUILD
A MUCH BIGGER ZOMBIE ARMY.

TOWN MAY BE SAFE FOR NOW –
BUT NOT FOR MUCH LONGER!

LOOK OUT FOR THE THIRD
PERFECTLY SPOOKY STORY,
COMING SOON...

If you liked

THE TROUBLE WITH PERFECT

you might also like

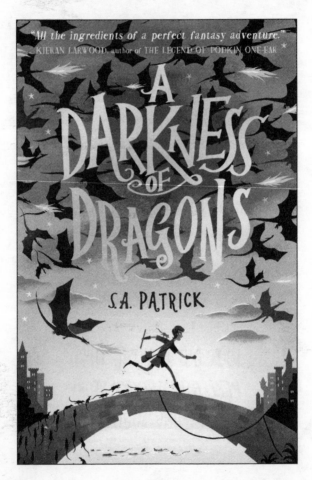

In a world of dragons, song-spells, pipers and battles, Patch Brightwater is a boy in disgrace. Thrown in jail for playing a forbidden spell, he is no one's idea of a hero. But only he knows a deadly truth – the evil Piper of Hamelyn is on the loose.

With the help of Wren, a girl cursed to live as a rat, and Barver, a fire-breathing dracogriff, Patch must stop the Piper sparking the biggest battle of them all.

Three accidental heroes versus one legendary villain... An epic adventure is born.

IF YOU LOVE MYSTERY AND
ADVENTURE STORIES
GO TO:
WWW.USBORNE.COM/FICTION

🐦 @USBORNE
📷 @USBORNE_BOOKS
📘 FACEBOOK.COM/USBORNEPUBLISHING